Secrets Revealed

By
Katie McKnight

Eternal Press
A division of Damnation Books, LLC.
P.O. Box 3931
Santa Rosa, CA 95402-9998
www.eternalpress.biz

Secrets Revealed
by Katie McKnight

Digital ISBN: 978-1-62929-013-3
Print ISBN: 978-1-62929-014-0

Cover art by: Dawné Dominique
Edited by: Kim Richards

Copyright 2013 Katie McKnight

Printed in the United States of America
Worldwide Electronic & Digital Rights
Worldwide English Language Print Rights

This book is dedicated to my sister, Leigh-Anne Dunckley. This world became a better place when you were born. Thank you for holding my hand and walking with me in this fictional world.

I have been told writers live lonely lives. In my case, this is not true. This book would not have been completed without my family and friends.

I would like to acknowledge my husband Bill, who works hard to afford me the luxury to raise our three sons and to write. Love you. I would also like to acknowledge my sons, Bryan, Michael and Shawn.
You bring joy to my life. I am so proud of each of you.

Thank you to my parents, brothers, sisters, nieces and nephews for your love and support.

Pat and Walter Hetzel, thank you for chasing people for feedback.

To my family and friends who read pieces f this story, I am eternally grateful for your help. Special thanks to Barbara Esposito, Susan Petrou, Jeanne Grieshaber, Andrew Dunckley and Risa Katz for tightening my pitch.

I would also like to thank Rosie Stauber, Megan Hetzel, Alex Bevinetto, Denise DeGiovanni, my Facebook friends and the Farmingdale Divas (ka kaa) for your encouragement. Thank you to the Farmingdale Writer's Group, Long Island Writer's Guild and Fanstory.com for your guidance. Walter Hetzel, Jr. I have the most fun editing with you.

Finally, thank you Kim Richards-Gilchrist and Erin Lale for the opportunity to publish through Eternal Press. This is a dream come true. Your talent makes me look good.

xoxoxox
Katie

Prologue

Six weeks was a sufficient amount of time to observe a person's daily routine. Waiting fourteen months to execute the plan sounded ridiculous to him. He was tired of the excuses his client gave. They needed to move forward with the plan. The longer they waited, the more difficult it was to get close to Melanie O'Shaughnessy.

He wanted the half-million dollars he was promised. The measly five hundred dollars he received so far was a joke. What a fool he was for agreeing to wait on payment until after he finished the job.

More importantly, he needed to satisfy the tingling sensation in his chest, fingers, and jaw. At one time, he feared the sensation was the onset of a heart attack. Now, he understood it indicated a desire to inflict pain on others. The last fourteen months fueled that desire.

He arrived at the diner and sat across from his client. The small talk annoyed him even though this client was also a close friend.

The tingling sensation was intense. "I want to execute the plan now. No more delays."

"Do you have a plan in mind?"

"Of course I do," he snapped. "She has dinner with her friends every Tuesday night. On the way home, she passes an alley. I'm going to wait for her there."

"What makes you so sure she'll walk? It's been a cold December. She could take a cab."

He sucked his cheek in annoyance. "She has eaten in the same restaurant with the same group of friends for the past year. When the evening ends, she always walks home."

"There's one problem with your plan," the client told him. "She and Ryan are spending the holidays in Pennsylvania."

He groaned.

"Don't be angry. I meant to tell you. It will be easier for you to handle matters once they leave New York. I can get close to her there."

He considered this. "Easy would be nice."

"I realize the enjoyment you get from tormenting people. Don't do it this time. Stay away from her until you hear from me. She's destroyed my family. I do not want this plan to fail."

"You focus on getting me close to her. Let me worry about the tactics I use."

He supported the client's need to destroy Melanie. After all, he *had* witnessed the impact of her actions over the last few years. At the same time, Melanie had become a big part of his life. He spent a huge chunk of the day following her. No one had the right to tell him he had to stay away from her, especially not someone who wasn't brave enough to terminate the problem on their own.

He needed to monitor her. Monitoring helped him remember that behind the beautiful face was an ugly woman.

The phony smile plastered on Melanie's face whenever photographers were around, filled him with rage. A sincere woman wouldn't allow theater security guards to accuse photographers of harassment after she encouraged their behavior.

He pegged her as the type of woman who would slap a restraining order against a man who loved her. A man who spent every dime he earned to buy gifts for her. She probably enjoyed hurting men. She was no different from the women *he* knew and loved. Someone had to teach Melanie the proper way to behave. He would be that person.

After lunch, he walked to the theater. Melanie's show would end soon and he wanted to be in place when she exited the building. He enjoyed the nervous expression on her face each time she spotted him standing there. It satisfied the tingling sensation...at least for a little while.

Chapter One

Melanie

Once the curtain call concluded, I hurried backstage to slide out of my costume and remove the heavy makeup. Jane, our company costume designer, removed the ponytail clip from my long, brown hair and used a flat iron to straighten the sections in need. For the past year, my hair has been dyed for this acting role, yet it still shocked me to see the dark locks of hair in the mirror's reflection.

The cast didn't include me for our usual Tuesday dinner plans, nor did they ask me to join them for cocktails afterward. Everyone knew it was a big day for me and I was anxious to get home. It took every ounce of discipline to remain in character for the afternoon performance. I danced a little lighter and sang with more excitement than I have in a long time. Having the role of a high school cheerleader, the enthusiasm enhanced my performance rather than hindered it.

For the past two weeks, my husband has been in California filming his latest movie role. While it is never easy living apart, I have found this separation especially difficult. The director summoned him to work a few days after our wedding and I have not seen him since he left. That is going to change today because he is coming home.

I waved goodbye to my friends in the cast and crew and exited through the stage door. I hoped the paparazzi had someone more important to harass than me. That wish vanished when a rush of photographers surrounded me. I was unsure which was more shocking to my system, the frigid temperature or the photographers bombarding me. Buttoning my cream-colored coat with gloved hands, I stepped around the men and their blinding flashbulbs.

"Hi Melanie," one addressed me as if we were friends. "How's married life?"

"Great," I responded with a smile.

"Will you and Ryan spend Christmas together?" another asked. He probably hoped we would be apart so his website could run articles suggesting marital problems. I could see the headlines: *Hollywood Heartthrob Ryan Carlisle and His New Wife Spend Christmas Apart.*

"We'll be together."

"You didn't go on a honeymoon. Are you planning an exotic getaway?"

"Will you join Ryan in Georgia when he films his next movie?"

"When does your show close?"

I waved goodbye to the men indicating I was finished with their line of questioning, but stopped dead in my tracks when I saw...*him*. A feeling of uneasiness hovered at the sight of the tall, blond-haired man standing across the street. I have noticed him hanging around the theater over the last several months. He never approached me or acted in a threatening manner. He just stands there...staring.

The sound of a siren startled me. "Get out of her way," a police officer yelled from his cruiser. When they ignored his order, he climbed out of the car and pushed through the crowd of photographers, moving one out of my face. "Gentlemen, leave Mrs. Carlisle alone." He wrapped his large hand around my shoulders shielding me from the men.

I looked across the street hoping to point the blond man out to the police officer but couldn't find him.

"How about a ride?"

I nodded.

Up until last year, I was able to walk around New York City without a soul recognizing me. When Ryan and I first met, no one would have recognized him either. We were both small-time, struggling actors. My claim to fame was a nine-month soap opera stint working as an extra.

Last year, Ryan landed a lead role in a low-budget film about zombies. The film went straight to number one and by the time it closed, Ryan was famous. His face graced the cover of numerous magazines, he appeared on television talk shows and he currently holds the title of most handsome man. Now, Hollywood producers want him in their movies.

The downside of his newfound fame is that he is never home and we are targets of tabloid articles. Everyone knows

Ryan. Because I am the woman in his life, most recently becoming his wife, everyone knows me too. Crowds of people swarm whenever he is around. The paparazzi are always snapping pictures and trying to break stories about him, regardless of whether or not the information is factual. Ryan is not a fixture in Hollywood's nightlife, so the paparazzi follow me hoping to pick up a juicy story.

"Where would you like me to drop you Mrs. Carlisle?" The officer interrupted my thoughts.

I looked at my watch. Ryan's plane was not due to arrive for another few hours. I knew I would go mad waiting in the apartment so I decided to buy last-minute Christmas gifts. "Would you mind dropping me off at the toy store on Sixth Avenue?"

The officer parked in front of the store and opened the car door. At five foot three inches, I felt small next to his tall, muscular frame.

"Call me if there are any further problems." He handed me a business card that listed his name, rank and telephone number. "Enjoy your day."

I wished the officer a nice holiday and headed inside the store in search of a robotic gerbil for Ryan's nephew and my niece.

A few shoppers eyed me wearily but I am convinced having appeared from the back of a patrol car was the cause of their concern. An elderly man wearing a vest with the store logo on it directed me to the second floor for robotic toys. Not only was the store crowded, it was warm. I unbuttoned my coat and slipped my gloves into the pockets while riding the escalator upstairs. Shoppers bumped into me as they shuffled along the crammed main aisle. Frustrated, I stepped into a quiet corner, removed the cell phone from my messenger bag and sent a text to my sister.

Did you honestly expect the store to be empty seven days before Christmas? Jessica responded to my complaint.

I was sort of hoping it would be. I typed.

Ryan will have to make a few more blockbuster films before stores close down for your shopping pleasure.

I was tempted to remind her that I have found my own success, but decided not to be petty. Besides, we both know Broadway actors do not receive that kind of special treatment. I typed *LOL* in response to her text and placed the phone in my coat pocket. Sliding back in line with the other shoppers, I worked to find the toys I came to purchase.

"We don't have 'em in stock." A plump, older woman laughed when I asked her about the gerbils. She straightened a display of toys while speaking to me. "People are lined up outside the store every morning, trying to get those things. I hope you didn't make any promises to your children."

I twisted my lips in disappointment. Veering off the main aisle, I huddled against a display cabinet and typed a text to my sister seeking alternate gift ideas. She suggested a doll, dress up clothing and computer games, and then closed the text by informing me that her daughter Lori would be disappointed the gerbils were not available. Just to be mean, I suggested buying a live gerbil for Lori. The phone vibrated in my pocket and I knew it was her warning me not to buy a live gerbil. I ignored the text leaving Jessica to worry.

I was searching through racks of computer games when I heard a high-pitched screech and felt someone grab my arm. "Are you the woman who just asked me about gerbil pets?"

I nodded, hopeful she had found some.

It takes a moment or two for her to catch her breath. "I just realized who you are."

It is not too often people recognize me and I must admit my ego received a boost. "You're Ryan Carlisle's new wife."

I chuckled as my head deflated back to normal size.

"You're a Broadway actress, aren't you?"

My head expanded.

"My granddaughter tells me we should go to your show." She beamed. "She says it is the only way she will meet your husband."

Deflation in progress, I couldn't wait to tell Ryan this story.

"We're expecting a shipment of robotic gerbils tonight. I will put a few aside and meet you outside the store tomorrow at noon. That's when I take my lunch break."

"Can you get in trouble for doing that?"

A look of annoyance crossed her face. "I'm not going to inflate the price or nothing."

"I'm not implying..." I placed my hand on her arm. "I just don't want you to lose your job doing a favor for me."

The smile returned to her face. "The store allows me to purchase them. Since my grandchildren are too old for these toys, I'd be happy to buy them for you."

"Maybe we can meet for lunch tomorrow," I suggested.

"Murray's pizza is down the street. I eat there a lot."

"What about Leone's around the block?"

The brightness in the woman's face disappeared. "I can't afford Leone's."

I glanced at her name tag. "You are doing me a huge favor Carol. The least I can do is buy lunch."

"Can you bring an autographed picture of your husband to lunch?" She scrunched her face as she asked the question. "It would make my granddaughter's Christmas."

I nodded in response, then told her I would make a noon reservation under the name Melanie O'Shaughnessy. O'Shaughnessy is my maiden name and the name I use even though strangers assume I go by Carlisle.

Deciding I had tortured my sister long enough, I updated her on Lori's Christmas gift then bundled myself up for the walk home. Three minutes in the cold and my face began to sting. Shielding myself with the collar of my wool coat, I walked up Seventh Avenue. Along the way, I stopped to admire the Christmas windows in the different department stores.

I was sixteen when I moved to New York City to attend a high school for performing arts. Twelve years later, I am still in awe with the city at Christmas time. My holiday excitement increased when I reached my apartment building. The door attendant informed me that my Christmas tree had arrived. I tipped him before heading upstairs. By the time I stepped off the elevator, I had convinced myself that Ryan was home. He often gives me false flight information then surprises me with an early arrival. I felt around the inside of my messenger bag for the key. When I found it, I unlocked the door and swung it open, finding a dark apartment.

Fighting off disappointment, I turned the lights on. The smell of pine needles invited me home. So did the sight of the eight-foot Douglas Fir Christmas tree nestled in the corner of my living room.

I glanced at the clock and smiled knowing Ryan was on his way home. I figured he would be hungry so I heated the oven and slid a tray of vegetable lasagna inside, along with the loaf of bread I prepared in the morning. I listened to Christmas music in the shower and sang along while applying makeup. Afterward, I slipped into the red halter dress Ryan bought me last Valentine's Day. While I strung the tree with lights, my stomach felt as though butterflies had taken flight.

This time tomorrow, Ryan and my family would be in the audience for my final performance. The show continues until June but my contract ends December 19.

Having chosen a December wedding date, I decided against renewing my contract for an additional six months. Instead, I begin rehearsals in February for a new Broadway show.

We planned to get married on December 23. Those plans changed when Ryan's mother found out. She was furious with us for planning a wedding two days before Christmas and even more furious that we didn't plan to spend the holiday with her.

Despite Nancy's objection, Ryan was against delaying the wedding. Since I didn't want to begin our married life as an enemy of his mother, I suggested we exchange vows in early December, aware Ryan had to return to work days later.

After a year of living apart, except for two weekends a month, it is going to be great having him all to myself for the next few months. We will celebrate Christmas in Pennsylvania with his family before flying to Hawaii for our long-awaited honeymoon. His parents were delighted with our arrangements. I, on the other hand, was a little apprehensive spending the next eight days with a mother-in-law who disapproves of our career choice, our living arrangements and our weight (or lack thereof).

Standing in my living room admiring the lights on the tree, I reminded myself not to dwell on the past. This was a new chapter in our lives. It would be a great Christmas. I just could not figure out what was causing the uneasy feeling in the pit of my stomach.

Chapter Two

Ryan

Thrilled the plane had finally touched down in New York, I gathered the movie script I had been reading on and off for the last six hours and placed it into my messenger bag. The last two weeks have felt like a year. The closer I got to home, the more excited I became.

Life would be perfect if we were leaving for our Hawaiian honeymoon this week rather than driving to my parents' house. I am still pissed over the drama my mother caused during the wedding planning. I thought she would be happy when my relationship with Melanie became serious, knowing Melanie is the reason I relocated from California to New York. Melanie's work schedule doesn't allow us to visit them too often, but there is no reason my parents cannot take the two-hour car ride into the city. Over the past year, we had invited them to visit a dozen times. They never came. My mother claimed it would be too difficult for her to witness us living in sin. My father was afraid to leave his car in the city overnight. Neither of them allows me to pay for a car service and they refuse to stay in a hotel. Therefore, I do not see my parents very often, which they somehow blame on Melanie.

I checked messages left on my cell phone. The first message was from my agent. She wants an answer on the two roles I am considering. I want Melanie's input before committing, especially since the role I am most interested in will film in Germany. The second message was from my mother. Not intending to return either call now, I slipped the phone into my messenger bag, threw the strap over my shoulder, stood up and stretched my long legs.

The pilot advised us the temperature in New York was twenty-two degrees, which meant I wouldn't bring attention to myself wearing my black ski hat in the terminal. During the flight, I signed autographs for passengers traveling in first class and for a few of the flight attendants. Provided the other passengers have not learned my identity, I should be in the car on my way home in ten minutes. It seems so pompous to think about such things. Since the release of *Zombie Wars*, I have no choice. Life has been strange since then.

Once the pilot permitted passengers to vacate the plane, I thanked the flight attendants and hurried down the corridor. Luckily, only a couple of photographers waited in the terminal. I promised to pose for pictures outside if they allowed me to gather my bags without causing a scene.

Keeping true to my word, I spoke with the paparazzi, signed autographs and posed for pictures. After fifteen minutes, I apologized to the crowd that had formed for not sticking around. "I haven't seen my wife since I married her. I'm sure you understand why I'm anxious to get home."

The crowd chuckled, but didn't stop thrusting paper and pens in my direction. The security guard who escorted me to the limo acted as a human wall allowing me to get into the car. The paparazzi and a growing number of fans encircled the car and continued taking pictures. The limo driver beeped his horn while inching forward until the last of the group moved out of the way.

"Do you ever get used to the craziness?" the driver asked.

"Nope. It's one part of my job I don't like."

"I've been driving famous people around for thirty years. Photographers used to take a few pictures and step aside. They're crazy nowadays."

"You can thank the internet for that," I admitted. "Pictures are more in demand now than ever before."

I settled into the backseat, removed my hat and coat then leaned my head against the headrest. It felt good knowing Melanie and I would be together for the next few months. I have not spent more than three consecutive weeks at home in over a year, which is another job aspect I don't like. My ringing cell phone shook me from my thoughts. By the time I found it in my bag, I had missed the call. There were four missed calls from my parents' number. My mother will not stop calling until she speaks to me. Before returning her calls, I dialed Melanie. The sound of her voice sent a thrill through me.

"Hey babe. My flight is delayed. It'll be a few more hours before I get home."

"Don't you dare lie to me Ryan Carlisle. I've been checking your flight information all evening."

"I'm in the limo on my way home." I laughed. "I can't wait to see you."

"I've made a delicious dinner for us."

"That sounds great."

"I'm counting the minutes. Love you."

After ending my call with Melanie, I took a deep breath, preparing myself for an unpleasant conversation with my mother

"Hi Rye."

"Hey Mom. The plane landed and I'm on my way home."

"To Pennsylvania?"

I shook my head in annoyance. "To my apartment in New York."

"Oh." She laughed.

Following an uncomfortable silence, I asked about my sister's plans. Marcy lives in Florida with her husband George and their two-year-old son Frankie. Twice a year they return to Pennsylvania to visit my parents—once in the summer and again for Christmas. When Melanie and I changed our wedding date to early December, my mother worried Marcy and her family wouldn't return for Christmas.

"They're flying in tomorrow morning and are leaving the day after Christmas. George doesn't have enough vacation time after the visit for your wedding."

"I'm happy they were able to join us for both the wedding and Christmas."

"Me too." She sighed. "I'm so excited you'll be on the East Coast for the next few months."

"So am I." The ease of our conversation caused me to wonder if she had been sipping the eggnog. "I'm almost home so... I'm going to say good night. I'll speak to you before we leave for your house."

"Bye sweetheart. Give Melanie our best."

Her last comment stunned me. She usually doesn't acknowledge Melanie during our phone calls, except for when she wants to complain about her. I hope this means her feelings toward Melanie have changed.

Slipping the phone into the breast pocket of my coat,

my finger brushed against the velvet box I placed there for safekeeping. Inside the box is a sapphire and diamond ring. Melanie fell in love with it while on a shopping trip with her sister. Jessica took a picture of the ring with her cell phone and e-mailed it to me. Unable to purchase the original ring, I called my jeweler to have it duplicated. The only difference between the ring she saw in the store and the one in my pocket was the inscription: *You are my life, my love, my everything.* The message choked me up. It is not like me to get emotional, which leads me to worry that acting has softened me.

When the limo pulled up in front of our apartment building, I realized acting has not softened my heart; it was the woman on the fourteenth floor waiting for me to come home.

I thanked the driver, gave him a generous tip and grabbed my messenger bag. The door attendant welcomed me home and offered to bring my bags upstairs. My heart exploded with excitement as I rode in the rickety elevator up fourteen floors. I could hear Christmas music coming from our apartment as I walked down the hallway. Slipping my key into the lock, I opened our apartment door. Melanie was at the sink washing dishes and singing along with the music.

The door squeaked as it closed, causing her to turn. Her blue eyes grew as wide as her smile and she ran over to me. The force of her tiny body jumping into my arms, legs wrapped around my waist, nearly sent me toppling into the wall. It took a moment or two to steady myself. Once I did, I took a few steps into the apartment and dropped my messenger bag on the floor. My arms held her in place while her lips welcomed me home.

"I've missed you so much. I have so many things planned for us tonight, but don't want to leave your arms now that you're home."

"I don't need to be entertained." I nestled my face into her neck.

Without breaking the embrace, she lowered her legs to the ground and led me toward our bedroom.

"My luggage is on its way up." I moped.

"Tell them to hold it." She unbuttoned my shirt. "We'll call for it later."

I was about to tell her it was a bad idea when she unbuttoned my jeans. At that point, I decided I would just buy new things if someone stole my belongings.

Undressing Melanie with one hand, I searched my coat pocket with the other, trying to remove my cell phone without revealing the ring box. "Hi Tom; it's Ryan Carlisle. Please hold my luggage. I'll call for it a little later."

Melanie removed the phone from my hand and tossed it on to the couch. She then slid the coat and shirt off my body, letting them fall to the ground. In response, I scooped her into my arms and carried her into our bedroom.

Chapter Three

Melanie

I love waking up in Ryan's arms. His chest is always warm against my cheek and having his arm draped over my body makes me feel secure. When he is home, I am not bothered by the strange noises my old apartment building makes or the loud sounds on the street below.

I slept soundly last night, despite the television being on. Ryan was still on west coast time and had difficulty falling asleep. I didn't want him to leave the bedroom, so I offered to let him watch TV, even though I prefer the room to be dark and silent.

I stayed in bed watching my husband sleep. Selfishly, I wanted to wake him up so we could spend every minute together before I had to leave for work. For the first time in my life, I dreaded going, which is silly considering Ryan will be in the audience. I imagined I would be sad leaving this role behind. Maybe if my contract ended last week I would be upset. Who knows, I might be sad tonight when it is over.

I mentally reviewed my to-do list, which made me fidgety. Careful not to disturb Ryan, I slid out of bed and left the room, closing the door behind me. While the coffee brewed, I removed presents from the closet and carried them to the kitchen table to wrap.

The apartment was cold, which irritated me considering the building is normally hot all winter long. Of course, the first morning Ryan is home, I'm forced to trade my T-shirt and boy shorts for an oversized robe and matching fuzzy slippers.

Tonight after the show, we will have dinner with my family. Since Jessica decided against bringing her two-year old daughter Lori along, we will exchange gifts tomorrow morning at my parents' house. While it is inconvenient for us to travel to Long Island then turn around and drive to Pennsylvania the same day, I would never refuse the opportunity to be with my family.

After high school, I performed on cruise ships. When my contract ended sixteen months later, I began working with theater companies that traveled from city-to-city. Neither job awarded me the opportunity to go home for the holidays. My mother refused to mail my presents, so we held off gift exchanges until I returned home. At that time, we held a party celebrating holidays and missed birthdays.

When I landed a stand-in role for an off-Broadway show, my family traveled to the city to celebrate holidays with me. Our celebrations took place within ten blocks of the theater just in case a performer got sick and I had to step in. They never complained about traveling to the city to be with me, nor did they mind attending holiday performances once I landed roles that didn't leave me waiting in the wings.

Ryan's family is not as accommodating. His parents have hosted Christmas Eve and Christmas Day in their house for the past thirty-five years. They are not willing to change their family tradition, especially now that they have a grandchild. I cannot fault them for not wanting to spend Christmas in New York, I just feel bad that Ryan doesn't get to see them very often.

I wrapped my Christmas gifts in candy cane paper and stacked them by family. My family's presents went under the tree so we wouldn't forget any tomorrow morning. I packed the gifts for Ryan and his family in a large box and addressed to the *Fowler family*. Ryan's real last name is Fowler. Carlisle is his stage name. He adopted the name from a distant relative on his mother's side, legally changing it a few years ago.

I cleaned up the leftover scraps of wrapping paper and then went to the kitchen to make pigs in the blanket and mozzarella sticks for my family to enjoy before the show. While I prepared the food, I downed three cups of coffee. I noticed a huge chunk of lasagna missing when I placed the appetizers in the refrigerator, and felt guilty for forgetting to feed Ryan dinner. I had been so excited to have him home that I forgot about dinner. I removed the lasagna from its tray and placed it in a plastic bowl with the intention of sending it home with my parents tonight. I would hate for it to go to waste while we are away.

Feeling a rush from the coffee, I dusted, washed and

straightened everything in my way. When I was finished cleaning, I decorated. I organized the nativity set on the tall stereo speakers, hung the quilted advent calendar between the two large windows in our apartment (the spot our wedding portrait will be hung), then placed Christmas nickknacks on the built-in shelving in the living room.

As the minutes ticked away, I stared at the tree and considered decorating it by myself. In the end I let it wait, deciding it was something Ryan and I should do together. Instead, I went into the bathroom to shower.

The hot water had the reverse effect of all the coffee I had consumed. I considered crawling back into bed when a blast of cool air shook me from my sleepy trance.

"You want company?" Ryan closed the door behind him then stripped out of his boxers.

"Come on in."

He stepped into the tub, wrapped his arms around me and leaned in for a kiss. "I was disappointed you were gone when I woke up."

"If I were able to shut my brain off, I'd still be there."

He took the soap from my hand and washed my back. "What has your brain racing this early in the morning?"

"The laundry list of things we have to do before leaving for Pennsylvania."

"Now that I'm a big star, I don't work off laundry lists." He flashed a pompous smile.

"Don't make me deflate that Hollywood head of yours, Ryan Carlisle." The teasing made me recall the conversation I had with the woman from the toy store the afternoon before. He laughed as he listened to my story, saving the hardiest laugh for her comment about wanting to attend my show just to see him.

"She's crazy. You are my absolute favorite actress."

"I'm your wife. You're supposed to say that."

"You became my favorite actress the first time I watched you perform. I fell in love with your voice and your talent before we were introduced." He kissed me again. "Your personality and beauty was just the icing on my Melanie cake."

"Melanie cake?" I wiped water from my face and shot him a shameful look. "That's very corny...even for you."

"Is it corny for me to carry you back to bed?" He kissed my neck.

"Absolutely not."

* * * *

An hour later, we were still in bed with our bodies entwined. When I shared the activities of the day with him, he groaned. "I guess staying in bed all morning is out?"

"We have to pick up the toys from the saleswoman I met yesterday."

We got up, dressed and took a cab across town to meet Carol for lunch.

She was at the table when we arrived. I entered the restaurant through the front door, while Ryan waited by the back door, out of view. I didn't tell Carol he would be joining us for fear she would bring half of New York to the restaurant with her. At the same time, I didn't want her to pass out at the sight of him.

Her mouth hung open when she learned he was joining us. Once she promised to remain calm, I sent a text inviting him to join us.

Wearing his signature ski cap and a black tweed jacket, he appeared from his hiding place. He walked in with his head lowered and his hands shoved deep into his jean pockets. To avoid a mob scene, he sat with his back to the other patrons. It often bothers me that he hides his beautiful face and hair for fear of fan reaction.

Carol shook Ryan's hand. "My granddaughter is going to scream when she finds out her old grandmother had lunch with Ryan Carlisle." She gushed.

"My niece and nephew are going to be thrilled with the toys you scored for them." He smiled.

An unenthusiastic waiter came to our table. His eyes widened in disbelief when he noticed Ryan. He scribbled our order on the pad with shaking hands. Ryan begged him not to make a big deal. When he returned several minutes later with drinks and an order of mozzarella sticks, he was more composed. We ordered lunch right away so Carol could return to work on time.

"I brought you the gerbils and some of the toys we sell for this particular item. Take whatever you'd like and I'll return the rest." She held out a large brown bag with the store emblem on each side.

Placing the bag on my lap, I checked out the toys and decided to take them all. Carol handed me a receipt for the purchase along with gift receipts. In return, I handed her cash to cover the bill plus a little extra for her time. "Thank you for getting these gifts for us."

I removed two of Ryan's headshots and a pen from my messenger bag and slid them to Ryan so he could autograph them. "I hope this will make your granddaughter happy."

"She's going to be ecstatic." Carol smiled; unaware that tomato sauce coated her teeth.

"Thank you both."

In the short time we had been in the restaurant, Ryan drew an audience. Despite his best effort to conceal his identity, six women stopped by our table with their cell phones in hand, requesting pictures.

Our lunch was enjoyable and I was appreciative of Carol's generous act, but sitting in the restaurant for over an hour left me feeling antsy. We had an appointment with our wedding photographer, still had to pack for our vacation and I wanted to decorate the Christmas tree before leaving for work. As soon as Carol finished her sandwich and Ryan freed himself from his admirers, we walked her to the store and then continued to the photographer's studio.

* * * *

It was close to three thirty when we completed our errands and returned to our apartment.

"Let's decorate the tree." Ryan offered. "I will unpack my suitcase and wash my clothing after you leave for work. You can finish packing your suitcases in the morning."

I was delighted with the plan.

We sang Christmas carols while placing ornaments on tree branches. Ryan wanted to open a bottle of wine, but I refused for fear I would get drunk. Instead, we settled on hot chocolate with marshmallows.

Decorating the tree turned out better than the image I had conjured in my head. The only disappointing part was how quickly the time passed. Before I knew it, it was time for me to leave for the theater.

After a slew of kisses, I slipped into my coat and hat. Before leaving, I gave him directions on heating the appetizers for my family's visit.

"I don't want you to go." He pulled me into his arms.

"I don't want to go either, but I have to. Besides, *you* have laundry to do."

"A nice wife would do the laundry for me."

"I guess you shouldn't have married a big-time actress then." I smirked. "I'm too famous to do your laundry." I placed a final kiss on his lips before hurrying out the door. Had I spent one minute longer in his arms, I just might have called my understudy to take my place tonight.

Chapter Four

Ryan

I spent the next two hours doing laundry, packing for our trip, and stacking Christmas boxes on the floor of the living room closet. In order to have enough time to style my hair before Melanie's family arrived, I had to take a fast shower. Although my hair usually looks as though I have just rolled out of bed, it takes a great deal of time to perfect the look. I considered a simpler hairstyle, but feared changing something as insignificant as my hair would stall my career.

When the doorman called to announce the arrival of Melanie's family, I tossed the appetizers into the oven.

"Ryan!" Melanie's Mom, Diane, hugged me. "How are you darling? It's so good to see you."

"I'm good. Happy to be home."

Aside from the dark hair Melanie has been sporting for her current role, she and her mother look very similar. Both women have brilliant blue eyes that sparkle when they are happy and round faces marked with deep dimples.

Melanie's father, Phillip, is a broad man who stands several inches shorter than my six-foot frame. He has been a high school baseball coach for twenty-three years and likes to remind me that he is as fit as the kids on his team and can kick my ass if need be. Melanie assures me his comments are in jest, but I'm not so sure.

"How's Hollywood treating you?" Phillip shook my hand.

"Good. Scripts are still coming in."

"I thought you were booked for the next few years?"

"My movies are consistently coming out over the next three years however; there is room in my schedule to film more." I explained while hanging their coats in the closet.

"I hope you'll pick movies that film on the East Coast."

Diane raised an eyebrow at me. "My daughter misses you when you're away."

I decided not to tell them about the movie I was considering and was relieved when the doorman interrupted the conversation to announce Jessica and Lewis' arrival.

"Parking in the city sucks," Lewis complained the moment he entered the apartment. "Hey Ryan."

Jessica greeted me with a hug.

"Something smells good," she said.

"Thanks for reminding me. Melanie keeps calling to make sure I cook the appetizers properly. She'll kill me if I burn them."

I invited my guests to take a seat in the living room while I fetched the appetizers. Lewis followed me offering to make drinks. Despite my galley kitchen being too tight for us to work in together, I am grateful for the help.

"How was Melanie feeling when she left for the theater?" Diane asked.

"She's excited for us to begin our vacation. I just hope my crazy life doesn't ruin her vision of what our marriage should be."

"I think the paparazzi gave her a sneak preview of your future together." Phillip reached for a mozzarella stick from the serving tray. "Did she tell you a squad car rescued her from a group of photographers yesterday?"

"No," I groaned. "I swear I'm going to murder one of those people."

"She wasn't upset or hurt," he assured me.

Jessica attempted to make light of Melanie's ordeal. "She thought for sure her picture in the back of the police car would have been in the paper today."

"I didn't tell you that story to upset you," Phillip added. "After the fact, Melanie thought it was funny."

"I don't like her being harassed. They're forcing me to hire security to escort her around."

"She will *not* like that," Lewis warned while delivering drinks to Diane and Phillip. "Why don't you hire a limo service to drive her instead?"

"That's not going to thrill her either." Phillip laughed. "My daughter loves walking around the city. She refuses to accept her new-found fame."

I was unable to share their humor in this situation.

Lewis returned from the kitchen a second time balancing three drinks in his hand: a white wine for Jessica, a scotch and soda for me and something for himself. Guessing from the dark liquid in his glass, he was drinking his usual Jack and coke. In an attempt to diminish the anger building inside of me, I swallowed my drink in one gulp.

* * * *

Two hours later, we were in the theater awaiting the show to begin. It took most of the first act for me to calm down. It was not until intermission that my anger subsided and that was only because hunger pushed it aside. Now I understand why Melanie made such a big deal over the appetizers. Without them, I would be famished. Her family used the break to run to the restroom. While they were gone, I slipped backstage to visit with Melanie and the cast.

"The show is great baby." I presented her with a bouquet of roses I bought on the way to the theater.

"One more hour and our vacation will begin. I can't wait." She beamed.

"Enjoy the rest of your show. You're going to miss it when it's over."

"Probably...but I'm going to love every minute spent with you." She threw her arms around my neck and kissed me on the mouth. When the kiss ended, my lips felt sticky. I removed the substance with my fingers and groaned when I saw red lipstick. "I hate wearing makeup when I'm not working."

"That comment would be very disturbing to most wives."

"I guess I'm lucky to have such an understanding wife." I kissed the bridge of her nose.

Blinking lights indicated the second half of the show was about to begin. On the way back to my seat, a few people approached me for an autograph. Out of respect of the performers, I refused to sign anything, but promised to make myself available after the show.

Phillip tossed me a bag of chocolate covered peanuts when I sat down. "We were a little hungry and figured you might be too."

After the show ended, Melanie sent a text letting me know she would be ready in thirty minutes. Since I promised to sign autographs outside, I invited her family to go ahead to the restaurant. The fact they didn't argue told me they were hungry too.

"Why don't you join my family?" Melanie suggested when I passed her backstage on my way out of the theater.

"Not without you," I responded. "I'll meet you outside."

A long line formed outside the stage doors. Based on the number of people waiting, it was safe to assume news of my presence spread to passersby. Much to my dismay the paparazzi was also waiting. I don't know why this surprised me. To be fair to the people I offered an autograph to earlier, I invited anyone with a playbill to come to the front of the line.

The lightweight tweed jacket I wore didn't provide relief from the frigid temperature. My teeth chattered and my handwriting was shaky. I decided to end the autograph session once Melanie materialized, but realized she had her own fans. I scolded myself for thinking she would walk out of the theater without a single person asking for her signature. It disgusted me for thinking, even for a second, that I was more important than her.

An elderly couple knocked me off my pedestal moments later. After waiting in line for an autograph, they expressed annoyance when they found out I was not one of the performers from the show. To appease them, I asked Melanie to sign their playbill.

Melanie and I stood back-to-back signing autographs when another wave of hunger washed over me. I asked the security guard, sent by theater management, to close my line. After signing the final autograph, I turned and wrapped my arms around Melanie's waist. "Are you almost ready for dinner? I'm starving."

"Me too." She peeked around the couple standing in front of her to survey the line. "There are only a few more people waiting, let me finish these last few autographs then we'll get going."

She didn't appear to be as chilly as I was, but I figured she was still on a high from her performance. I signed a few more autographs and posed for pictures while I waited for her. When other performers materialized from the theater, we waved to the crowd and hurried into an awaiting SUV.

"What's that?" I pointed to an envelope in her hand.

"A fan slipped it to me." She grinned. "It may be my first love letter."

"Open it. I want to know who my competition is."

"No one could replace you." She leaned in for a kiss. "I am thinking this person *could* keep me entertained while you're away."

"Ha ha."

"I'm sorry to interrupt," the driver said. "There's a large crowd outside the restaurant. Looks like photographers. What do you want me to do?"

Dozens of paparazzi were huddled on the sidewalk awaiting our arrival. How they knew where we were dining was beyond me, although it wouldn't be below them to have followed Melanie's family.

"I don't know any other way into the restaurant. We'll have to fight through the crowd."

Bright flashbulbs blinded us the moment the car door opened. To make matters worse, photographers blocked the restaurant door, preventing us from passing.

"I spoke to you yesterday when I was in the airport and chatted with you outside the theater a few moments ago, now I'm asking that you give us some space."

"Melanie, how does it feel to be out of work?"

I got in one photographer's face. "I think one of you asked that question yesterday, right before the cops came to rescue her."

"That's not how it went down. We just happened to be sitting outside the theater."

"You just happened to be sitting there?" I pointed my finger in his face. "Back off."

The photographer held his hands up as if he was surrendering to me and stepped aside. I heard the men mumbling about my attitude as we entered the restaurant.

"Your show was wonderful, darling." Diane hugged Melanie as she made her way around the table to greet her family members. "I'm going to miss that character. She's been a part of our family for so long."

"I think I've spent more time with you in character than I've spent with the real Melanie in the past six months," Jessica added.

"I can spend more time visiting with you now that I'm on vacation." Melanie reached across the table for the bottle of red wine and poured us each a glass. "I'm so hungry. I can't wait for the day my stomach stops doing nervous flip flops and

I can eat something substantial before going on stage."

"You know the role backward and forward. Why would you be nervous?" Lewis asked, rubbing his shaved head.

"I'm afraid I'll have to go to the bathroom in the middle of the show." She chuckled.

"I felt that way the first week Lori started nursery school," Jessica admitted. "My stomach would twist and turn the whole time she was gone. The moment I picked her up, I felt better. It's funny how nerves can mess up our whole body."

"Are we almost finished with the bathroom conversation?" Lewis asked with a good-humored eye roll behind his thick glasses.

"We are," Phillip answered. "I'd like to congratulate my daughter on a successful Broadway run." He lifted his glass. "May you have many fulfilling roles."

"Thank you. I have enjoyed every moment of my time with this show. It beats waiting in the wings for one of the actors to puke so I could take over."

Lewis rolled his head around his shoulders in response to Melanie's last comment.

There was a lull in the conversation when dinner arrived. Melanie was the only person not devouring her food, which surprised me considering she just admitted she was hungry. I followed her gaze to a tall, blond-headed man standing by the bar.

"Is that your boyfriend?" I teased.

She shook her head. "He's been hanging around the theater. Now he's here tonight. The situation creeps me out."

"He's probably paparazzi. I'll check it out."

Her family was enthralled in their dinner until I stood up to leave the table. The scrapping of my chair against the ceramic tile knocked them out of their eating stupor. Phillip's face burned when Melanie shared the story. He joined me in speaking with the man.

* * * *

"What did you say to him?" Diane asked when we returned.

"He left the bar, disappearing into the crowd of photographers before we could reach him. It would have been stupid of us to go outside into that mess," I told her.

"I hoped to get his name from a credit card slip or

something." Phillip shrugged. "The bartender told me he paid cash for his drink. No one knew his name."

"Maybe we should call the police," Diane suggested.

"Do you know for sure it's the same guy?" Lewis asked.

Melanie shrugged. "I'm pretty sure."

"Could he be paparazzi?" Lewis asked.

"I have never seen him with camera equipment."

"Has he ever approached you?" Jessica asked.

Melanie shook her head. "He hasn't done anything more than stand across the street from the theater and stare."

"Based on the stories you tell us about the paparazzi harassing you after work, it's no wonder he stares. I'm sure the ordeal each day is entertainment for him." Jessica removed her glasses and cleaned them with her cloth napkin.

Melanie considered this option.

"Is there a possibility he works on the block?" Jessica asked. "He may take a cigarette break the same time each day."

"What are the chances of him showing up here tonight?" Diane asked. "It scares me."

Jessica ignored Diane's question. "Have you received any strange items in the mail or has anything been left for you at work?"

"No."

"Any strange or threatening phone calls to your house? Any hang up calls?"

"No."

"He hasn't broken any laws. The police are not going to arrest a man for standing on the streets of Manhattan." Jessica told us in her lawyer tone.

"What about him showing up tonight?" Diane asked again.

"This restaurant is only a few blocks from the theater. It isn't too much of a coincidence—at least not from a legal standpoint."

"You should keep a record of each time this guy shows up—whether it be the theater, the store or a restaurant," Lewis advised.

I put an arm around Melanie's shoulders and gave her a reassuring squeeze. "Try to relax. He's gone now."

"Why don't you guys come to our house tonight rather than waiting until morning?" Diane suggested.

"I'm not done packing," Melanie told her. "I'd much rather

get a good night's sleep in my own bed and drive out tomorrow morning."

"I thought you could use a night away from the city and the craziness." She stuck her bottom lip out like a spoiled child.

Melanie gave her mother a pleading look. "I'd like to keep the plans we've already made."

Diane sulked.

No one was interested in dessert, so Phillip requested the bill. I excused myself under the pretense of going to the restroom, when in fact I wanted to settle the bill before anyone was the wiser. Of course, when Phillip learned what I had done, he was upset and I spent the next five minutes refusing the cash he thrusts in my direction.

In an effort to avoid the crowd of photographers gathered by the front entrance, we left through the back door and slipped into an awaiting SUV. Together we drove to the parking garage to retrieve Lewis' car. Once the family settled inside and Lewis drove away, we headed home to our apartment.

After a short but good night sleep, we woke at dawn and finished packing. Afterward, I waited in the lobby for our rental car to arrive.

We had an insane amount of luggage to stuff into the midsized car. Between the gifts for Melanie's family, five suitcases and a bag of shoes, I began to wonder if there would be room for Melanie.

I did the best possible job cramming everything into the car when Melanie appeared with three additional bags filled with makeup and toiletries.

* * * *

Driving in the city has always been stressful for me. Honking horns and aggressive cab drivers stress me out. Today was no different. I cannot tolerate tailgaters, especially since pedestrians tend to dart across the street against the light. I was unable to relax until after we crossed the bridge and were traveling on the Cross Island Parkway en route to the Southern State.

"What would you think about moving to Long Island?" I asked.

"Can you imagine my commute every day?" Melanie laughed at the idea.

"That guy in the restaurant last night freaked you out." I glanced in her direction. "Don't even get me started on the fiasco outside the theater the other day. I was just thinking a move out of the city might make us both feel more comfortable."

"You don't think the paparazzi can afford the bridge toll?"

I laughed. "I just think the suburbs would afford us more privacy."

"I'm happy in the city. Don't you like it?"

"I am a country boy at heart but I do enjoy the city. I was just thinking it would be nice to own a house in the suburbs. We could have a large backyard with a pool and maybe a tennis court."

"You have never mentioned wanting to move out of the city before. What's going on?"

"Nothing is going on. I was just thinking how nice it would be to have some privacy. I'm not looking to relocate."

She settled back into her seat appearing to be satisfied with my answer. The tension no sooner left my shoulders, and then she brought up another uncomfortable topic. "I read the scripts you sent me. I think the army film is perfect for you but...any idea where you'll be filming?"

"Germany," I admitted.

"Oh."

"Filming overseas prevents me from jumping at the opportunity. That and going from leading man to a supporting role."

She shrugged. "I like the character in the supporting role better than the lead."

"I thought it would be fun to play a nasty character for once."

"I think the supporting character has potential to be an award-winning role. I wouldn't want you to miss out on that opportunity to play someone mean."

"Considering I haven't been asked to audition for the lead, it's a decision I do not have to agonize over."

She took a deep breath and exhaled. "I think you should call your agent and let her know you're interested."

"I don't know that I am." I exited the Southern State and circled the ramp leading to South Peninsula Boulevard.

"You are. You're just letting the location scare you."

"What did you think about the love story? Most of the

filming would take place in Connecticut."

"That script stinks. It would be selfish of me to talk you into that role."

I took her hand in mine. "If I get the army film, I'll be home less than I am now. I'm not happy about that."

"By the beginning of August I'll have accumulated at least seven vacation days. I'll spend a week with you in Germany. If you're lucky I'll give you some acting tips." When I looked in her direction, she burst out laughing.

I smiled even though the conversation had brought my mood down.

Chapter Five

Melanie

Ryan had grown quiet by the time we arrived to my parents' stone-sided colonial home. He was not very talkative during brunch either. Jessica and Lewis *did* spend a good part of the meal bickering back and forth. Their argument began when Lewis commented on how relaxing it must be for Ryan to get away for months at a time. Jessica invited Lewis to pack his bags and take a first-class trip to California off the end of her foot. Needless to say, lunch was awkward.

Afterward, my mother, sister and I cleaned the dining room. The men and Lori retired to the living room to watch a football game my father recorded the night before. With each hoot and holler, my mother warned the men not to get too involved in the game, reminding them that we would be opening Christmas gifts shortly.

When I joined the others in the living room, I noticed Ryan was still not himself. He has never been a fan of football, much to my father's dismay, but he knew enough about the sport to fake interest. Lewis and Dad were on the edge of their seats waiting for their favorite team to score, while pleading with their wives to hold off gift exchange for another three minutes. Ryan was sitting in a blue armchair in the corner of the living room staring out the window.

Each time my father and Lewis leaped up for a game play then dropped back down onto the leather sectional sofa, the legs scuffed my mother's beloved cherry wood floor. I knew this would anger my mother, so I discretely pointed the scratches out to my father on the way over to Ryan.

"Are you okay?" I dropped onto Ryan's lap.

"I'm tired."

I raised an eyebrow recalling our lovemaking late into the night. "Why don't you take a nap after we open gifts?"

"I'm fine," he growled.

"If you don't get a smile on your face, I'm going to call my backup guy."

"Who?"

"The guy who wrote me that note." I realized I never did get the chance to read it—thanks to the paparazzi. "Speaking of my secret admirer, I wonder what I did with that letter."

"I don't remember seeing it after we got out of the car."

"I finally get fan mail and it's lost before I even had a chance to read it."

I pouted.

My mother entered the room, prompting Ryan to nudge me off his lap. After years of saving money, my parents redecorated their house this past summer. My mother has since become obsessed with keeping her house in pristine condition. What she doesn't realize is how uncomfortable her guests feel when they visit.

Dad turned the television off after receiving a nasty look from my mother. I fetched a chair from the dining room and nestled it between Ryan and the Christmas tree.

The next thirty minutes were spent exchanging gifts with one another. My family prefers to open one gift at a time so we can watch the expression on our loved-ones' faces. For the most part, the Christmas celebration was a success. I loved the boots from my parents and the sweater my sister bought.

Ryan and I bought Lewis a new leather jacket. We also purchased him a watch that turned out to be the same watch I bought for his birthday three years ago. We gave him the cash value and offered to return it to the store. My father was pleased with the pajamas, the dress shirts and the bookstore gift certificate we bought him, but the Major League Baseball season tickets were his favorite. Thrilled with the response from my father, I couldn't wait for my mother and sister to open their gifts.

"That's a very nice gift, Melanie and Ryan." My mother was less than thrilled with her gift certificate.

"You and Jessica have talked about a spa weekend for years now. I thought you'd be thrilled."

Jessica's uneasy gaze shifted from our mother to Ryan and then to me.

Realizing Jessica was most likely concerned about leaving Lori for the spa weekend, I told her that Ryan and I would baby sit for Lori while she was away. That information did nothing to appease her.

I was feeling a mixture of annoyance and confusion by their reaction to the gift. Hoping for a better response from Lori, I fetched her present.

Lori shredded the festive gift-wrap and squealed in delight with the gerbil pet and its accessories. Out of the corner of my eye, I caught sight of my mother leaving the room. I considered following her, but anger held me in my seat. Besides, I was trying to enjoy Lori's reaction to her new toys. Ryan squeezed my shoulder when he noticed a tear escape from the corner of my eye.

My hands shook with anger as I gathered the gifts Ryan and I received from my family. Ryan took the packages to the car and encouraged me to speak with my mother. I found her in the kitchen emptying the dishwasher.

"What happened back there, Mom?"

She turned, leaned her hip against the kitchen counter, and let out a long sigh. "Your gifts are generous, but you know we don't spend that kind of money on one another." She paused. "We agreed after your father's birthday that our gifts wouldn't exceed a certain dollar amount."

Ryan and I enrolled my father in a two-day, race car-driving course for his birthday. While my father was thrilled with the gift, my mother demanded we get our money back. She had looked into buying the same gift a few years earlier, but decided it was more money than she could afford. Lucky for my father, it was a non-refundable program. I think he would have cried if we canceled his reservation.

"When I first started acting, I accepted generous gifts from each of you, knowing I could not return the gesture." I bit my lip. "You told me it was the thought that counted rather than the price tag. Why can't it be that way now that the tables are turned?"

"Because I am the parent and you are my child."

"Don't you think it would be selfish of me not to lavish you with gifts now that Ryan and I are doing well?"

"I am thrilled you and Ryan make a healthy living doing something you enjoy." She walked over to me and pinched my chin between her thumb and pointer finger. "You are a young couple just starting out. I want you to save your money and use it to build your life together. Dad and I appreciate the thoughtful gifts you buy, but we'd rather you stay within the price range we have all agreed upon."

"Can we take you away on vacation every once in a while?"

"As long as the trip is within the gift budget."

I rolled my eyes. "Are you going to use the spa weekend?"

She nodded. "As long as you will join us."

"I did promise to baby-sit."

"I'm sure Lewis' Mom will baby-sit. It would be fun for the three of us to enjoy the spa weekend together."

"Ryan has to travel to California one weekend in January. Let's schedule it for when he's gone."

"I will make you a reservation." She kissed my cheek. "Speaking of Ryan," she began. "I don't think he liked the sports jacket we bought him."

"I don't think it's the jacket, Mom." I stood and slid the stool under the island. "He has a lot on his mind."

"He seemed all right yesterday. What's going on?"

"Between the paparazzi harassing me and the man who showed up at the restaurant last night..."

"I'm upset about that too." She interrupted.

I acknowledged her concern by nodding. "He also has to make a decision about a movie role he's been offered. It's proving more difficult than he thought."

My mother made a face. "I hope he works everything out before you leave for your honeymoon. You both deserve to relax."

She hugged me.

Ryan joined us in the kitchen. "We'd better get moving if you're going to get your hair done before our trip."

"Pennsylvania is expecting snow today," Mom told Ryan. "Do either of you know how to drive in the snow?"

Ryan laughed at her question. "Have you forgotten that I grew up in Pennsylvania? Six inches of snow is nothing there."

Since we didn't plan to return after my hair appointment, I spent the next few minutes talking with my father and brother-in-law. I thanked them both for our gifts, apologized to Lewis for the duplicate present and scooped Lori into my arms, smothering her face with kisses. We discussed Santa's upcoming visit and I listened to the list of gifts she hoped he would bring.

My mother and sister followed us to the salon so we could spend more time together. Lewis had to return to work, so my father agreed to look after Lori as long as he could continue watching the football game.

Ryan dropped me off in front of the salon. Rather than join me inside, he remained in the car reading the newspaper.

My mother and sister looked through the wedding proofs while Miguel stripped my dark hair and applied a lighter shade.

Two hours later, my hair was colored and styled. My sister, mother and I kissed and hugged one another goodbye at least four times. After they drove away, I sat in the rental car admiring my curly, light-ash-blond hair in the mirror.

"Your diva is showing." Ryan teased as we pulled away from the curb. "I don't remember you being so vain when we first met."

"When you're married to one of America's most handsome men, you have no choice but to worry about your looks." I continued to finger-style my hair in the mirror before flipping the visor shut. "Besides, a husband should never be more beautiful than his wife."

"You're crazy. I was smitten with you the moment I met you."

"You always say it was my talent that mesmerized you. You can't change the story now."

"Correction my dear," he waved his long, slender finger in the air. "I was mesmerized by your voice the moment you walked on stage that night. When we met after the show, your beauty astounded me. You cannot deny I have said that."

"I *have* heard you say it a few times." I couldn't help but notice his mood remained melancholy. "What's going on with you today?"

"Hum?"

"Something's bothering you. What is it?"

He shrugged his shoulders. "I feel like everyone is pressuring me into taking the job in Germany. I don't know that I want it any more than I want the romantic comedy."

"We established the romantic comedy is out because the script is horrible."

"Not to mention all of the nudity," he added. "You know how I feel about that."

I did. He didn't believe in stripping down for movies, regardless of the dollar amount attached. Four years ago this belief cost him a part in a movie that turned into a blockbuster hit. Despite Ryan being at the lowest point of his career and completely broke, he was at peace with his decision to turn the role down.

"The war film means I'll be in Germany for months. I don't want to be that far away from you. Why am I the only one bothered by that?"

His comment stung. "That was not a nice thing to say Ryan. You know how depressed I feel when you're away. The thought of you living in another country sickens me. That doesn't give me the right to stifle your career by asking you to pass on the opportunity."

"My gut tells me if we continue spending time apart, it will eventually hurt our marriage."

"I'd be lying if I didn't admit it scares me too," I confessed.

He lifted my hand to his mouth and kissed it. "I consider giving up acting everyday just so we can be together. The only thing stopping me is my fear of not being able to support you any other way."

"There is also the chance you'll regret that decision one day. You are Hollywood's hottest commodity. You would be a fool not to ride its coattails. We just need to spend our time together wisely." I pulled my seat belt away from my chest and stretched across the console to kiss him.

A sharp pain just below my ribcage caused me to withdraw. I unfastened my seat belt to investigate the pain and found the envelope I received the night before in a pocket on the inside of my coat.

"My love note," I exclaimed and tore it open. I reached inside and removed a piece of paper wrapped around a small piece of satin. I unfolded the material revealing a pair of thong underwear. "Gross." I tossed them on the floor and opened the attached note. *Would you model these for me? I pay very well.*

Ryan laughed. "Your first pair of underwear. Do you plan on saving them?"

"It isn't funny, Ryan." Tears streamed down my cheeks. The thought of Jack Boucher slithering back into my life horrified me.

"Why are you crying?"

"This gift is upsetting."

"I get crazy fan gifts all of the time."

"This is different." I continued to sob. *Ryan had no idea*

what Jack did to my friends and me. I hoped he would never find out. If this package were from Jack, Ryan and my family would find out what I had done. The thought terrified me.

"Baby," He kissed my fingers. "I know the changes in our life are crazy. Please don't let it upset you. I have received at least ten pairs of women's underwear and even a few pairs of underwear from men. I get all kinds of crazy things in the mail. At first, it freaked me out too. Now I know it's part of the job."

The muscles in my chest and shoulders relaxed. A week ago, I would have been horrified to learn that women mail my husband their underwear. Under the current circumstances, I was relieved. Maybe the gift *was* innocent; at least I prayed that was the case.

We sat in silence for several long miles. Unable to stand the silence or the thoughts in my head any longer, I turned the radio on and listened to Christmas music. During commercials, Ryan and I played the license plate game and told jokes. Before long, I was in a better mood.

My parents called every thirty minutes asking for a weather report and to make sure we were safe. Ryan's family called once to notify us that the snowfall was heavy by their house and suggested we spend the night in a hotel. We were only thirty miles away when the call came in. Ryan was tempted to lie about our location and spend the night in a hotel, but informed his father we were nearby and asked him to have drinks ready for our arrival.

"My parents must have lost faith in my driving if they're suggesting we pull over because of the weather. I walked to school in five inches of snow when I was a kid. Now they're worried."

"I guess they're afraid the California sun has dried up your ability to drive in bad weather." I teased.

When we exited Interstate 80, I asked to stop at the supermarket to buy a few items. Once inside the store, I set out to find an apple pie. When my search came up empty, I called Ryan on his cell phone looking for another idea.

He joined me in the store hidden beneath his hat and the collar of his coat. While I understood his need to shield his face from the other shoppers, I thought the disguise made him stand out more—if not as a celebrity, then a criminal. He laughed when I shared my thoughts.

We decided on a banana-cream pie smothered in whipped cream. I included a case of water to our shopping cart, remembering that Ryan's parents drink faucet water. Ryan assured me it was safe to drink water from the faucet, but I cannot get used to the idea. We also bought fruit, low-fat yogurt, seltzer water, a case of beer and a box of cookies Ryan claimed were calling his name from the shelf.

"Your parents won't be insulted that we're bringing our own groceries will they?"

"They didn't ask me what we like to eat." He rubbed my shoulders as we waited in line to check out. "You need to relax. We're going to have a great visit."

I want to believe him but something in his tone is less than convincing.

Chapter Six

Ryan

We drove up the winding road leading to my childhood home. The twinkling lights that framed the white, ranch-style house, its windows and front door gave a festive look to the place. The old-fashioned light bulbs were in perfect alignment thanks to the time my father gave to the project. I paused for a moment to admire the large pine tree in the front yard blanketed in colorful lights. It evoked memories from my childhood. I helped my father decorate the bottom of the tree when I was young. When I reached my teenage years, my father handed me a ladder and told me to decorate the whole tree.

As a kid, I wanted to help my father decorate the roof and the front of the house, but my mother wouldn't allow it, claiming I would get hurt. I have often wondered if the real reason they wouldn't allow me to help, was my haphazard decorating practices. Several times I spied my father re-arranging the lights after I hung them on the bushes. Despite my father's obsessive-compulsive behavior, I have fond memories.

Melanie opened the car door. I stopped her before she got out. Cupping her cheek with my hand, I guided her face in for a kiss. "Thank you for talking me into coming home for Christmas."

Beyond the colorful lights, my mother stood in the doorway waving us in. "Are you going to get out of the car today? We're having appetizers."

The smell of cigarette smoke was a telltale sign that my brother-in-law was smoking again. I do not know why my parents permit him to smoke in the house.

"I hope the drive wasn't too bad for you." My mother threw her arms around my neck, squeezing me. Her dark hair returned to a salt-and-pepper color in just a matter of weeks.

"Not bad at all. The Interstate was empty. We just drove a

little slower." I ended the embrace with my mother and greeted my sister Marcy with a hug.

"How long was the ride?" George crushed his cigarette into a nearby ashtray before shaking my hand and kissing Melanie.

"It took us a little over four hours, but we left from Long Island, which adds another forty-five minutes to the ride." Melanie held her coat outside the door, shaking snow from it.

"Let's get out of the foyer and go back into the living room." My mother instructed everyone.

My father took our coats and rattled off a few drink options. Melanie chose a glass of white wine and I requested a beer.

"I guess there won't be any baby news this visit." My Mother sat down in a beat-up armchair by the fireplace.

"I don't know, Mom?" I turned to my sister. "Marcy, do you have any baby news you'd like to share with us?"

"No Ryan, I don't." She laughed. "How about you?"

I rested my arm on the back of the couch stroking Melanie's shoulder with my fingers. "We've only been married for two weeks. Even I can't work that fast."

"It's not like you haven't lived together for the two years prior to your *winter* wedding." My mother shot a disapproving look our way. "Your father and I wouldn't have dreamed of living together before marriage."

I felt Melanie tense.

"I could have followed your way of thinking only I would have been living in a cardboard box."

"Ryan, you weren't hard up when you met Melanie. You could have rented an apartment. Or even better you could have come home to Pennsylvania."

"Coming back to Pennsylvania was never an option." My comment did exactly what I intended it to do—hurt my mother's feelings.

I lifted Frankie onto my lap and asked him to show me the dinosaur he was playing with. Melanie smiled at him and waved, but didn't attempt to touch him. She learned during their visit to New York that Frankie needed time to warm up to new people.

"You used to come home before you and Melanie met," my father added, much to my surprise. He normally avoided the bickering between my mother and me.

I do not want to spend the week fighting with my parents. The way I see it, the only way we will get through the week without killing one another is by steering negative conversations into another direction, which is what I decided to do.

"No tree, huh? Does this mean I haven't missed chopping our Christmas tree down?"

"I know how much you enjoy finding our Christmas tree, son." My father handed Melanie a glass of wine and me a cold beer. "We've been waiting for you. If it doesn't snow too badly tonight, we'll go in the morning."

I waved my hand to dismiss the thought of snow stopping us. "No matter what, I wanna go. Give me a blanket and a saw and we *will* have our Christmas tree tomorrow." I turned to Melanie. "Once you cut down your own Christmas tree, you'll never want to buy from a corner tree salesperson again." I was excited to share this tradition with her.

"Where do you get your tree, Melanie?" George smoothed his mustache and dark goatee.

"I buy it from a tree lot set up on the street. I used to drag the tree back to my apartment leaving a trail of pine needles from the lot to my living room." She laughed. "Then I would decorate what was left of the tree. This is the first year the tree was delivered in one piece."

"If it isn't too cold we'll all go," my mother added. "I just don't want Frankie to get sick. His Florida blood may not be used to Pennsylvania weather."

"Melanie, if this is something you're not into, you can stay home with Frankie." Marcy offered.

"Did you just hear how excited I am for Melanie to join us?" I snapped at her. "Why would my wife want to stay home to watch *your* son?"

"I'm sorry. She just didn't seem interested. I...I thought I was doing her a favor."

"You're in for a treat Melanie," George scoffed. "When I say a treat, I'm being sarcastic. You are in for frozen toes, cold hands, and hours of looking at trees that are identical to one another. After an hour of searching for the perfect tree, they always decide to buy the first tree they looked at."

"Shut up George." Marcy punched him in the arm then whined when one of her long, manicured nails bent the wrong way. "You're from Florida and grew up with aluminum Christmas trees. What do you know about Christmas?"

"I know enough to stay home tomorrow." George took a swig of beer. "I'll stay with Frankie."

"We make a big production out of decorating our Christmas tree, Melanie," Marcy explained, still examining her damaged nail. "We play Christmas music, string popcorn for the tree and get drunk on eggnog. Decorating the tree has always been special for us."

"It's the only time these two chose staying home over going out with friends." My mother thumbed her nail at Marcy and then me. "We all love decorating the tree."

"Speak for yourself," George interrupted. "I can live without the tree decorating ceremony too."

Marcy punched George again.

"Before your sister beats her husband to a pulp, bring your luggage in from the car." My mother directed. "Dave and George, please help Ryan with his luggage while Marcy and I get dinner on the table."

"I'll help you, Ryan," Melanie offered.

"No you won't," My mother told her. "There are three men in this house to carry those heavy bags. You finish your wine and relax."

"You're not wearing the most sensible shoes for this weather." Marcy commented on the high-heeled boots peeking out from beneath Melanie's dress pants. "The last thing you need is to be laid up with a broken ankle."

"Those heels must be three inches high." George leaned down to examine her shoes. "How do you walk in them?"

"Years of practice." She laughed. "I've always hated being so much shorter than the rest of the world. As soon as my mother permitted me to, I wore heels. I gradually went from a small heel to a high one."

"You hate being the shortest person in a room yet you married a guy who is over six feet tall." George laughed. "I would have thought you'd be on the prowl for some short guy."

"That's why I wear three inch heels in the snow." Melanie chuckled. "If no one minds, I'm going to call my parents to let them know we've arrived safely. Then, I'll join you in the kitchen to put our groceries away."

George, my father and I paraded up the stairs with suitcases from the trunk of our rental car. All of the suitcases were heavy, but my father wound up with the heaviest one in the group. "What the hell did your wife pack in here?"

I shrugged and rolled my eyes as if I was agreeing that my wife packs too many things. Truthfully, he carried my suitcase and there were fourteen pairs of pants, twenty T-shirts, five sweaters, ten pairs of pajama bottoms, a bathrobe, slippers and four pairs of shoes inside. I know if I admitted it was my suitcase, I would never hear the end of it.

"What happened to my bedroom?" The floral wallpaper and pink rug horrified me.

"A bedroom belongs to those who reside in the house. Once you stopped coming home, it became a guest room. We redecorated last summer." Carrying the luggage upstairs winded my father. He sat down on the bed and rubbed his round belly with his hand.

"I never stopped coming home." I reminded him. "I moved out. Since we are on the topic, would you ask Mom to lay off Melanie while we're here? Her big complaint is that we don't come around. Well, we're here so maybe she can try to make this an enjoyable visit."

George did his best to avoid arguments—probably because his marriage was eighty-five percent drama. Sensing our conversation was about to grow serious, he excused himself leaving my father and me alone.

"She only gives you a hard time because she misses you."

"She must miss Melanie too." I pursed my lips together.

"Melanie's complained?" I am undecided if the redness forming across his cheeks is embarrassment or anger.

"She's never once complained to me about any of you." I'm honest. "She's so tense when Mom is around. It's obvious she feels the resentment Mom harbors toward her."

"Your Mother harbors no resentment. Melanie is a nice girl. Not the girl your mother would have picked for you, but she's still a nice girl."

I made a face.

"I'll speak to your mother." After taking a deep breath, he stood, slid his thick arm around my neck and guided me downstairs to the dining room. The table was set with my mother's best china. In the center of the table was a spiral ham, sweet potatoes and carrots.

"We brought our wedding proofs." I announced while taking a piece of ham off the platter.

"I can get them from my bag after dinner." Melanie offered. "I'm hoping you'll be able to pick pictures for your parent album this week, along with any portraits you'd like to order."

"With Christmas a few days away, I don't know..." My mother paused when Dad raised his eyebrows at her. "I'll do my best to look over the pictures a few times before you leave."

"Thank you." Melanie smiled either oblivious of the nasty response she almost received or choosing to ignore it. "I still have to pick the pictures for our wedding album. There are so many beautiful pictures of your son. I'm having a difficult time eliminating some."

"I have to ask you something, Melanie." Marcy slid a piece of ham into her mouth and pointed the fork in Melanie's direction. "You had dark hair at the rehearsal dinner. Your hair was blond on your wedding day. A few days ago, I came across a picture of you on the internet and your hair was dark. Today you're blond. How is it possible that you have changed your hair color four times in a matter of weeks?"

"Hollywood." Melanie laughed. "Even though I absolutely hate wearing wigs, I wore one the day of our wedding. Earlier today I had my hair colored blond, ridding myself of the brown hair for good."

"Why would you wear a wig on your wedding day?" George asked.

"I wanted the pictures to be of *me* rather than my character. My friend found a beautiful wig made with real hair that matched my texture and color."

"I didn't know it was a wig until she took it off that night," I teased. "I freaked when she pulled it off her head."

My family chuckled.

"It doesn't bother you coming home to a wife who changes her appearance with each role?" my mother asked.

"My appearance changes more often than Melanie's." I turned my attention to Marcy. "To answer your next question, my hair was completely natural the day of our wedding." I shook my hair in Marcy's face.

"Get your sloppy hair out of my face." Marcy pushed me away. "I don't know what America finds so appealing about that hair of yours."

"You're just jealous." I lifted a strand of her long, dark hair then released it pretending to be disgusted.

"Stop playing with hair at my dinner table, you two." My mother shook her head in disgust.

"Frankie is behaving better than both of you."

My dark-haired nephew smiled as if he were gloating.

"I just thought of something," Melanie's eyes widen. "Will you have to shave your head for that army movie?"

"I imagine so." I considered this. "It'll be weird. I'll have to add that to the list of reasons why I should turn the role down."

"We'd probably save money if you shaved your head." Melanie laughed.

"Lucky for me, Marcy has no reason to spend money on her hair," George added. "She sits home all day taking care of Frankie."

It came as no surprise to anyone when Marcy reached across the table and slapped George.

"Are you going to let her get away with hitting me?" George asked my mother, rubbing his head.

"If she didn't hit you, I was going to walk around the table and smack you myself." My mother laughed. "My daughter gives you a beautiful son and you act as if she is sitting home all day doing nothing. There is no job more important than a mother."

"Maybe Marcy should dust off her nursing degree and get a job."

"You couldn't handle being home with Frankie," Marcy told him.

"Enough you two," My father admonished my sister and her husband.

"Ryan, eat something." My mother held the platter of ham out to me. "Neither you nor Melanie have eaten very much. I'm not sure it's healthy for you two to be so thin."

"We eat plenty Mom," I assured her. "We are the perfect weight for our profession."

"You're not exactly in the healthiest profession, son," my father added.

"I'm sure you are going to fatten me up this week."

"We're going to try." My mother shook her head. "I'm surprised *your* family isn't concerned about your size, Melanie."

I could tell from the flush of pink on Melanie's cheeks that my mother managed to embarrass her once again.

"They do manage to squeeze a meal into our plans whenever we get together." She smiled at everyone, appearing pleased when they laughed in response.

Of course, my mother could not give Melanie the benefit of laughing. She swallowed a spoonful of vegetables then shared one last remark. "You will learn that I'm not as tactful." She stared at Melanie. "When I'm concerned or unhappy with the way one of my children is been taken care of, I do not hesitate to discuss it openly."

I held Melanie's hand in mine and gave her a reassuring squeeze. When she glanced over at me, I could see sadness in her eyes. On our wedding day, I promised Melanie's father I would always protect her. I am not doing a very good job tonight.

The only time Melanie's face brightened was when I suggested we go ice-skating. I am sure the idea of getting away from my family was more appealing than actually skating.

"N-o-w?" My mother growled when she learned my plan. "You just got here."

"We used to love ice skating when we first met. There is no chance of doing that in New York any more. I've been thinking about it all day."

"You have all week Ryan." My father handed me a beer. "I was looking forward to sitting by the fire tonight and catching up with you."

"Besides it's snowing out. You'll freeze," my mother added.

"We're going." I put the full bottle of beer on the table next to my father knowing it wouldn't go to waste. "Dad, we'll appreciate that fire when we get back. We can stay up all night and talk if you'd like."

He nodded. I didn't dare look in my mother's direction, but imagined she was not smiling.

Melanie and I went to my old bedroom and changed into snow pants and boots. She tied her hair up and slipped a fur headband on her head while I removed gloves from the suitcase. I kissed her before wrapping a winter scarf around her neck.

"Thank you." She grabbed my coat and pulled me in for another kiss.

"Can George and I come along?" Marcy stopped us on the staircase.

"Can you treat my wife properly?"

Marcy appeared hurt by the comment.

Melanie placed a hand on her shoulder. "We'd love for you and George to join us."

Marcy looked in my direction. When I nodded in agreement, she requested a few minutes to get Frankie into bed.

My father walked us to the door, begging us to drive carefully. My mother was noticeably absent. Dad remained in the doorway waving until we drove away. I know he would have enjoyed coming along to watch us skate and take pictures. I hoped he would use the time alone to speak to my mother. If I have to confront her, there will most likely be a huge blowout.

There was about four inches of snow on the ground and it left the pavement slick. To avoid an accident, I reduced my speed on the curvy mountain roads leading to the outdoor ice rink.

We parked the rental car in the lot and walked along the path of Christmas trees covered in fresh snow and colorful holiday lights. In spite of living in a city with beautiful Christmas decorations, Melanie was in awe of the lighted trees. For the first time since we arrived in Pennsylvania, she appeared relaxed.

"I feel so bulky in this winter coat." Marcy complained on our way to the rink. "I wish I looked as good as you guys do in your winter coats and snow pants."

"That's why they're movie stars and we're not," George told her.

"It's our lack of weight," I teased. "The coat and snow pants make us look like normal people instead of the anorexic actors we are."

Marcy and George laughed at my joke. There was a hint of a smile on Melanie's lips, but she refrained from laughing.

"Mom always has something to say," Marcy confessed as we waited in line to rent skates. "She scolded George at your wedding because his goatee was messy looking. She keeps asking if I'm going to have another child."

"You can expect to go through an initiation process, Melanie," George told her. "No one gets into the Fowler family without a little suffering."

"I don't remember my mother treating you poorly," I told him.

"I went through hell for years after moving your sister a thousand miles away from home. You just don't remember."

I do not remember George having a difficult time fitting into our family. Then again, George met Marcy right before I moved to California. I was too busy fanning the flames on my own parental problems to take notice of their tribulations.

I laced up my rental skates, then helped Melanie tighten hers. The snowfall tapered off, so the Zamboni cleared the ice.

Pennsylvania nights are known to be dark. Tonight was no different thanks to snow clouds. One thing I miss about living in Pennsylvania is looking up at the night sky and watching millions of stars twinkling above. The white Christmas lights hanging overhead from one candy-cane-decorated pole to the next provided the only twinkling in the night sky. Christmas music played from speakers hanging on large poles at each end of the ice.

Melanie has only been in skates a handful of times and had a difficult time when we first began skating. She used the guardrail as a crutch the first few laps around the ice. Once her confidence increased, she abandoned the wall and reached for my hand.

As a kid, I played hockey on organized teams, so I am comfortable on skates. Before long, we glided along together. The four of us sang and laughed as we skated around the rink.

A man dressed in a blue ski jacket and a colorful knitted hat donning a pompom on top caught my attention. He sat on the bleachers across the ice from us staring in our direction. I don't think I will ever get used to people gawking at us and am relieved he appears to be the only person taking an interest in Melanie and me. It had been a long time since the two of us have enjoyed ourselves in public without people bombarding us. It made me long for life before *Zombie Wars*.

I enjoyed the time skating with Melanie, Marcy and George. It has been years since I have *really* hung out with my sister. For the second time today, I am grateful Melanie planned this visit with my family.

Swept up in the moment, I lifted Melanie's hand above her head attempting to twirl her. The move caused her to lose balance. Without warning, her feet tangled and she fell on the ice, bringing me down on top of her. Her expression went from horror to a huge smile.

"Have you forgotten who you're skating with?" She laughed as George helped us both to our feet. Two rink employees skated over to check on us. When we assured them we were all right, they instructed us to move out of the way of the other skaters.

Melanie and I skated into the center of the rink to catch

our breath. I wrapped my arms around her. "I'm sorry baby. I didn't mean to make you fall."

She kissed me. "You'll have to teach me how to twirl so next time I'm ready."

George skidded in front of us, splashing ice on our clothing. "We're going to get hot chocolate. You two want some?"

Melanie shook her head. "I'm good."

George skated off to join Marcy in line at the food shack.

Melanie and I skated for another hour before we stopped to rest our feet. On our way to the bleachers, I noticed the man in the colorful hat still watching us.

"Would you mind getting me coffee?" Melanie asked.

I considered pointing the man out to her before heading over to the food shack, but feared my paranoia would upset her. She had enough stress the past few days between the paparazzi, the blond man who showed up at the restaurant and the envelope she received. We were having a great time and I didn't want to ruin the evening. Instead, I kept an eye on him while I waited on line.

In an effort to keep my identity secret, I placed my hand across my face pretending to rub my temples while I ordered the beverages.

"Has anyone ever told you that you look like Ryan Carlisle?" the girl behind the counter asked.

I was careful not to make eye contact with her. "No, but thanks for the compliment." I placed a ten-dollar bill on the counter.

"Here's your change."

"Keep it."

The man with the colorful hat disappeared at some point between the time I ordered the coffee and left the counter. I was thrilled he was gone.

I hummed along to the music as I walked back to Melanie. When I reached the bleachers, she was gone. I scanned the ice to see if she had joined George and Marcy, but could not find them in the crowd of skaters. Abandoning the coffee on the bleachers, I hurried to the ice to search for them.

"Have you seen Melanie?" I asked when I caught up with them.

Marcy looked around. "I haven't seen her in a while."

We moved to the center of the ice to talk.

"I went to buy coffee. When I returned she was gone."

I checked the bleachers a second time to make sure I hadn't missed her, and then scanned the area around the ice rink.

"We'll help you look for her," George said.

An image of the man in the hat entered my mind, causing my heart to race. "Some man has been watching us the entire time. He and Melanie are both gone, and that has me concerned."

George hurried off to the parking lot, still wearing his skates. Marcy walked the perimeter of the rink and I backtracked to the food shack.

I sprinted around the outside of the rink calling out to Melanie. For the first time in a year, I didn't care if I brought attention to myself.

Marcy grasped my arm when I passed her. "George just called. She's not in the parking lot. I can't find her either. I'm heading to the ladies' room to search."

"Call the police if you don't find her there," I told her.

Fear gripped me as I continued jogging around the property in my ice skates calling my wife's name.

An announcement interrupted the Christmas music. "Ryan Fowler please report to the restroom area."

A security guard pointed me in the right direction. I moved as quickly as my skates permitted, while praying Melanie was safe. My knees weakened when I saw a crowd of people gathered around a woman lying on the ground—a woman with long, ash-blond hair.

Chapter Seven

Melanie

Lying on the snow-covered ground was more painful than the actual fall. If it weren't bad enough that the man who tossed me to the ground took off, the one who did help insisted I remain lying down.

"We should have someone check you out before you move," he told me when I requested assistance.

I was relieved when I heard Ryan call my name. I couldn't imagine what took him so long to reach me.

"Are you all right?" His face lacked color despite the chill in the air.

"I hurt my ankle."

"Who did this to you?"

"Some guy grabbed her around the waist and started walking off with her," The man caring for me told Ryan. "She flailed her arms and legs around so hard that he dropped her. Then he took off."

"I think he tried to move me out of the way." I down-played the incident. "He might have been in a rush and I was moving slow."

Ryan looked to the man for answers. "Was he moving her or dragging her somewhere?"

The man shrugged. "It looked like he was dragging her off, dude."

"Why would he kidnap her with all these people around?" Another chimed in. "He was probably some jerk in a rush and physically moved her out of his way."

"What happened, Melanie?" He looked to me for answers.

"He moved me out of the way."

To be honest, I wasn't sure what the man's intentions were. It did seem like he tried to carry me off, yet, it would be stupid to kidnap a person with a crowd of people milling around. The parking lot *was* a good distance away so it wasn't as if he could drag me unnoticed. I wondered if the events of the past forty-eight hours were making me paranoid. If that was the case, the last thing I wanted to do was add to Ryan's paranoia.

"Are you okay Melanie?" Marcy walked up behind Ryan.

"What took you so long?" Ryan asked her.

"I couldn't find the ladies' room," she said. "I *did* call the police."

"Why are the police coming?" I asked.

"I couldn't find you...I wanted to tell you about the man, but...I thought you were..."

"I sent you a text." I interrupted his rambling. "I had to go to the bathroom."

"I didn't get it."

Marcy leaned down and examined my ankle. Pain radiated up my leg when she moved the foot.

"Can you move your toes?" Marcy asked.

"Yeah."

"How about the ankle?"

"It hurts, but I can."

George appeared with our boots. Ryan shoved his feet into his boots then worked my good foot into mine. Marcy suggested he leave my injured foot free.

"You look pale, Ryan. Are you okay?" I asked.

He nodded. "I didn't know where you were and was afraid someone took you."

"I'm fine. I'm sorry I scared you."

"I don't think it's broken." Marcy announced. "You gave it a good twisting though. We'll elevate that ankle and get some ice on it once we're home.

"I knew it!" A teenaged girl stopped in front of us. "You're Ryan Carlisle... Oh, my God. Ryan Carlisle is here!" She bounced with excitement. "Can I have an autograph?"

The excitement of the teenaged girl turned the group's attention from me to Ryan. She also caught the attention of nearby skaters. Young women pushed and shoved one another in an attempt to get close. George fought against the mob to rescue a child knocked to the ground by a group of girls. Security took the child from George and reunited him with his frantic father.

Rink attendants and additional security guards rushed to

the scene to force the crowd back from the spot I was still sitting. Marcy hurried to the parking lot to get the car while George and Ryan helped me to my feet.

"It looks like you're going to have to trade your heels in for sneakers. Do you own sneakers?" George asked me.

I smiled in response, but was in too much pain to answer. Together, George and Ryan pushed through the crowd of people and carried me down the tree-lined path to the car. Security guards continued to shield us from the crazed crowd.

A police cruiser pulled into the parking lot. Thanks to the mob scene, it wasn't difficult to find us. Ryan apologized to him for the false alarm, explaining his concern over the man who had been watching us throughout the evening.

"It looks like you need my help with another matter." He hitched his chin toward the crowd forcing its way past ice rink personnel to reach us.

"I would appreciate it. My wife is hurt and I want to get her out of here."

The officer requested back up and then assisted the security members in moving the crowd back. We sat in our car waiting to leave. Once it was safe, the officer directed us out of the parking lot.

"Do you go through this every time you leave the house?" Marcy asked as we drove away.

"It's been bad for the last six months," Ryan told her.

"It is the second time this week police have to rescue us," I admitted.

"What a crazy life." Marcy shook her head in disbelief.

"Who would have thought your creepy little brother would become a Hollywood heartthrob?" George laughed. "Apparently these people haven't seen you in those one-piece pajamas. I'll show you some pictures Melanie."

We laughed at George's description of Ryan's younger self with the Dutch-boy haircut, the pajamas that covered him from neck to toe and the big dinosaur he carried for years.

"No matter how much of a geek I thought you were as a kid, I do look forward to meeting my niece or nephew." Marcy's face grew serious. "I really hope you *both* protect yourselves by hiring security."

"It's not the first time that suggestion has been made," he told her. "The last few days have me seriously considering hiring a security guard to protect Melanie."

I wasn't happy with this revelation. "I would move to Long Island before I allowed someone to follow me around. We both know I have no intention of moving out of the city."

"A conversation for another time ," he told me. "Marcy, let's stop off at the liquor store. I need a drink."

* * * *

Dave was kneeling in front of the fireplace diligently working on a fire when we arrived home. "Frankie woke up after you left," he told Marcy. "Your Mom took him into our bed."

"Thanks Dad. I'll move him into his bed."

"Don't wake him. I'm going to sleep on the couch tonight. Let him sleep."

Reluctantly Marcy agreed. She assisted Ryan in hanging our wet clothing in the mudroom while George helped me into a chair by the fire.

"What happened to you?" Dave asked.

"I twisted my ankle."

"You should have seen her skating around on those high-heeled boots," George joked.

"Do you think it's broken?" Dave asked.

I shook my head. "I just gave it a good twisting. I'm sure it will be better in a day or so."

Marcy placed an ice pack on my ankle and handed me a glass of red wine. "This will make you feel better."

"Don't worry about me," I told her. "My husband needs something to calm his nerves."

Ryan poured himself a shot of liquor and washed it down with a beer. The fear had yet to leave his eyes.

"I'm fine Ryan." I patted the oversized chair inviting him to sit with me. "I don't think we were the reason that man was at the ice rink tonight." I meant it this time. After rethinking the events of the evening, I do believe it was an unfortunate coincidence.

"Who would have known you were going there?" George asked. "It was a last-minute decision."

Marcy filled her father in on the background story. "He was probably there watching his kid skate and thought he recognized you. Who hasn't stared at a person and wondered why they look familiar?"

"Fame is making me paranoid. I hoped this trip would

allow Melanie and me to feel like normal people." He rolled his eyes. "How sad is it that I can't relax. I am so used to living with cameras in my face that I don't fully believe they're gone."

"After tonight they may be back," George told Ryan. His comment caused him to receive another elbow to the ribs.

"Don't hit him," Ryan admonished his sister. "He isn't telling me anything I don't already know."

"If the media shows up, we will have to skip the Christmas tree hunt tomorrow." Dave made a face displaying his disappointment.

Ryan wasn't any happier with the idea of skipping the family's tradition.

"We don't have to make a decision tonight," Marcy told her father and brother. "Let's see what happens tomorrow."

George refilled our drinks. The conversation changed to family stories that I hadn't heard before. I learned more about Ryan's family in that hour than I have in the past few years. The most shocking discovery was that Marcy was a retired New York City police officer. If I were to guess her occupation, police officer would never have entered my mind. I viewed her as a diva, not someone who would risk her life for another person. Of course, I kept those thoughts to myself.

"What made you decide to be a police officer?" I asked.

"The father of an old boyfriend of mine was a detective. He used to talk about work during family dinners. I felt a thrill of excitement each time he described a car chase or arrest he had made."

"After her second year of college she secretly took the police test," Dave added. "She was in the academy for three weeks before breaking the news to us."

"A black eye forced me into confessing." Marcy smirked.

"How did your mother react?" I asked, already knowing the answer.

George lit a cigarette and took a drag. "She came close to walking out of the living room with two black eyes that night. We were equally furious with her."

"Our children never fail to surprise us." Dave shook his head. His eyes glazed over as if he was remembering the moment Marcy described.

"I'm guessing everyone came to terms with it?"

Marcy shook her head. "Never. My mother cried for the

two years, two months, ten days and eight hours I was on the force. She had a huge party the day I quit."

"Why did you quit?"

"My partner was stabbed while trying to break up a fight between two teenagers." She divulged. "I spent the night in the emergency room speaking to detectives." She shook her head at the memory. "Once I found out he would be all right, I left the hospital, walked to my precinct and handed my gun and shield to the lieutenant."

"Quitting that job changed my relationship with Nancy," George told me. "I was no longer the man stealing her daughter away by marrying her. I was now the man she quit the force for."

His comment sobered me. If forcing Ryan to quit acting and move to Pennsylvania is the only way she would accept me into the family, then we will be adversaries forever.

"That love fest lasted until the two of you announced your plans to move to Florida." Ryan snickered.

"That's not true." Marcy poured herself another glass of wine. "She turned against George the Easter he spilled red wine on her new yellow tablecloth."

"Don't pick on your mother. She loves each one of you." Dave looked around the room at us. "You just need to live by her rules. After thirty years of marriage I've learned and now my life is easy."

"Is that why you're sleeping on the couch tonight?" George's teasing got him another elbow to the ribs.

Dave began telling a story about his first date with Nancy. Between the beer and the late hour, he had a hard time staying awake. As a result, nothing he said made sense. He drifted off a few times; only to awaken moments later asking where in the story he had left off.

"You and mom were in the corn field..." Ryan teased.

Dave waved his hand dismissing the ridiculous statements before drifting again.

George was the first to retire. A few minutes later Marcy stumbled to the hall closet to retrieve linens, and made up the couch for her father. As we prepared to go to bed, Marcy hugged Ryan and then me. "I'm so happy you and Ryan are spending Christmas with us."

A lump formed in my throat. It felt good that his sister accepted me.

Ryan woke his father, who was sleeping in the recliner, and assisted him to the couch. Dave tapped Ryan's face and told him he loved him before drawing the covers to his neck and drifting back to sleep. The affection between father and son made me happy we were spending Christmas with his family.

The consequence of drinking five glasses of wine hit me hard when I stood up. My head had a hollow feeling and spun. I was grateful Ryan and Marcy were assisting me. On the way up the stairs, Ryan missed a step. He unsuccessfully reached for the banister, banging his stomach against the wood steps. Marcy and I were hysterical.

George appeared at the top of the steps and admonished us for making so much noise. He made his way down the steps, past Ryan and me and assisted his wife to their room. He then returned to carry me upstairs.

* * * *

"I had a good time tonight." I dug my toes into the pink shag rug in our room. "I'm sorry your evening was ruined."

"It wasn't ruined. I had a nice time too." Ryan removed my nightgown from the dresser and tossed it on the bed beside me. "The fear something had happened to you was horrible. It made me realize we have to make changes in our life."

"What kind of changes?" I wasn't sure I liked where this conversation was heading.

"We need to hire bodyguards or a car service to drive us around."

"We'll look into both options after our honeymoon. In the meantime, let's try to relax." I was anxious to get off the topic. "Didn't you tell me this was your bedroom?"

"It's changed a lot since I've moved out." He looked around the room and shook his head. "I'm going to take a shower."

"I can use a shower too. Want me to join you?"

He laughed. "As exciting as that sounds, I'm thinking you'd better rest that ankle." He kissed my nose. "I'll be back. Do you need anything before I go?"

"Help removing my pants."

I grimaced while he freed my sore ankle from my form-fitting pants. "I might also benefit by having the garbage pail by my side of the bed."

He smirked and fetched the pail.

"You want me to bring you to the bathroom?"

I shook my head and slipped under the warm blankets. I was sound asleep before he returned to bed.

I would like to say when I woke up the next morning I was rested, but I would be lying. My stomach was queasy and my head ached. The last thing I wanted was to be nursing a hangover during breakfast. I looked at the alarm clock on the nightstand. It was five-thirty. I slept a total of six hours. I sat up and slid my legs over the side of the bed, hugging the garbage pail. It took a few minutes before my stomach was strong enough to stand and a few more before I could walk around the dark room to the door. On a positive note, my ankle was better. Other than a pinching sensation when I put pressure on it, the pain was gone.

I removed Ryan's robe from the back of the door and wrapped myself in it. Creeping down the stairs past the living room where his father was still sleeping, I tip toed through the dark dining room into the kitchen. Once the door closed behind me, I searched the wall for the light switch and flipped it on.

I remembered from past visits where the coffee and the filters were stored. Placing a clean filter into the pot, I scooped five heaping spoonfuls of coffee in before flipping the switch. Snacking on a roll left over from last night's dinner, I stared out the window waiting for the coffee to finish perking. Unlike the city streets that are lit up and busy regardless of the hour, Pennsylvania was dark and quiet. I could not imagine having to navigate my way through the city streets at night in the dark.

On the other hand, the stars do not twinkle this bright in New York. Now that the snowstorm was behind us, the stars were magnificent. I imagined how beautiful it must be during the summer and hoped we would be able to return just to sit in the yard and enjoy their beauty.

When I grew bored of staring out the window, I brought my half-eaten roll to the table and admired the kitchen. Unlike my parents' modern home and my mismatched apartment, the Fowler's house had a country motif. I have always favored the country design but never had the money to redecorate. For now, I live with boring white walls and furniture acquired from relatives who had moved on to newer and better decor. Once we return from our honeymoon, we will renovate, provided Ryan drops the idea of moving to Long Island.

I liked their crème-colored walls and the apple border. There were enough dark wood cabinets around the U-shaped work area of the kitchen to store dishes, food and to keep most of Nancy's appliances out of view. The only items found on the tidy kitchen counter were a rooster cookie jar and some country-themed knickknacks.

I longed for more cabinets in my apartment. I only have five kitchen cabinets: two long cabinets to the left and right of the sink, two short ones overhead and a base cabinet below. They do not provide much storage space. I love my apartment and hope to stay for years, but secretly have a list of things I would like to change about it.

While I waited for the coffee to finish perking, I was tempted to view the family pictures hanging in the hallway. I have passed the photos mapping Marcy and Ryan's childhood several times over the past two years but never had the chance to examine them. Not wanting to chance the light waking Dave, or better yet Nancy, I limped to the front closet to retrieve my messenger bag. By the time I returned to the kitchen, the coffee was ready. I poured myself a cup, took two aspirin I found in the cabinet, removed the script Ryan sent me to read and limped back to the table. I was enthralled with the story when Ryan entered the kitchen and startled me.

"I was worried when I awoke to find you and the garbage pail gone." He kissed my head. "I thought you don't read the end of scripts?"

"I'm making an exception this time. It's too exciting to put down. I have one page left. There's coffee if you want some."

When I finished reading the story, I closed the script and smiled at my husband. "I love it. Have you called your agent yet?"

"I still haven't decided if I'm taking it."

"Not this again." I rolled my eyes at him. "Do I have to call her myself?"

"I'll call." He leaned against the kitchen counter and grinned at me. "How's your ankle?"

"Well enough to walk over to the phone and call your agent."

"You might piss her off considering it is only 3 am in California." He smirked. "Does your offer to shower together still stand?"

My eyes widened at the thought. "No way. Your family will hear us."

"You weren't worried about my family last night." He put his coffee mug down and walked over to me wearing a funny expression on his face.

"I was drunk then."

"Since you're not drunk now, I don't have to worry about you giggling." He kissed my neck. "How about a nice relaxing bubble bath?"

"What if they come looking for us? How do we explain the two of us in the bathroom together?"

"You've never done your hair while I'm in the shower?"

"So you plan on leaving the hair dryer on while we're in a bubble bath?" I laughed. "Your mother might be tempted to throw it in the tub and electrocute us."

He chuckled. "The only people using the upstairs bathroom are my sister and George. They were pretty toasted last night, so I doubt we'll hear from them for a while."

"You're a bad influence." His hands wandered across my body. "Lucky for you, I'm easily persuaded."

"I'm undecided if that response is a turn on or something I should worry about." He wrapped his arm around my waist and guided me toward the door. On the way out, we shut the kitchen light, crept through the dining room and up the stairs. At this point, I was excited for this intimate time with my husband and prayed his family didn't awaken and disturb our romantic interlude.

We remained in the tub until the water cooled, then headed to the bedroom, one at a time, to make love. Afterward, I slept peacefully in his arms. When I woke this time, I felt refreshed.

We walked hand-in-hand to the kitchen and found Ryan's family enjoying a pancake breakfast.

"Were you two in the kitchen during the night?" Nancy asked.

"I couldn't sleep so I came down and made myself coffee. I'm sorry I left a mess." I omitted the part where Ryan seduced me, making me forget to clean up the dishes.

"It's okay." Nancy smiled. "The coffee tastes good. I am the only one in the house who likes strong coffee. It was a pleasant surprise to find it the way I like."

Her compliment delighted me.

"I *would* question your decision to drink coffee when you're having difficulty sleeping, Mrs. Carlisle, but considering the amount of wine you drank last night, I figure you needed it." George smirked over his coffee cup.

My face flushed. "I remember having some company finishing off the wine last night."

"That's what all the giggling was about?" Nancy shook her head. "You are very lucky you didn't wake Frankie."

"I wish I wouldn't have stopped Marcy from taking him to his own bed. My neck is killing me. That couch isn't as comfortable as it used to be," Dave complained.

"Who told you to sleep on the couch?" Nancy shot back.

"I'm not blaming anyone else, it was my stupid idea." Dave stretched his back. "What time are we going tree hunting today?"

"There is no sign of the paparazzi, so we're good anytime you want," Ryan told him.

"I'd like to go early so we have time to decorate before the church Christmas party tonight." Nancy poured pancake batter on to the warm griddle.

"Please tell me you're not going to drag us to that thing again this year," Marcy whined.

"For the first time in years we'll all be going together. I want to show my family off. They are having a DJ and Santa will be there with a gift for Frankie." She peeled bacon from the wrapper and placed on the long griddle next to the pancakes.

"Give your mother a break. She's been excited for this dinner dance ever since Melanie and Ryan said they were coming home for Christmas." Dave glared at his children.

"I didn't say anything," Ryan responded as if he was a child wrongly accused of bad behavior. "Except for our wedding, Melanie and I haven't hit the dance floor in ages."

"You should have seen the crowd gathered around Ryan last night when we were leaving the ice rink," George said.

"Tonight will be different. These people have known Ryan from childhood. They won't be as impressed as strangers who meet him," Nancy responded while sliding plates of pancakes and bacon in front of us.

I have often wondered if Nancy is ignorant or intentionally belittles her family members. Ryan didn't seem affected by her comment so I decided not to dwell on it.

"Melanie, we will be walking through the woods today

in five inches of snow. I think you should fore-go your high-heeled boots and wear something more sensible," Nancy told me.

I tried to ignore the fact she spoke to me like a child.

"Melanie manages to dress herself every single morning. I think she'll pick the right shoes." Ryan barked.

"I was just trying to be helpful."

"You're being facetious," Ryan said under his breath.

* * * *

Dave removed the rear bench of his minivan so the tree could slide inside the car. He didn't want to strap it to the roof. This left room for Nancy, Frankie's car seat and one other person to ride with them. George volunteered to drive with Dave and Nancy while Marcy opted to ride with Ryan and me.

The ride to the farm took forty-five minutes. When we arrived, the family stood in the parking lot discussing the type of tree they should buy. Dave wanted a fat tree, Nancy a Douglas fir. Ryan wanted a nine-foot tree and George wanted them to pick a tree as quickly as possible, because he was freezing.

The large crowd of people on hand left Ryan feeling anxious. Before anyone recognized him, he set out with his parents and George to find the perfect tree, while Marcy, Frankie and I trailed behind.

"I wish my brother and mother wouldn't butt heads all the time." Marcy admitted as we swung a bundled up Frankie by his arms like a swing between us. "We were a close family when Ryan and I were kids. Every weekend we watched him play hockey at various ice skating rinks. My father was convinced Ryan would grow up to be a professional hockey player. He was so disappointed when he hung up his skates to act during High School."

I nodded as I listened to information I already knew.

"Mom watched his games between her fingers." She positioned her free hand over her own face to demonstrate. "Yet she was disappointed too. I can't blame them. They spent a fortune on hockey lessons, ice time, equipment and traveling for games. I was happy when he quit. Traveling every weekend killed my social life." She snorted. "When my parents and I went to Ryan's first theater performance at his school, there was no denying he had found his calling. They supported him throughout high school, driving him back and forth from rehearsals and singing lessons four times a week. My father even agreed to let him take dance classes. Of course, that didn't last long. Some of the jocks made his life miserable when they learned he left hockey to dance."

"It's a shame he didn't stick with it," I added. "He's a terrible dancer."

We both laughed.

"When the time came for him to look at colleges, he would only consider schools with theater arts programs. My parents were furious. They had hoped by the time he graduated high school, his acting career would end as abrupt as his hockey career had. He was into computers and they assumed that would be his major. After months of fighting, my parents gave him an ultimatum. He either went to college to study a real career or would have to get a job and support himself. A year later, when he graduated, he packed his things and moved to California."

I was not sure where she was going with the story but I wished we would catch up with the others. We were missing everything.

"My parents were devastated, yet they were convinced that Ryan would return home within a couple of months with his tail between his legs, ready to live in the real world."

"Then you moved?" I asked.

She nodded while looking down at Frankie who continued acting as a human swing.

"I thought it was going to be bad. I was petrified to tell them we were moving. Surprisingly they didn't react as bad as I expected. They considered buying a house in Florida and becoming snowbirds. In the end, they decided against it."

"How long had Ryan been in California when you moved?"

"A few years, and he was beginning to get some small roles at that point." She smiled. "My parents were thrilled when he met you."

"They were?"

Frankie grew tired of swinging and wrangled free of our grip. Marcy permitted him to play in the snow on the side of the trail.

"She figured the glamour of Hollywood had worn off when he started visiting you on tour rather than working. She assumed it was only a matter of time before he returned home or settled in New York. She could handle him living in New York. As soon as she learned you were encouraging him to find work, she made it her mission to break you up. Every time he came to visit, she'd invite another girl from his past to dinner, hoping one of them would spark his interest and he'd return home to reality."

I felt as though someone had punched me in the gut. He never told me about the match making dinners thrown in my absence. The revelation both angered and hurt me. I shoved my hands deep into my pockets. "Why are you telling me this, Marcy?"

"So you'll understand why my mother is so angry." Marcy touched my arm. "She worries about Ryan and the harsh lifestyle of being an actor. She didn't want this life for him. Had you been a teacher or a nurse or a secretary, she'd love you."

"His dream became a reality. Why can't she be happy for the success he's found?"

"In her mind Hollywood is full of hardship which eventually leads to drugs, alcoholism, divorce, and overdose. What happens one day when producers lose interest in him? How is he going to return to a normal life without cameras in his face and women worshiping him? She's afraid he's going to face the hardship many actors have suffered when their star fades."

I was speechless. I could not deny people *have* succumbed to Hollywood's dark side over the years, but wishing for the demise of our marriage because of my career path was ridiculous.

"That's why it is so important for the family unit to remain close. It keeps us grounded," I told her, trying to keep resentment out of my tone. "That's why I brought him home for Christmas."

"We appreciate that you postponed your honeymoon to be with us," she told me.

"I know firsthand how much your mother misses him. I'm devastated every time he flies off to shoot a movie, knowing weeks will pass before I see him again." I confessed. "He loves his job. To demand he quit acting would be selfish."

She nodded in agreement. "I've only met you a few times and to be honest, I let my mother's feelings influence me." She smiled. "I'm so happy we spent last night getting to know one another. It allowed me to form my own opinion."

I wrestled with anger when she hugged me. I didn't understand how she thought this conversation would *help* me understand his mother better. All she managed to do is cause me to feel even more resentment toward her.

"You are the perfect match for my brother." She stopped walking and took my hands in her own. "Try not to let my mother's comments upset you. I am confident that she is going to love you. Just give her time to get to know you."

"She makes it difficult to keep coming back." I was honest. "For Ryan's sake, I will."

Ryan motioned for us to join them. When Marcy called Frankie over, he was not pleased having to leave his snowy playground. While Marcy dealt with her angry son, I caught up with the rest of the family.

"The three of you missed the whole thing." Nancy moaned.

"We were standing right over there watching you," Marcy informed her. "Frankie wanted to play in the snow."

"Do you like the tree?" Ryan twirled it for me.

I nodded.

"Is everything all right?" he asked me.

I shrugged. "Marcy and I were talking about your mother." He sighed.

I was about to ask him about the dinner dates his mother had set up in the past, but decided against it. He is not responsible for his mother's actions and I don't know that I would have confessed something so sinister if the tables were turned. I suppressed the urge to lash out at him and decided to deal with my own insecurities.

Dave bought hot chocolate for the adults and a hot pretzel for Frankie. We huddled around a fire pit and toasted marshmallows, courtesy of the staff, while Ryan and George carried the Christmas tree to Dave's van.

Frankie was transfixed with the idea of cooking over a fire. The moment his mother took a bite of her toasted marshmallow, he tossed his half-eaten pretzel back to his grandfather and grabbed a stick.

Nancy snapped pictures of Marcy holding Frankie while he toasted his marshmallow and then the unpleasant expression on his face upon learning marshmallows are sticky. When Ryan and George returned, she turned the camera on us. I tried not to think ugly thoughts about her capturing phony pictures of a happy family unit.

"Ryan, I hope you know you're hanging the star on top of the tree. I don't want your father climbing any ladders."

"I'm willing to risk my life to place the star on top of our tree. There is nothing better than a nine-foot Christmas tree."

"I prefer our little tree that sits on a table in front of the window," George admitted. "We bought it already strung with lights."

"In early December we take it out of the box and sit it on the table and in January we return it to its sad little box," Marcy added.

"I should have done the same," I admitted. "It was silly for me to buy a tree this year. The only reason I bought it was because it was our first Christmas and the thought of not having a tree was upsetting." I pulled my hood up trying to protect myself against the cold chill running down the back of my neck.

"I'm just sorry you and Marcy stayed back with Frankie. You didn't get the full effect." Nancy pouted.

"Next year."

I noticed a spark in her eyes. Her mouth moved as though she planned to say something, but thought better of it. After a brief hesitation, she turned her attention back to the marshmallow she was helping Frankie toast. For the first time since our arrival, she looked peaceful. I figured the two words I spoke gave her hope that we would be back again next Christmas.

"If we are going to get this tree trimmed and arrive to the dinner dance on time, we'd better get going." Dave got up from the bench and threw his cup away.

"George and I are going to drop by the mall on the way home," Marcy told them. "We still have to pick up a couple of things for Frankie's s-t-o-c-k-i-n-g." She spelled the last word.

"You still have three days before Christmas. Please don't rush out on me." Nancy pleaded.

Marcy looked at George and twisted her lips. He sucked his cheeks in anger. On our way back to the car, Marcy and George fell behind the rest of the family while they argued. In the end, they headed to the mall with the understanding that they would be back by the time Ryan and Dave finished stringing lights on the tree.

When Nancy was not directing Dave and Ryan, she was in the kitchen preparing appetizers and eggnog for the decorating party. Since she didn't need my help in the kitchen, I went upstairs to unpack our suitcases. Afterward, I returned a text my sister sent earlier in the day.

Hi. I couldn't chat before. We were picking out a Christmas tree with Ryan's family. How is everything?

Lori has a cold so we're keeping her indoors so she isn't sick for Christmas. How is your visit with Ryan's family?

We had a rough start to the visit but things seem better today. Ryan and his father are putting up the tree. Shortly, we are going to decorate it and then go to a Christmas party.

Mom is here and wants to know how you are making out.

I chewed my upper lip while typing. *I'm getting along with everyone except for his mom. She is not a likeable person. I hope that each day will be a little better. She has been pleasant this afternoon. Tell Mom I miss and love her.*

She sends her love. Keep your chin up. I hope that you will experience a Christmas miracle and walk away best friends.

I smiled at the text. *I'll settle for tolerating one another. LOL. Talk to you soon. Hope Lori is feeling better. I'll check in tomorrow.*

I erased both the incoming and outgoing messages and left the phone on the nightstand. One by one, I slid the suitcases under the bed.

From the staircase, I overheard Ryan and his parents talking about me. He was expressing his disappointment over the way his mother had been treating me. I turned and tiptoed back upstairs to our room. I was annoyed that Ryan picked now to have this conversation with his parents. I had been looking forward to decorating the tree. Now the evening is most likely going to be uncomfortable. I lay across the bed playing with my cell phone. A half hour later, when he did come up to the bedroom, he seemed happy.

"Is the rest of the day going to be awkward?" I glowered at him.

He appeared taken back by my question. "We aired our grievances. Hopefully now things will be better."

I waited a few moments hoping he would share the conversation with me. When he didn't, I asked. "What are her grievances?"

"The usual. We don't come around often enough." He lay down on the bed next to me.

"Your sister says your mother resents me because I support

your career. She feels now that we're married you'll never stop acting."

He shook his head in disgust. "We've had that discussion a hundred times. My decision to act came long before I met you. It's in my blood. I told her she should be happy you're ambition is to remain on Broadway, otherwise I would have asked you to move to the West Coast with me." He stood up, took my hands into his, and helped me up from the bed. "How's your ankle?"

"Good." I moved it around to show him. "Your Mom is nervous that your career is going to end and the rejection will lead to drugs and alcohol."

"If I turn to drugs or alcohol, she'll be to blame." He kissed me. "Now let's go decorate the Christmas tree."

Chapter Eight

Ryan

Christmas music filled the house as we decorated the tree while snacking on popcorn, homemade cookies and caramelized walnuts. My mother thought she was sly preparing a plate for me to eat while I fixed a section of lights that had blown out. I wasn't too concerned that the giant bowl of candy and twelve dozen cookies would disappear in the time it took me to fix the tree. My father snapped pictures of us laughing and acting the way a family should when they are together.

Two occurrences almost turned our family celebration into a battle zone. The first was when Frankie's bouncy ball got away from him. He chased it, lost his footing and slid head-first into the tree. Two minutes earlier, his father instructed him to put the ball away. Rather than heed the warnings, he threw the ball one last time. Ornaments smashed on the wood floor. Since each ornament on my parents' tree was a memento of important events throughout our lifetime, my mother could have gone berserk. I guess being a grandchild protected Frankie from the beating Marcy and I would have received had we broken the ornaments as children. Instead, my parents gathered the broken pieces and made plans to glue them together.

Drama also ensued when my mother announced our traditional tree-trimming gift exchange. Melanie's cheeks flushed while fire burned in her eyes. I forgot to tell her about this tradition. Assuring her things would work out did nothing to calm her down during the gift exchange.

My parents gave us an ornament shaped as a wedding bell with our names and wedding date engraved into it. The ornament we received from Marcy and George was of a woman dressed in a black, glittery gown singing into a microphone. Regardless of the thought my family put into the gifts,

Melanie allowed her embarrassment to get in the way of her appreciation.

"I was not aware you had this tradition...I didn't buy..."

"Anything for the tree," I finished Melanie's sentence. "Considering Marcy's tree is the size of a bread box, we thought we would do something different this year. We purchased tickets for each of you to come to New York and attend the opening night of Melanie's new show."

"I appreciate the offer, but George has used all of his vacation time." Marcy pouted. "He won't accumulate enough hours until the summer."

"I purchased round-trip airline tickets for the three of you to come for the weekend. Your flight leaves late Friday night and will get you home Sunday evening." I removed two envelopes from my pocket and distributed them to my family. The envelope for my parents contained two tickets to the show and a reservation for a car service. My sister's envelope included show and airline tickets "I have booked three rooms in a beautiful hotel so we can spend the weekend together." I looked at my mother. "You haven't had the pleasure of hearing my wife sing. Her beautiful voice will bring tears to your eyes when you hear it for the first time."

My sister was excited to attend Melanie's show. My father wrapped his pudgy hand around my neck and pulled me in for a hug. Even my mother thanked us, although it took effort on her part.

"Thank you," Melanie whispered in my ear before kissing me. "Next time let me in on your secret so I'm not humiliated."

Despite the earlier mishap, my mother permitted Frankie to hang the final ornament. It was a round ornament with seven snowman faces. Printed below the faces were each of our names, followed by my family surname and the year.

My father lit our Christmas tree following a countdown. My parents posed in front of the tree for pictures, followed by my sister and her family, then Melanie and me. Afterward my father attached the camera to its tripod, set the timer, and took a few family pictures. My mother planned to use the best picture as this year's family Christmas card. My father and I carried the empty ornament boxes down to the basement while Marcy and Melanie cleaned up the living room. Once the house was clean, we showered and dressed for the dinner-dance.

The catering hall, located behind the church, was transformed into the North Pole. Inside the front door was a small, white picket fence with snow-filled scenes of Santa's village. Different Christmas scenes continued throughout the hallway with motorized dolls working on toys, Mrs. Claus removed cookies from the oven and Santa waved his mechanical arm as he flew in his reindeer-guided sleigh. Inside the ballroom were colorful lights strung along the ceiling. Silver and gold tablecloths covered the tables. To the right of the DJ booth was an oversized green, felt chair that would undoubtedly be utilized by Santa. The people and the decorations overwhelmed Frankie. His excitement caused me to fear he was going to have a stroke. George calmed him by giving him a candy cane off the huge Christmas tree located in the center of the dance floor.

"I don't think he should be given sugar," My mother reprimanded George.

Initially, I believed George was foolish for giving Frankie candy, but it worked. Frankie stopped running. Instead, he admired the tree while sucking on the candy. His little bottom wiggled back and forth to the beat of the music. When the other children entered the dance floor, Frankie lost interest in both the tree and the candy and broke into his own dance routine.

Watching him with the other children got me thinking about the family Melanie and I will eventually have. The prospect of creating a life with my wife excited me. The contentment on her face while watching Frankie indicated her thoughts most likely matched my own.

My mother disrupted my pleasant daydream by requesting Melanie and I pose for additional pictures. She positioned us in front of the tree and snapped away with her camera. Once the other one hundred or so people noticed us, they photographed us too. We spent the first hour of the party taking pictures and signing autographs for most of the guests. Daggers shot from my mother's eyes, warning her friends not to make a big deal over us. The friends complied, until later in the evening when my mother was in the ladies' room. Playing it cool, they asked about our wedding, how long we would be visiting and if we planned to attend Mass on Christmas Day. When they could not think of anything else to ask, they removed their cameras and included Melanie and me in their group photos. My mother was livid when she returned. She ended the photo shoot by escorting us to our table.

We enjoyed salad, followed by our entrée. Melanie ordered prime rib and I chose Chicken Marcella. Neither of us was able to empty our plate. When my mother noticed our half-abandoned dinners, she made a face but said nothing. I guess even *her* nagging takes a holiday.

I escorted Melanie to the dance floor once the music changed to a quicker beat. She was radiant in her red-strapless dress and matching high heels. People gawked at us as we danced to the upbeat music. While our careers intrigued the women and teenagers, Melanie's beauty captivated the men.

"Thankfully my son wants to dance with me, otherwise I'd be a lump sitting at the table all night too." Marcy chastised George from the dance floor. George had never been much of a dancer. As usual, he spent the entire evening sitting at the table. "I don't know why you prefer to sit there watching other people have a good time, rather than dancing with me?"

My mother interrupted their loud discussion to introduce Marcy and me to people we knew, but had long forgotten. The small group made a big deal over Frankie, but quickly steered the conversation toward Melanie and me. Lana, a friend of my mother, questioned my long-distance relationship with Melanie. She then proceeded to share a story about her daughter's recent divorce, which was a result of the husband's constant business trips.

"He was always so attentive and loving toward her, so we were shocked to learn he had been having affairs most of their ten-year marriage. It just goes to show you, long-distance relationships don't work out."

Melanie's body stiffened as she listened to Lana share the details leading up to the divorce.

"Just because her daughter's marriage fell apart doesn't mean ours will." I told Melanie as we walked to the bar located in the corner of the room. "We are only hearing her mother's side. We're not hearing all of the circumstances."

My father waved us over from the bar. "This is my son Ryan and his wife Melanie." I shook hands with the tall and slender older man. "Ryan, do you remember John Barkley? He has been an usher with this parish since you were a boy. One time you helped him with the collections. You thought it was the greatest job in the world."

I remembered him well. Not only was he an usher, he also made repairs around the church property. To listen to the man speak one would think he was the holiest of people. Meanwhile the inside of his toolbox contained pornographic pictures of young women. I made that discovery one summer when my parents volunteered my services to him. "Hello Mister Barkley. How are you?"

"Not as good as you." He nudged me and put his arm around Melanie. "You're a movie star and have a beautiful wife. God has been very good to you."

"I'm a lucky man."

The man has always made my skin crawl. The fact he has wrapped his arm around my wife's shoulders, made me sick. "It was nice to see you again. We were just on our way back to the table to keep my brother-in-law company."

"Would you mind getting your old man a beer before you go?" my father asked. "Do you want anything John?"

"I'll take a beer too. While you're gone, I'll keep your wife warm."

I pulled Melanie from the embrace of my father's perverted friend a little harder than I intended to.

"Ouch!" She complained.

"I'm sorry." I rubbed her arm as we walked back to the bar. "That man is a pervert. I couldn't stand watching him rub his wrinkled hand up and down your back."

"What makes him a pervert?" She leaned her arm on the bar while we waited for the bartender to finish with another customer.

"Two beers," I requested when he approached us. "I worked with him one summer and found naked pictures of women in his toolbox."

She shrugged. "I know a lot of people who have pictures of women hanging in their garage or workshops. What's the big deal?"

"When I say pictures of women, I really mean teenaged girls. When he found me looking in the toolbox, he accused me of trying to steal something. I think he was embarrassed I had found the pictures and was trying to scare me out of telling anyone."

"Did you tell your parents?" Melanie gulped the white wine she had ordered during our first visit to the bar and asked for a refill. I almost laughed but figured she needed something to relax her. This trip has been stressful for her. My mother's friends haven't made matters any easier.

"I told them that he accused me of stealing something but was too embarrassed to tell them about the pictures." Melanie took one bottle of beer and her refilled wine glass while I slipped money in the tip jar. "To be honest, at the time I was more upset about the accusation. I didn't give the pictures much thought until I was older."

She made a face indicating the story sickened her.

"Thank you, son." My father removed one bottle of beer from my hand then motioned for his friend to do the same. Melanie held the bottle out to John Barkley.

"We'll see you later." I took Melanie's hand and turned to walk away.

"You look very familiar to me." John Barkley touched Melanie's arm prompting her to stop walking.

"Ryan and I have been on the cover of at least ten sleazy magazines in the past six months. You probably recognized me from your last supermarket run."

"No, that's not it."

"She's a Broadway actress. Maybe you've seen one of her performances," my father suggested.

"No, that's not it either." He scratched the white hair on his head. "Now it's going to drive me crazy. Are you from around here?"

"No. I must have a twin." Melanie's response had an edge to it that caught me by surprise.

He turned to my father and laughed. "You know I'll remember at four in the morning when there's no one around to tell. I've been slipping lately. Last week I could not remember where I had left my watch, only to find it…"

We walked away from the conversation and returned to our table. The DJ turned the music down and created excitement by announcing Santa's arrival. My sister parked Frankie in front of Santa's chair to make sure he didn't miss anything.

"How do you think he's going to react when Santa arrives?" I asked George with a chuckle. "Melanie's niece freaked when we brought her to the mall last year to see him."

"He liked him last year, but that doesn't mean anything." George removed a camera from his coat pocket and stood up. "I'd better get over there to take pictures or else your sister will kill me."

Melanie excused herself for the ladies' room. On the way out, she bumped into Santa and his twelve elves, as they rang bells and handed out candy canes. You would think he was handing out money the way the parents pushed and shoved in order to get their child a piece of candy. Some kids were crying when Santa came near them, while others cried because they couldn't see him. I would think as a parent with a child frightened by Santa you wouldn't force them to go near him, but that was not the case. These parents placed their frightened children on his lap, and then pleaded with the child to stop crying long enough for a picture or two. I am not sure who I pitied more, the child or Santa.

When Melanie returned from the ladies' room, I told her about the craziness she had missed. "Promise me we will not force our children to do something that frightens them."

"Mm hum."

"It just looks so wrong." I turned to look at her and noticed her pale skin and red eyes.

"Are you all right?" I put the back of my hand up to her cheek and then her forehead. Her skin felt cool.

She slipped something into her purse. "Yeah, I guess...I'm fine.

"What's that?" I asked about the envelope.

"My ankle is bothering me a little. Can we go home?"

I eyed her wearily. "Yeah, I think we've both had enough."

Chapter Nine

Melanie

Nancy was not pleased that Ryan and I left the party early. She pleaded with us to stick around until dessert ended. I had no interest in pleasing my mother-in-law and was happy Ryan hadn't backed down.

I leaned my chair back and closed my eyes during the car ride home. My thoughts were on the envelope tucked away in my purse. Unlike the first envelope, there was no denying the contents of this one were meant to scare me. Someone at the party slipped it under the bathroom door. They wanted me to know my past mistakes were no longer secret.

Other than Nancy and her friend Lana, I was not aware anyone else was in the ladies' room. Based on the unfavorable comments they made about me, I doubt they knew anyone was there either-including me.

I remained in the stall for several minutes after they left trying to console myself.

"The conversation about Lana's daughter has you *this* upset?" Ryan interrupted my thoughts. He was shaking his head in what appeared to be annoyance.

I have spent the last two years trying not to cause problems between Ryan and his family. I've had my fill of wearing phony smiles and pretending to miss nasty comments shot in my direction. Now he's going to give me attitude?

"The conversation about Lana's daughter annoyed me," I snapped. "Learning that your mother put her up to sharing the story infuriated me."

"Why do you think my mother made her tell the story?"

"I overheard them talking in the ladies' room. You should also know that your mother is hoping to end our marriage before we have kids. According to your sister, the plan has been in motion since we met." I glared at him. "Did you enjoy the dinners at your mother's house with the ex-girlfriends she invited?"

"Melanie, I...don't..."

"I don't want to hear excuses right now, Ryan. I need some time to think."

He didn't say anything else.

Once inside the house, I climbed the stairs, grabbed my nightgown and a towel, and then locked myself in the bathroom.

I hate fighting with Ryan and normally don't give him the silent treatment, but I needed space. He would hover if I hadn't started a fight with him. I planned to speak to Ryan about his mother after I spoke to my sister about the contents of the envelope.

My hands shook as I typed the text message to Jessica. While I waited for a response, I turned the shower on, stripped out of my dress, stepped into the shower and washed myself. The warm water felt good against my cool skin.

The pinging sound of my cell phone indicated I made contact with Jessica. Turning the water temperature down so only cold water was running, I leaped out of the shower, wrapped a towel around myself and grabbed my phone.

I'm here. We've been in the house all day. Lori is still sick. Her message read.

I'm sorry to hear that. I responded out of courtesy, before charging forward with my problem. It wasn't that I didn't care about my niece, I was just anxious to get answers.

I need your help.

What's wrong? she responded.

Ryan introduced me to a man who keeps naked pictures of teenagers in his toolbox. He kept telling me he's seen pictures of me, but insisted they were not in magazines or on television. Then I received an envelope. Inside were naked pictures of Amanda.

Was she one of the girls photographed with you that night? She typed.

Yes. That's not all. Earlier this week I received an envelope containing a pair of underwear and a note asking me to model them. Ryan thought it was a gift from some crazed fan. I'm not so sure anymore.

Someone was moving outside the bathroom door. Fearing

it was Ryan, I turned the volume of my phone down so he wouldn't hear the pinging sound of incoming text messages.

That is suspicious. I think it's time you come clean about that night.

The thought of telling my parents horrified me. I couldn't imagine what Ryan would think.

A story Ryan once told me popped into my mind. It happened six months after he arrived in California. His job at a local car wash left him with enough money to pay his rent, but not a penny left for food. One day a customer offered him five hundred dollars to escort her to a party. She was older, but attractive and he was strapped for cash. With no acting prospects, he accepted her invitation. She rented a tuxedo for him and they attended the formal dinner together. The evening was pleasant and he enjoyed her company, so he agreed to go back to her house for a drink rather than going home to the dingy room he had been renting.

One drink turned into three and it soon became evident the woman was looking for more than conversation. She kissed him a few times, ran her hand up the inside of his leg, and unbuttoned his tuxedo. He moved her hand to a safer location and told her while he was enjoying her company, he didn't intend to have sex with her. She threatened not to pay him if he turned her down. Without a second thought he left without the money, admitting it was worth living on crackers and water for the next two weeks.

I would have shared my experience with him had I not traded *my* morals for cash.

After the honeymoon I'll tell him. Is there anything we can do to stop this without Ryan finding out?

After your honeymoon you'll find ten more reasons not to tell him, she responded. *I don't think you can wait any longer, Melanie. You have to tell Mom, Dad and Ryan before they read about it in the paper. I know you think you did something horrible, but you are not to blame.*

I did some stupid things that night.

Melanie, stop beating yourself up. She typed. *I'll take care of the legal aspect. You speak to Ryan.* I felt sick. *I'll call you tomorrow to check on Lori. Thank you for listening. Love you.*

Love you too.

I erased the text conversation, closed my cell phone and

placed it on the pile of clothing I gathered. Using my toes, I picked the wet towel up off the floor and threw it into the hamper.

I could see a shadow moving under the door. I figured it was Ryan waiting for me to emerge. The thought irritated me. I was not sure what, if anything, I was going to say to him.

Relief washed over when I opened the door and saw Marcy heading downstairs. She was most likely milling around waiting for Frankie to fall asleep.

I pretended to be sleeping when Ryan came to bed. At some point, I drifted off into a restless slumber. Around four in the morning, anxiety awakened me. I lay in bed trying to slow my breathing and push the nightmare of John Barkley and the pictures out of my head.

The dream aroused my fears once again. My thoughts drifted back to Jack Boucher. We met ten years earlier, when I was eighteen and he was in his mid-twenties. He had dark, straight, shoulder-length hair and piercing blue eyes. He liked to show off his toned chest by keeping most of the buttons on his shirt undone. His jeans were expensive and fashionably torn—every bit as stylish as I imagined a fashion photographer to be. It's funny how he had impressed me at the time. Now the thought of him made my skin crawl.

I rolled onto my side and wiped a tear as it ran down my cheek. Feeling alone, I slid closer to Ryan and placed my head on his chest. In response, he wrapped his arm around me, kissed my head, and asked if I was all right.

"No," I whispered, not expecting him to hear me.

"What's the matter?"

I regretted my off-the-cuff decision to answer him. "Nothing. Go back to sleep."

He awakened himself by rubbing his hand over his face. "Please talk to me. I don't want my family to come between us. We'll pack our things and leave now if you want."

I shook my head. "Ryan, I have a problem much larger than your mother."

He sat up. "What's going on?"

"Your father's friend John…"

"Did he do something to you?" He interrupted.

"I don't know." The emotions I wrestled with all night spilled out of my eyes. Without asking further questions, Ryan enveloped me within his strong arms, allowing me time to sob. For the first time in my life, I feared something far worse than those pictures resurfacing. Rejection horrified me. I craved his arms around me. Since I hadn't shared this experience with anyone except Jessica, I could not even begin to imagine the reaction I would receive from him. *What if he is disgusted with me and asks for a divorce?* I was angry with myself for opening my big mouth. I should have left the secret locked away in my head.

"You're scaring me Melanie." He combed his fingers through my hair. "What did he do to you?"

As painful as it was to end the embrace, I pulled away from the warmth of Ryan's chest and sat Indian style on the bed. "Something horrible happened to me when I was a teenager. It was after I had enrolled in the theatrical high school in Manhattan."

"What does this have to do with tonight?" he asked.

I removed the pictures I received from my purse and handed them to him. "John insisted he had seen pictures of me. Then tonight these were left in the ladies' room. The envelope was addressed to me."

Ryan looked confused. "Who is this?"

"A girl I went to high school with. These pictures were meant to scare me. So was the underwear I received the other night."

"I don't understand. Why would someone send these pictures to you?"

"They know a secret about me."

He stared open-mouthed. I could tell his brain was working hard to figure out the cryptic conversation we were having. Before I lost my nerve, I started at the beginning. "I promised my parents if they allowed me attend the high school in the city, I would pay my own living expenses. Between school, studying, acting lessons and auditions, I had little time for a steady job. One day after dance class, I overheard two of my classmates talking about a modeling job they had been offered. As usual, I was short on cash and jumped at the opportunity to work with them. The job paid two hundred dollars, which was enough to cover my expenses for a couple of months. We went to the photographer's studio, which doubled as his apartment. You'd think that would have tipped us off."

Our eyes met briefly, before embarrassment forced me to I look away.

"What happened, Melanie?"

"Jack, the photographer, offered us drinks to ease the discomfort of posing in skimpy underwear. Three drinks later, the photo shoot began. Each wardrobe change resulted in less clothing and more provocative poses."

"So you kept drinking?"

I nodded. "One of my last memories was Jack threatening to fire us because I refused to unhook the latches on the corset I was wearing. I remember my friend Amanda yelling at me. She planned to buy a car with the money and freaked over the possibility of being fired." I paused to swallow a lump in my throat. "I barely remember getting home that night. I do recall the cab pulling over so I could throw up. Somehow, I got back to my dorm room in one piece. He never did pay us."

Ryan's jaw tightened as he processed the information. Taking a deep breath, he asked if Jack did anything to me.

His words awakened an unanswered fear deep inside of me. "There were pictures."

Anger burned in his eyes. "What pictures, Melanie?"

"Horrible ones." I sobbed. "We called him a few times. When he didn't respond, we went to his apartment looking for our money." I wiped a tear as it ran down my face. "The professionalism he displayed the evening of the photo shoot was gone, as were his manners."

"What part of intoxicating minors did you find professional?"

The question felt like a slap across the face. "I was eighteen, Ryan. I thought adults acted this way." I hugged a pillow against my body. "Jack's friends were there the night we returned. They made crude comments, which Jack found amusing. It left me with an uneasy feeling. I wanted to leave, but Julie and Amanda wanted the money, and we were all curious to see the pictures. After some prodding, Jack walked us into his bedroom. I came close to vomiting when I saw the pictures taped up on the wall. I have no memory of posing for the pictures he had on display. They must have been taken after we passed out." I spent years trying to forget the pictures. Now, they were fresh in my mind. "The pictures were of the three of us in bed with him. They were sexually explicit." My words were barely a whisper.

Ryan punched the bed, stood up and walked out of the bedroom. I wanted to follow him, but couldn't. I was too frightened and sick to move. Many different emotions ran through my head, yet anger was the most overwhelming. I was angry with my sister for insisting I tell Ryan, angry with Jack Boucher for taking advantage of my friends and me, angry with Ryan for not assuring me we'd get through this and angry at myself for making one dumb decision after another throughout the entire ordeal.

The sound of someone heaving pulled me out of self-pity and had me sprinting to the bathroom. I tapped my fingernails against the door. "Ryan, let me in."

It took a minute for him to unlock the door.

"Are you all right?"

He nodded.

Neither of us spoke for several agonizing minutes. Tears streamed down my face while I waited for him to say something.

He brushed his teeth, wiped his mouth and pulled me close to his body.

"I want to punch someone." He said, "The thought of that man touching...I can't handle it."

"He did some awful things, but I wasn't raped."

"You passed out. How would you know?"

Humiliation swept over me. I was unable to look my husband in the eye while sharing intimate details of another relationship, so I focused on my polished toenails. "I was twenty when I slept with someone for the first time. Evidence pointed to it being *my first time*."

"Oh." He craned his neck to the side, indicating the conversation was uncomfortable, yet his eyes signified relief. He took my hand and led me back to his childhood bedroom. Once behind closed doors, the inquisition resumed.

"I assume you never went to the police."

I sat down in the middle of the bed. "Jack threatened us not to. He said he would tell the police he paid us for sex. He said he had the pictures to prove we were prostitutes. When Julie told her brother Tommy, he said a defense attorney would rip us to shreds. I couldn't handle my parents hearing lies about me. I went to Jack's apartment believing I was going to be a model."

Ryan paced the floor.

"Julie's brother Tommy planned to visit Jack with a few of his martial art buddies. He said he was going to teach Jack a lesson," I admitted. "I suggested we speak to Jessica instead. She was in law school and was interning for a law firm."

"No one suggested you go to the hospital to get checked out?" He looked appalled.

"Jessica demanded I go, but a week had passed before I called her. It was too late by then."

Anger seeped out of Ryan's eyes.

"I didn't want my parents to know. I was afraid they would make me leave the school. Jessica's boss called Jack and threatened to go to the police if he didn't produce the pictures. Jack was frightened enough to turn the pictures and negatives over to Jessica. He also signed an affidavit swearing that he had destroyed all copies."

"Did you ever tell your parents?"

"No. I didn't discuss any of this for six years," I told him. "While working for the cruise line, a passenger left a note with the cruise director inviting me to model for him. The description of the man matched Jack's description. I waited days for the pictures to show up. Thankfully, they never did. It took months to push that memory to the back of my mind and it's been locked away ever since."

Ryan continued pacing. "How would Mister Barkley have gotten his wrinkled hands on those photographs?" He stopped walking and gnawed on the side of his finger while deep in thought. "We need to press charges against the photographer."

"My sister is ready to take legal action should the pictures turn up."

"I want to end it *before* the pictures turn up."

"No, Ryan."

He stared at me in disbelief. "Why would you let him get away with a crime?"

"I don't want to face it."

"You want to worry about those pictures every day of your life?" He hissed at me. "We are on the cover of dozens of magazines every month. If these pictures do exist, they *will* eventually show up. I don't want to be blind-sided when they do."

"This is why I'm telling you now. If I had my way, you would have never found out about the pictures. I was petrified of your reaction." I lowered my face into my hands, once again allowing the tears to fall. Ryan pulled me into his arms and consoled me.

"What are you thinking right now?" I asked.

"I'm sick over the thought of someone violating you. I want to kill the man who did this," he said, "I want to erase your pain and the torment you've endured for so long." Sadness was present in his eyes when he released me. "I am also...I'm not sure if I am feeling hurt or...embarrassment." He cupped my cheek in his hand. "Why were you afraid to tell me about this? I love you, Melanie. I love you *so* much. This is something horrible from your past. You have done nothing wrong. You were a child who was taken advantage of by a piece-of-shit human being," he whispered in my hair before kissing my head.

"I should have handled things differently that night. I was so foolish."

"At twenty-eight years old, you would have done things differently. An eighteen-year-old doesn't have the experience to know better. Don't blame yourself."

"What are you going to say to your father's friend?"

"Mister Barkley? I'm not sure. I can promise you, he will be one sorry old man if I find out he has those pictures." He slid into bed and invited me to lay with him.

I nestled in his arms. "I'm sorry I never told you."

"Now that I know, we'll take care of this together."

Chapter Ten

Ryan

My mind raced the rest of the night. I could not believe my wife didn't trust me enough to confide in me. What had I done-or failed to do-to make her believe I would turn my back on her?

Rushing out of the room to vomit could not have helped matters. Nevertheless, I couldn't help it. I couldn't deal with the realization that someone violated my beautiful wife. Learning it happened when she was a child, sickened me that much more.

I squeezed Melanie closer to me and kissed her head. Even in slumber, concern crept into her features. I wanted to take the pain away. We needed to take care of Jack Boucher for once and for all. I planned to begin by visiting John Barkley.

Before I did anything, I had to finish what started last night when my parents returned home from the dance. I slipped out of bed, careful not to awaken Melanie, and went downstairs. The smell of coffee told me someone was up. I was sure I would find my mother in the kitchen. At least I hoped I would.

"Good morning Ryan," my mother greeted me with unease.

"Melanie and I are leaving."

"Ryan...please..."

"I've given it a lot of thought," I interrupted her. "You're never going to change."

"I admitted I was wrong," she said. "I told you I only act-ed out of concern for your wellbeing. I didn't want you to get hurt."

"You hurt me Mom," I admitted. "And you've hurt my wife. I won't stand for that."

"I didn't understand. The way I saw it, you two put your-selves in a tough position by spending so much time apart."

"You don't know anything about us."

"Long-distance relationships don't last Ryan. Is she willing to give up her career to follow you around the country?"

"If I asked, she would," I said.

"Why hasn't she thought to do it without you having to ask?" She waited for an answer. "I don't think either of you are willing to sacrifice your career for one another."

"You have no right judging my marriage."

The kitchen door opened and Melanie stepped inside. The conversation paused when we noticed her.

"I love your son," Melanie said.

I wondered if she had been listening by the door or if she overheard us on her way into the kitchen.

"I have thought of leaving my job every single day since meeting Ryan."

"Neither of you have answered my question," my mother reminded us. "Why haven't you quit your job and moved to California to be with Ryan."

"We weren't married," Melanie told her. "Until recently, neither of us had enough money to support ourselves. Forget about supporting one another."

"Had she quit her job after I found success with *Zombie Wars*," I added, "you would've accused her of being a gold digger."

"What are your plans now that you are married?" My mother pressed on.

"To take life one day at a time," Melanie said. "For the next month I plan to spend every second with Ryan. In February I will return to work."

Marcy entered the room in search of coffee. When she realized what she had walked in on, her face dropped. She stood in the middle of the kitchen, probably trying to decide whether she should run.

"Magazines say terrible things about your relationship. How can I have faith in your relationship when every week I read stories about infidelity within your marriage?" my mother asked.

"They are all lies," Melanie told her.

"Explain the pictures," she demanded.

"Photoshopped," I said. "You can't believe half of the things you read in magazines."

"You have to admit, the pictures look real."

"Why do you believe articles written by strangers, but you don't believe us?" Melanie asked.

"She decided that our marriage will fail and refuses to believe anything else," Ryan said. "Here is the sad part, Mom. Melanie means more to me than you do."

"Ryan!" Marcy cried out.

"Don't start!" I yelled at Marcy before turning to my mother.

"What a foolish woman you are." I shook my head in disgust. "You have a family who loves you. Instead of basking in that love and maybe returning some of it, you have managed to destroy this family. You should have accepted me for who I am. Instead, you have pushed me away. You have made things so bad that I hate coming home."

"How dare you speak to me this way?"

She slapped me.

* * * *

I tossed the suitcases on the bed, pulled our clothing out of the drawers, and packed them. All the while, Melanie stood in the corner of the room reeling from the argument with my mother.

"What happened down there?" she asked.

"You can't reason with my mother."

"I didn't expect things to get so messy."

"How long do we sit back and allow her to treat us badly? I've allowed it for too long now."

Melanie straightened the crumpled clothing in the suitcase. "I thought we'd be able to talk things through. I never should have told you the things she said."

"Will our entire marriage be filled with secrets?" The words shot out of my mouth before I could stop them.

She turned from me and bolted for the door.

"Melanie...stop. I'm sorry." I grasped her arm to prevent her from leaving. "I didn't mean it that way. Please don't walk out." I sat down on the bed and lowered my head into my hands. "I don't want you to keep things from me. I'm your husband. I want to be the person you turn to."

She sat down next to me and rubbed my back. "I've complicated your life."

"Don't say things like that." I leaned over and kissed her

temple. "You've made my life better. Now, let's go home."

We changed out of our pajamas and grabbed the suitcases. I braced for another argument with my family, but was pleased the living room was empty. Without bothering to look for anyone, we continued out to the car.

"Ryan," Marcy called from the house. "Please reconsider your decision to leave."

"Marcy, stop wasting your breath."

She followed us to the car. "Stay for Dad's sake. He's devastated."

I stopped walking. I never considered what this would do to my father.

"He threatened to leave if she didn't straighten things out with you."

"She deserves to be alone. It might teach her a lesson." I lowered the suitcases to the ground and unlocked the trunk.

Marcy clucked her tongue in disapproval. "You're angry with her for trying to destroy your marriage. Do you want to be the reason our parents' marriage ends?"

"It won't be my fault."

I threw the suitcases in the trunk, one at a time.

"Melanie, please talk some sense into him."

I shot forward and pointed my finger in Marcy's face. "Don't you dare put this on Melanie. Mom caused her own problems. She destroyed our family. Now she has to suffer the consequences."

Melanie pulled me back. "We don't have to stay, but we should talk to them. Let's try to work things out."

"Please Ryan," Marcy interjected. "Dad is crying."

* * * *

My father had gone to bed last night after the Christmas party, so he missed the heated conversation between my mother and me. The hour-long screaming match this afternoon filled him in on the details. His face turned bright red when he learned my mother had been working to destroy my marriage.

Twice my mother threatened to leave the room. Both times my sister promised to pack her family up and return to Florida if she didn't work things out with Melanie and me. While my mother didn't appreciate the threats, she remained in the chair with her arms folded across her chest. I figured the thought of losing her entire family frightened her.

Once she finished defending her actions, my mother apologized and promised to change her attitude toward Melanie and me. I don't believe the discussion will change anything. My mother will never accept my career choice, nor do I see her welcoming Melanie into our family. If anything, she will blame Melanie for this fight.

Her words meant nothing to me, but Melanie accepted the apology.

"Does this mean you'll stay here?" Marcy asked.

"No," I told her. "We're staying in a hotel."

"Christmas is two days away, Ryan," Mom interjected. "Please stay."

"We will spend Christmas Eve and Christmas Day with you, but we will not stay here."

"That's a fair compromise," George told them.

* * * *

We checked into a hotel twenty minutes away from my parents' house. Red wallpaper with thin black lines covered the walls. The rugs were black with tiny red dots and the bedspread was a brilliant red. A mirror hung above the bed. Chandeliers, dripping with crystals, lit the room.

"I'm guessing this is the honeymoon suite." Melanie laughed.

"I wouldn't want to stay anywhere else."

The bathroom walls were a pale shade of pink and the floors were gray. Candles and flower arrangements surrounded the soft-pink Jacuzzi bathtub, which was nestled in the corner of the room. Directly across from the tub was a glass shower wide enough to fit two people. In the opposite corner were steps leading to the swimming pool. Another short staircase led to a sauna.

Melanie remained in the poolroom while I waited for the bellhop to drop off our suitcases. By the time I joined her downstairs, she was sitting on the side of the pool with her jeans rolled up to her knees.

"The warm water feels good against my legs," she told me. "But the dry heat is causing me to sweat."

"Why don't you get out of that heavy sweater and join me

in the pool?" I stripped out of my clothing and tossed them on to the rug so they wouldn't get wet.

"Is the suite locked?"

I nodded. "The water's warm. Are you coming in?"

Melanie slipped out of her clothing and tossed them on top of my pile. Goose bumps covered her skin as she entered the water. I swam over and wrapped my arms around her waist. We floated around the pool with our bodies entwined. For the first time since we arrived in Pennsylvania, the muscles in Melanie's shoulders loosened and the crease between her eyes was gone. I was equally at peace. The intimate time with my wife erased the anger and frustration that had consumed me over the past few days.

Chapter Eleven

Melanie

Christmas Eve dinner at Dave and Nancy's house was awkward. We plastered phony smiles on our faces and did our best to keep the conversation going, even though the evening felt strained. Thankfully, David's sister Janet, who was spending the holiday with us, livened up the evening by suggesting we play cards. The friendly competition got us joking and laughing with one another. Even Ryan loosened up a bit.

I asked Ryan about Janet once. He told me that she was engaged to three different men, yet she was never a bride. She ended the first engagement six months before their chosen wedding date when she realized she was no longer in love with him. The second engagement ended when she learned her fiancé was cheating on her. Her third fiancé, the love of her life, died in a car accident.

She was twenty-seven years old when her fiancé passed away. It was then she realized she would never marry and have children. The path of trying to find a mate just proved to be too painful, so she returned to school and focused her efforts on her career.

While Aunt Janet came across as an upbeat person, I have wondered if her decision to give up on love lead to a lonely life. Ryan claims independence has made her a happier person.

Janet tried to convince us to spend the night at the house this way the whole family would open presents together in the morning. Ryan refused. Shortly after dessert, he fetched our jackets and told his parents we would meet them at Church. He didn't intend to spend Christmas morning with his family.

I was pleased Nancy refrained from having one of her temper tantrums.

"Thank you for spending Christmas Eve with us." Her tone was cool. "We'll see you at Church. Mass begins at eleven."

"Try to arrive thirty minutes before. It's difficult to save seats," Dave added. Spending the night under Nancy and Dave's roof was not something I wanted to do, but staying in a hotel on Christmas Eve wasn't much better. The lack of decorations made it difficult to enjoy the holiday. I missed the Christmas tree in our apartment and wished Ryan and I were at home making love in the living room with the soft glow of blinking lights shining down on us.

Ryan disrupted my thoughts by leaving our bed. He walked to the closet and returned with a small box in his hand. "I planned to give this to you the day we got married, but it wasn't finished in time."

He flipped the box open revealing a sapphire and diamond ring. The familiar ring brought tears to my eyes.

"How did you know about this?"

He smiled. "Jessica e-mailed me a picture. I couldn't get the exact ring; I had my jeweler duplicate it. I hope you like it."

"I love it." I kissed him.

"This ring has something the one in the store lacks."

"What?" I beamed.

He slid the ring out of the box and showed me the band. "There's an inscription."

"You are my life, my love, my everything." Tears continued to flow.

"I mean every word. I cannot imagine life without you."

"I wouldn't *want* to live without you," I told him. "I love the ring and I love you. Thank you."

I admired my ring for the next several minutes. Then I realized something and pouted.

"That's not the face of a happy person."

"Your presents are at your parents' house. How do we celebrate Christmas morning without presents?"

"I can wait until after mass to open my gifts. That will give us more time in the morning to..." He raised his eyebrows.

I smiled. "This isn't how I imagined spending our first Christmas."

He turned on his side and propped himself up on his elbow. "We're together. That's all that matters. If it makes you feel better, I left most of your presents at my parents' house too."

* * * *

The next morning a knock at the door awakened us.

"Who is that?" I asked.

"Your next present." He grinned.

"What?"

He leaped out of bed and disappeared into the living room. I heard him thank our visitor before closing and locking the door. Moments later, he appeared before me holding a puppy wrapped in a large red bow.

"Merry Christmas." He lowered the dog into my arms. "I am not sure how much protection this little guy will provide, but he guarantees companionship when I'm away."

"He's cute," I rubbed the dog's head. "I'm just not sure the landlord is going to allow us to have a dog."

"Our lease provides for a dog less than fifty pounds. I would have preferred a larger breed but figured *you* would like a Yorkie. You can dress him up and stuff."

"I love him." I stretched the truth. A puppy was not something I wanted, but Ryan didn't need to know that.

"Thank you for my new roommate." I kissed his chest. "Why don't we lock our new friend up so you can unwrap your present?" I removed the bow from the puppy and tied it around my neck.

* * * *

"Are you sure you like the dog?" Ryan asked while we dressed for Church.

"I do." I was honest with him this time. "How can I not fall in love with this face?" I picked the dog up from his box and squeezed his face. "It will be nice having someone greet me when I return home from work each day. I hate walking into an empty apartment."

"Any thoughts on a name?"

"Holly was the first name that popped into my head, with it being Christmas and all. Then I noticed my new gift is a male." I chuckled. "So, I'm thinking Versace."

"I like it."

"What do you think about your name?" I nuzzled the dog against my face. He licked me with his tiny tongue, leading me to believe he was pleased with the name choice.

* * * *

The Church Nancy and Dave belonged to was beautiful. Considering we were in the mountains of Pennsylvania, I had imagined the Church to be rustic, but it wasn't. The white marble Altar matched the floor tile. High hats filled the church ceiling. Christmas trees stood on either side of the Altar and wreaths hung in between the long, stained-glass windows. The church made me feel at home and for the first time in my life, I rethought my decision not to participate in organized religion. This church called out to me and made me want to become a parishioner.

We met Nancy, Dave and the rest of the family by the back door. Together, we walked up the main aisle to our seats. Members of the congregation murmured as we passed. A few stood by their seats and stole a glance while others pointed. No one approached us.

The Pastor shook hands with Ryan's parents and then Marcy and George. When he reached Ryan and me, he stopped and smiled. For a moment, I thought he had some special priest power that allowed him to pick out the people who weren't practicing Catholics. I feared he would ask us to leave.

"We are honored to have both of you celebrating with us today." The Pastor extended his hand, and then held mine when I returned the gesture.

"Thank you Father," Ryan responded.

"Our lead singer has come down with a virus and cannot join us today." He smiled at us both. "We were hoping you would share the wonderful gift God has given to you by singing with the choir this morning."

I looked at Ryan and smiled, anxious to hear what excuse he would use to get out of this request. Horror set in when I realized the priest directed the request at me.

"I don't think so," I told him. "I...I wouldn't know the first thing about singing in Church."

"I don't expect you to lead the choir." He chuckled. "I hoped you would sing a song or two. Do you know *Ave Maria* and *Silent Night*?"

I blushed. "I do know the songs, but not well enough to sing them in Church today. I would have to practice with the band."

"The choir is downstairs practicing now. We have thirty minutes before Mass begins. That should be plenty of time."

"I...I don't think..." I looked to Ryan for assistance.

"Thank you for the offer, Father," Ryan began. "If it wasn't last minute we would be thrilled to participate."

The priest looked down at the floor for a moment or two before returning his gaze to my face. "No one is here to judge you, Melanie. Please do it for God. Grant him the simple request on this glorious Christmas morning?"

"Okay." I smiled despite anxiety racing through my veins. I could not believe I agreed to sing.

The Pastor's eyes danced with excitement. "Thank you. What a treat this will be for our congregation."

Ryan escorted me to the basement where the choir was practicing. It took effort on my part not to spew a few four-letter-words his way. "What the heck did I get myself into?"

"You'll be fine, Melanie," he told me. "Even on your worst day, you sound fantastic."

"You'll say anything as long as you don't have to sing," I snapped.

The choir practiced in an oversized room with cream-colored walls and a large crucifix hanging on the far wall. The band tuned their instruments while the choir practiced hymns.

Donald introduced himself as the choir leader. "Here are detailed instructions for you." He handed me a piece of yellow paper filled with written instructions. The notes directed me when to stand, kneel, and sit. It also instructed when and what I would sing.

He grabbed the attention of choir members by clapping his hands three times. "I would like to introduce you to Melanie..." He looked at me expectantly.

"Melanie O'Shaughnessy...Carlisle." I added my married name after a moment's pause.

"Melanie will be singing with us today," Donald continued. "Please grab your music so we can practice. We'll begin with *Ave Maria.*"

I glared at Ryan. "You should be singing. It's your Church."

"I sang with the choir once or twice when I was a kid," he told me. "Apparently I left a lasting impression–and it wasn't good. That's why they asked you."

I reviewed the music Donald gave me. Beads of sweat formed on my forehead when I noticed the song was in Latin. "Um...Donald, I don't know Latin."

"No problem." He smiled. "Here is the English version."

"Thank you."

"I'm going to return to the pew," Ryan told me. "Will you be okay on your own?"

"I'll be fine," I snapped. "You and I both know you can sing. This is the last time you pretend otherwise."

Donald blew into a pitch-pipe tuner then counted to three. The choir members mimicked the three-note scale by singing the word *Alleluia*, and then the pianist played the song introduction. At that point, Donald motioned for me to begin. The sheet of music vibrated against my hand. I missed my cue the first two times. The third time, I stumbled over the words.

The fourth time I closed my eyes. Instead of concentrating on the choir and the piano and worrying about my part, I felt the music in my soul. When it came time for me to sing, the words rang out of my mouth and the tune floated around the room like angels in flight.

When the song concluded, the room was silent. I looked up, fearing a negative reaction. There have been times a song sounded good to my ears but received horrible feedback from the director.

A few of the women dabbed their eyes. A couple more whispered back and forth. Donald's eyes were wide. "I have never heard anything so beautiful in my life."

My face grew warm.

"Now you know why she is on Broadway." A short woman with light red, curly hair smiled at me. "Nancy told me you and Ryan were visiting for Christmas. When Loretta came down with the virus, I suggested the Pastor ask you to join us."

I smiled, even though I wanted to strangle her for making the suggestion. Even after practice, I wasn't thrilled singing during Mass.

The woman walked over to me and extended her hand. "My name is Eve Austin."

"It's a pleasure to meet you." I shook her hand. "I have to be honest," I leaned over and whisper close to her ear, "I am more nervous about performing today then I am when I'm at work."

She waved her hand as if to tell me I was acting silly. "You are a successful actress. Why would you be nervous about small potatoes like singing in our Church?"

Donald told everyone to take a five-minute break while the guitar player fixed a broken string. Eve motioned for me to have a seat. We walked arm-in-arm to the chairs.

"This is my in-law's parish and they are fond of the community. I don't want to embarrass them by making a mistake."

"You are a very nice daughter-in-law. I hated my in-laws. My mother-in-law was an evil woman." Her facial expression displayed the disdain she felt for her husband's mother. "I am the mother of four sons. When they were born, I promised myself I would never be mean to my daughter-in-laws. When each of my sons married, I took their bride to the side and told them I wanted to be their friend."

I could not help but smile at the cute woman.

"You know...I wanted to be an actress. I took singing and dancing lessons from the time I was three. After years of watching Shirley Temple, I wanted to break into show business. Shortly after graduation, my boyfriend was drafted." She touched my hand every so often while she spoke. "He was stationed in Texas and I wanted to move with him. Back in my day, we didn't live with our boyfriends. So, two months after I completed high school, I married him and had my oldest son ten months later." She shrugged with a smile. "Singing with the Church choir is the only performing I have done. Here I am fifty years later still singing in Church."

I found myself resisting the urge to hug her. "How would you like to step out of the choir today and sing beside me on the Altar?"

Her cheeks flushed over. "I don't think the others would be happy. I'm new to this parish and don't want to make enemies."

I could tell from the twinkle in her far-off eyes that she was imagining herself standing in front of the congregation singing for them. "It can't hurt to ask. I'll speak to Donald."

He was conversing with a member of the choir. They smiled in my direction when they noticed me waiting for their conversation to end.

"Do you need something, Melanie?" Donald asked.

"It's no secret that I am uncomfortable singing at mass today. Spur of the moment plans unnerve me a bit." I smiled. "So...I was wondering if Eve could sing beside me."

"Grace would be a better choice," the woman standing with Donald said.

"I was just speaking with Eve." I directed the conversation to Donald. "She was telling me she wanted to be an actress and I thought it would be a nice treat for her to sing with me today. I'm a believer of paying it forward."

He stared at me for a few moments. I feared he thought I was another pushy actress, and waved my hands in the air as if the motion would erase the thought from his head. "I'm not trying to be difficult," I began. "I thought having Eve sing with me today would make her feel...as if she was living her dream too."

Donald smiled and touched my arm. "It's very thoughtful of you Melanie. Eve told me her husband passed away five years ago and she's been having a difficult time since his death."

"She's worried the others might become angry with her. Would you let them know I made the request?"

He nodded.

"Do you know if she has plans for Christmas?

He shrugged. "I'm not sure."

I removed my cell phone from my pocket and sent a text to Ryan. *Would your Mother mind a guest for dinner tonight?*

A moment later, he responded. *She said we could bring the dog.*

I never thought to ask permission for the dog and was glad Ryan mentioned it. *I would like to invite a member of the choir. I just found out Eve Austin is going to be alone today and would like to invite her to join us.*

She says to ask her.

I walked back to Eve and sat down beside her on the metal folding chair. "Donald loved the idea. He will tell everyone I requested your help."

She clapped her hands in delight. "This is so exciting. It is not every day I get to sing with a Broadway actress. As a matter of fact, I have never sung with a Broadway actress."

Donald gathered the group to practice *Silent Night*.

We sang the song through in one take and were invited to rest our voices until mass began.

"What are your plans for Christmas?" I asked Eve when we returned to our seats. "We're having turkey for dinner and would love if you joined us."

Her expression grew serious. "I'm feeding the needy tonight."

I acknowledged her duty. "Would you like to stop by after you finish at the shelter? Ryan and I can pick you up."

"I drive." She assured me. "I work until six. Can I come around six-thirty?"

"That would be wonderful." I smiled at my new friend. "My husband gave me a new puppy for Christmas. I would love you to meet him. His name is Versace."

"Even your dog has a great name." She laughed. "I have often wondered what my stage name would have been had I pursued acting."

"I like your real name," I told her.

"If your Broadway friends are in church today and want to whisk me away to New York, tell them my name is Eve Versace." She waved her arm and held her hand in a dramatic pose before breaking into hysterics.

Three sharp claps grabbed our attention. "It's time to move upstairs to the Church. Mass begins in ten minutes." Donald's voice bounced off the bare walls.

I entwined my arm in Eve's as we climbed the stairs, not because I thought she needed help. Lord knows she was too spunky to need help walking up a flight of stairs. I was holding her arm because she gave me the same warm feeling I had gotten from my grandmother when I was a child.

Grace and her friends didn't look happy when Donald invited Eve to sit in the front row next to me. I could hear the comments made under their breath about some new woman coming in and taking over. I hoped Eve's hearing was not as good as mine was.

Of course, I was wrong. Eve's hearing was as sharp as her mind. "I guess Donald forgot to mention the conversation you had with him," she told me. "Look at the scowl on Grace's face. She must be furious having to sit in the second row of the choir after ten years of coveting the front seat."

"I'm sorry, Eve. I don't want to cause problems between you and your friends."

"These women are *not* my friends."

One of the choir members hushed her when she responded a little too loud for church. "My best friend is Mabel Wright. We did everything together. She died a year ago."

"I'm sorry to hear that."

"We have seven children between us. They are scattered around the United States, so we kept one another company.

My sons are very busy men." She was quick to defend the absence of her children. "They have families to support. We talk on the phone, but they do not have much time to visit."

My heart broke for this woman. "Do you have grandchildren?"

She nodded and raised five fingers.

"Ryan and I planned a trip right after the holidays. Now that we have Versace, I'm thinking of canceling it," I lied. "The tickets cannot be refunded but you can exchange them for other locations. Why don't you use them to visit your family after Christmas?"

She glanced at me for a moment or two before looking away.

"I would hate to give the airline that money when they didn't earn it." I pressed on.

"I'm sure your in-laws can use those tickets to visit Marcy and her family in Florida."

"It sounds like you spend a great deal of time helping others. It's time you help yourself. Please accept my gift."

"Two live in Georgia, one in New Jersey and the youngest lives in Ohio. I can drive to see my son in New Jersey. The two in Georgia only live an hour apart. I'd be able to visit all of my sons." She was silent for a few minutes. The silence told me she was mentally planning her trip. "Are you sure you can't use the tickets for something?"

I shook my head. "My new show begins in February. There isn't time for a vacation."

She smiled and squeezed my hand. I looked over at Ryan hoping he wouldn't mind me purchasing tickets for this woman. Of course I was not about to give up our honeymoon, but figured Eve wouldn't accept the tickets if she knew I was buying them for her. I was confident Ryan would make the same offer.

When the first music note rang out of the organ signaling the beginning of mass, I leaned over and whispered, "Merry Christmas, Eve Versace. Are you ready to sing?"

Chapter Twelve

Ryan

Melanie took my breath away when she walked onto the Altar wearing the black vintage pencil dress I brought her back from Italy. I bought it while on the movie tour with *Zombie Wars*. It was the first time I could afford to buy an expensive gift.

My mother squeezed my hand when Melanie started singing the opening hymn. I looked over my shoulder at the priest who sang on his way to the Alter. His voice reverberated through the church thanks to the microphone attached to his vestments. I hated that his voice interfered with Melanie's, and wished he would stop singing.

"I welcome you this beautiful Christmas morning..." The priest spread his arms in a joyous welcoming after the song concluded.

"Who is the woman standing with Melanie?" Marcy leaned across me to ask my mother.

"She's too short to be heard through Melanie's microphone," George added.

My mother shrugged. "We've spoken a few times, but I don't remember her name."

"Wanna bet she's our dinner guest?" I asked them. "Melanie befriends all kinds of people. Last week we had lunch with some lady who works at the toy store Melanie shops in."

"What?" Marcy tried to stifle a laugh.

"We had lunch with the woman who sold her Frankie's Christmas present," I whispered back.

My father shushed us.

"She recently joined the choir. I can't imagine why she was picked to accompany Melanie," my mother said.

"Melanie was probably nervous and asked for assistance," I whispered back.

I had a difficult time paying attention to the Mass. Rather than participating in the service, I scanned the pews for people I knew from my childhood.

Right before Melanie's next song, Donald set up a second microphone for the older woman. That annoyed me. I wanted the congregation to experience Melanie's voice without amateur singers interfering. My mother would be embarrassed if she heard my sinful thoughts. Melanie wouldn't be happy either.

"If I had one Christmas wish, it would be that the woman's microphone be disconnected." George leaned over Marcy to tell me.

"You should be ashamed of yourself making fun of her." Marcy gave George her usual nudge in the ribs to shut him up. Then leaned over close to me and admitted she agreed with him.

I snickered but didn't share my feelings.

One song during communion was not enough. The band played the song Melanie and her father walked up the aisle to on our wedding day. The contented look on her face made me want to run over and kiss her. Visions of her walking into church in the antique-white, satin peacock wedding dress floated around my head.

My mother elbowed me, bringing my thoughts back to the present. "Are you receiving communion?"

Much to her dismay, I didn't plan to receive. She glared down at me as she passed. "All you have been given and you don't go to church?"

I made a face acknowledging I was wrong, and then rolled my eyes. Right or wrong, it drives me crazy when she treats me like a screwed up little kid.

Melanie returned to the microphone one last time to sing. This time the older woman remained seated. I could not recall the name of the familiar Christmas hymn even though it was one of my favorites. The beat was quicker than usual and Melanie swayed back and forth in front of the microphone as she sang. I wondered if she added her own spin to the song.

At the conclusion of Mass, the congregation applauded both Melanie and the choir. Someone behind me, who looked familiar, slapped his hand on my shoulder. When I turned in his direction, he told me how lucky I was.

"I sure am." I smiled over my shoulder.

After mass, Melanie motioned that she was going downstairs with the choir. I slipped my coat on and stood by my parents, who were immersed a conversation with a couple who sat next us during mass. Naturally, my mother had to introduce me to the couple. This led to a lengthy conversation about how their family and friends will never believe they sat next to Ryan Carlisle during mass.

"What a beautiful voice your wife has. Promise me you'll bring her to sing again." My mother's friend Janice said as she passed our pew.

"She should make a Christmas album," Janice's husband added.

I thanked them both before turning to Marcy. "I'm going to get Melanie. Where should we meet you?"

"Meet us here." She hitched her head in my parents' direction. "We'll be here for a while. Mrs. Jensen just sent her husband to the car to get pictures of their new granddaughter."

I rolled my eyes and headed for the stairs. There are two sets of staircases leading to the basement. One set requires people to walk across the Altar. The second is in the back of the church. I could not bring myself to walk on the Altar so I headed toward the back of the church. Several people stopped to congratulate me on my recent marriage. A few asked for autographs. One young girl held up her cell phone begging me to take a picture with her.

Once downstairs, I scanned the music room for Melanie, but didn't see her. Donald told me he lost track of her after mass. A group of women pointed to the seats Melanie and her friend had been using.

The woman who sang with her during Mass scanned the room. "She said she would wait for me to finish my phone call."

"Maybe she went to find me," I told her.

"She was supposed to give me your parents' address. Did she tell you I was joining you for dinner?"

I nodded. "She probably went to get their address. I doubt she has it memorized."

"Either that or she changed her mind. People have canceled on me before." She lowered her eyes in a pathetic way.

"One thing Melanie would never do is rescind an invitation." I wrote the address down and handed it to her. "I'm going upstairs. Should Melanie return, please ask her to call."

I checked my phone but didn't find a missed call or text from Melanie. A call to her cell went to voice mail.

My family was still looking at pictures of their friends' new grandchild when I caught up with them. No one had seen Melanie.

Marcy checked the ladies' room, while I returned to the music room.

"You still can't find her?" Donald glanced around in disbelief.

"One moment she was standing by her coat, next moment she was gone," Netty Cleary announced. "We thought it was a bit rude that she left without saying goodbye."

I could not decide if I was worried or angry. I dialed her cell a second time, but didn't reach her.

"What's taking so long, Ryan?" my father asked from the staircase. "Frankie's getting antsy."

"We can't find Melanie," Marcy told him. "A few people saw her come down here after mass, but no one noticed her leave. Her coat is missing."

"What about the woman she sang with?"

"I'm as puzzled as you are," the redheaded woman chimed in. "By the way my name is Eve. We spoke after mass a few weeks ago."

My father didn't pay any attention to her. "There's no way she left the Church without someone noticing."

"It's too late to find out. Most people are gone." I pressed my fingers against my eyes in frustration. "I'm going to check outside."

"That's a good idea." Marcy rubbed my back. "Maybe she received a call. You go outside. Dad and I will look around here one more time."

Frustration turned into panic. "I cannot find my wife. Have you seen her?" I asked a small crowd of people standing outside the main doors.

"Who's your wife?" a man asked with a laugh.

It frustrated me that the first time I wanted to be recognized, I wasn't. "The woman who sang during mass," I snapped.

"She's a talented singer," a woman standing in the crowd told me. "Does she sing professionally?"

Realizing I was wasting my time, I continued without answering. I questioned a few other people as I descended the church steps. No one recalled seeing Melanie. Although the second group appeared star struck, they didn't ask for autographs. The fear oozing from my eyes must have warned them against asking. I circled the building, but found nothing.

Donald was on the front steps by the time I finished my lap around the Church. "No one has seen her. Do you want me to call the police?"

"Why is he calling the police? Where's Melanie?" The look on my mother's face matched the horror in my chest.

"Ryan!" George called to me. "We've found her."

"Where the hell was she? Is she all right?" Both relief and anger replaced my fear.

He shook his head. "She's hysterical and not making a bit of sense."

George and I raced through the lobby and down the basement stairs with Donald and my family in tow. I pushed past the crowd of people encircling Melanie. "What happened? Are you all right?" I hugged her tightly in an attempt to stop the hysterical crying.

"He had a knife." She managed to say in between sobs.

"Who?" I looked around as if the knife-wielding man was standing there.

"Are you hurt?" I slipped her coat off and checked for blood. There was a long red mark on her neck, but the skin wasn't broken. I ran my finger over the abrasion, as though doing so would erase the injury.

"I'm calling the police." Donald took his cell phone out of his coat pocket.

"No!" A crazed look settled in Melanie's eyes. "I don't want anyone to call the police," she sobbed. "I just want to go home."

I held her limp body against me. Something digging into my stomach caused me to pull away in search of the source. Tucked under her arm was a large manila envelope. I grasped the envelope, attempting to free it from her hand.

"Please leave it." She hugged it against her chest. The terror in her eyes answered any question I had about the contents.

My Aunt slipped Melanie's coat on her shoulders. George and I each held one of her arms. We walked only a few steps when she stumbled. A few more feet, she stumbled again. Not wanting her to injure herself, I scooped her into my arms. She protested for fear someone would take a picture of me carrying her out of church and submit it to the paper.

"There's no one around to take your picture," I assured her. She shuddered. "They're everywhere. Just let me walk."

Marcy placed sunglasses on Melanie's face to hide her red, swollen eyes. George and I walked her out to the car and settled her inside. Once Frankie and the women were in the car, the rest of us walked the church grounds searching for Melanie's attacker.

"Why won't she let us call the police?" Donald asked. "The cops will have a better chance of catching this guy while the details are fresh in her mind. They can fingerprint the area she encountered him."

"She's too hysterical right now to provide anyone with the particulars." We walked inside to search each pew. "She fears becoming tomorrow's tabloid headline. Having the paparazzi follow your every move leaves you a little paranoid." I checked under the first few pews hoping to find the coward hiding. "I'll call the police once we're at my parents' house. I want to give her a few minutes to calm down."

"She can't let the paparazzi get in the way of keeping her safe. This man could attack another woman. She needs to think of the safety of others too."

I understood Donald's concerns, but didn't need a lecture from him. "No one wants this guy more than me. He held a knife to my wife's throat. Next time it could be my mother."

I realized I was shouting at the man, so I pinched the bridge of my nose and took a breath. When I spoke again, my words were less aggressive. "I intend to call the police; however, Melanie isn't going to be any help while she's hysterical. Let's finish searching the church, so I can get her home."

"Any chance the church can be locked until the police arrive?" George asked.

Donald shrugged. "This is the last mass of the day. I can ask the Pastor."

I shook Donald's hand and thanked him for helping.

My parents' internist suggested we bring Melanie to the emergency room. When she refused, he called a prescription into the pharmacy to calm her nerves.

I helped Melanie out of her coat and brought her upstairs to my old bedroom. My father drove to the only open drug store in town to pick up the prescription. Afterwards, he went to our hotel room to retrieve Versace.

I lay in bed next to Melanie until he returned. Without

releasing the envelope, Melanie stuck the pill in her mouth, washed it down with a glass of water and slid back down under the covers.

"Promise me you won't call my family," She begged.

"I promise," I told her.

"Please don't look in the envelope. The pictures are worse than I thought they would be." Her words were slurred.

"I'll keep them safe until you're feeling better."

The tranquilizers won the battle and Melanie drifted to sleep without answering.

"What *is* inside the envelope, Ryan?" my mother asked in the disapproving tone she often uses. "I warned something like this would happen. The magazines have been writing about it for months."

"You don't know what you're talking about. The contents of the envelope have nothing to do with me. Melanie is being blackmailed."

"Who would do such a thing?"

"I have no idea, but I'm going to kill the person when I find out," I told her. "By the way, was John Barkley in church this morning?"

"I didn't see him. Why do you ask?"

"I'm just curious," I told her.

"I can call him and ask if he was there," she offered. "It is a good idea to find out what people saw."

I shook my head. "Forget it."

"What makes you think Melanie is being blackmailed?" my mother asked.

"This note." I waved it in the air.

Her eyes were full of concern. "Have you called the police yet?"

"I'll call. I just want to sit with her for a little while longer. I don't want her to wake up and find me gone."

"She'll be asleep for hours." She kissed my head before heading for the door. "Is this really the life you want for yourself?"

"Don't start Mom. I have enough on my mind right now. I don't need you giving me a hard time."

She left the room without another word.

"Mom," I leaped from the chair and followed her into the hallway.

"You don't know anything about the situation, so don't go

downstairs judging Melanie. She's the victim...please remember that."

Without giving her the opportunity to respond, I turned and walked back into the bedroom to sit by Melanie's side.

Streaks of eyeliner stained her face. I brushed her cheek with my finger hoping to remove the stains. There were so many warning signs I ignored. I couldn't decide what prevented me from calling a security company. Most likely stupidity. I would never forgive myself for allowing this to happen.

Someone touched my shoulder, startling me. My body bolted from the chair and my eyes darted to Melanie.

"It's me, Ryan." Marcy squeezed my shoulder. "We're having lunch. Mom sent me up to find out if you were hungry."

"No." I returned to the chair and rested my head in my hands. The jolt awake made me feel sick. "Would you mind sitting with her?" I asked Marcy. "I need to make a few phone calls."

Marcy agreed. "Get something to eat while you're downstairs. I'm sure Mom won't mind if you bring your food up here."

I grabbed my cell phone off the night table. My first call was to the police station. The second call was to a local security company.

An hour later, I sat in the living room with a police officer. He wrote a report using as much information as I was able to provide, then told me to come by the station house with Melanie when she awakened."

I spent the next few hours sitting in the darkened bedroom that belonged to me as a child. The envelope Melanie was guarding, even in her sleep, fell out of her arms and dropped to the floor. I picked it up and placed it on the night table next to her. The last words she uttered before falling into a deep sleep haunted me. *The pictures are worse than I thought...the pictures are worse than I thought.*

I went downstairs to greet Donald when he stopped by to check on Melanie, and again when Eve showed up for dinner. Her visit was more of an inquisition. I felt bad interrogating the woman, but wanted answers.

Eve reiterated what she told us earlier. "Melanie said she would wait for me by the coats to give me the address."

"Where were you when the man assaulted her?" George asked.

"I received a call and slipped outside to answer it."

She repeated her earlier assumption that Melanie had skipped out on her. When asked, Eve told me there were many strange faces in Church today and it would be impossible for her to notice one person who didn't belong.

I had no appetite and little desire to celebrate with my family. I encouraged them to enjoy the holiday meal, and then returned to the bedroom to check on Melanie. Once again, I found myself sitting in the armchair staring at the envelope. *The pictures are worse than I thought.*

Time spent alone created horrible images in my head. Her words continued to haunt me. She said she wasn't raped during that modeling job in high school. Would she lie about that? Maybe she blocked the unpleasant memory.

A sickening thought crossed my mind. Was there a chance the pictures had nothing to do with the incident during high school? *The pictures are worse than I thought.* It took her two years to tell me about an incident in which she was the victim. Could the pictures reflect something less innocent? Possibly an event she willingly participated in? What else in her past don't I know?

Although I was angry with myself for doubting my wife's loyalty, I could no longer stand the unknown. I stared at the envelope for a long time before opening the clasp and removing the contents. Emotion consumed me as I viewed pictures of the teenaged version of my wife partaking in sexual acts with two other women.

Chapter Thirteen

Melanie

The first thing I did when I woke up was look at the clock. According to the red digital numbers, it was nine forty-five in the morning. I hoped to have just awoken from a horrible nightmare, but knew better. My dreams and reality were the same. Someone was blackmailing me and now my parents were going to learn about my past mistakes. Even worse, the tabloids were going to have a field day at my expense.

I felt around the bed for the envelope, but couldn't find it. Not wanting to face reality, I tried to force myself to fall back to sleep, without avail. I didn't notice Ryan sitting in the chair next to the bed. He startled me when he leaned over and stroked my hair.

"Hey, how are you feeling?"

I shrugged in response.

"Are you hungry?"

I shook my head. "Did you see the pictures?"

The guilty expression on his face answered my question before he uttered the word, "*Yes.*"

"Was it John Barkley who hurt you yesterday?" he asked.

A rush of emotion overcame me as I recalled the man who held the knife to my throat. "It was the blond man we saw in the restaurant the night we had dinner with my family. The same man who hung around the theatre. How did he find us here?" I sat up in bed, surprised to be wearing the dress from yesterday.

"I don't know." He shook his head. "The pictures in the envelope, are they from the photo shoot you told me about?"

"Yes."

"Do you remember posing for those pictures?"

"No. He must have hidden a camera in the bedroom and photographed us changing from one outfit to the next."

I referred to the two pictures of Amanda, Julie and me changing in Jack's room. We were all half-dressed, Julie was laughing at something and Amanda was speaking. "The rest of the pictures must have been taken after we passed out."

"He did a good job making it appear that you were all partying together."

"He signed an affidavit swearing that all of the pictures were turned over to the lawyer."

"He failed to include pictures he wasn't photographed in." His tone lacked its normal warmth. "Any chance the two girls in the pictures are behind this?"

"I doubt it. We were all pretty shaken up at the time." I scratched the back of my head with my nails until I could no longer take the burning sensation in my head. It was my way of self-punishing. "Julie's brother wanted to kill the men involved."

"When was the last time anyone contacted you about these pictures?"

"Yesterday was the first time." I picked the cuticle on my thumb. "I'd be lying if I told you I had forgotten about them. I'll never forget the experience. Until I met John Barkley the other night, I hadn't given them much thought."

"Did the blond man ever approach you before yesterday?"

"No. I was afraid he was a stalker. I never imagined he was involved with those pictures."

Ryan lowered his head and pressed his fingers against his eyes. "I'm going to call my publicist and ask her advice." He let out a breath of air. "We need to stop by the police station and give them a statement. The cop who came by the house yesterday was angry that I refused to turn the pictures over to him. He wants to check for fingerprints."

"This isn't going to remain a secret, is it?"

"I don't think our blackmailer is going to allow us to keep this a secret." Ryan picked the envelope of pictures off the floor and slid them into a plastic bag. "How did he get you into the bathroom without anyone seeing?"

"I was standing close to the restrooms waiting for Eve to return. He came down the back staircase and dropped his wallet on the way into the men's room. I followed him to return it. The door is out of view, so when I got close enough to him he grabbed me, placed his hand over my mouth and dragged me inside."

"You didn't notice him?"

"He had his back to me and was wearing a hat. I didn't see his hair."

"What did he say?"

"He wants us to drop money to him today. If he doesn't get it, he is going to sell the pictures to an internet site. He reiterated the information in the note."

"No amount of money is going to make him go away." Ryan's words dripped disgust.

"I have to call my parents. I don't want them to find out from the newspaper." I slid my hands through my hair and held it in my fists. "They're going be so upset with me."

"You were a kid."

"I went into a man's apartment for a photo shoot, drank alcohol and passed out in his bedroom. Do you believe people are going to be sympathetic?" I wished I could swallow another pill and sleep through this nightmare. "I have to warn my sister that I'm about to tell my parents. They're going to be just as furious with her for not telling them."

"She's a big girl," he told me. "The blond guy—is he the one who took the pictures?"

"No. Although I assume they're connected. He said something about payback for hurting Jack. Jack is the name of the photographer."

"What does that mean?"

"I have no idea."

"We'll go to the police station this morning, then go back to New York and talk to your parents."

Ryan opened the bedroom door and found Marcy standing in the hallway. "I promise I haven't been listening to your conversation." Her hands were in front of her as though she was swearing in court. "I only heard the last part about going home to speak to your parents." She sighed. "They left several messages on your cell phone yesterday. When you didn't respond, they called the house this morning. My mother told them about the man at church. Your parents are on their way here. They're freaked out."

Chapter Fourteen

Ryan

Diane and Phillip charged through the front door of my parents' house fueled with anger. They screamed at me, at Melanie and even turned some of their fury toward my parents.

Before they arrived, I explained to my family that Diane is protective of her daughters and begged them to ignore any negative comments she may spew at us.

"If the tables had been turned Ryan, I would have called you right away." Diane waved her festively manicured finger at me. "I can't believe the total lack of respect you have demonstrated."

"It's not Ryan's fault," Melanie yelled back at her mother. "I wanted to tell you, but wasn't in any condition to speak to anyone yesterday."

My father suggested we move to the dining room. "My sister prepared food for us. Let's sit down and discuss this."

Diane and Phillip followed my parents into the dining room and took a seat at the table. For the first time I noticed Jessica standing behind them. I hugged her when she passed. The alarm in her eyes told me she was nervous. I could not decide if she was worried about Melanie or feared her role in this nightmare would become known.

Aunt Janet moved around the room pouring coffee for everyone. Afterward, she invited us to eat fried chicken cutlet heroes blanketed with mozzarella cheese and roasted red peppers. Diane refused a sandwich claiming she was too upset to eat. Emotions didn't seem to affect anyone else's appetite.

"Why would you keep something like this from us, Melanie?" Phillip's tone had a hint of anger, yet he displayed a calmer veneer than his wife did.

"The incident in Church was more than some random assault." Melanie's voice quivered, but she didn't cry. "He was looking for me."

"Is he a stalker?" Diane asked in horror. "I hope you filed an order of protection."

"He isn't a stalker." Melanie corrected her mother. "He's a blackmailer."

"What?" They cried out together.

"He's threatening to publish...pictures of me if we don't pay him two million dollars by the close of business today."

"I knew something like this would happen. Our children spend way too much time apart." My mother folded her arms across her chest and glared at Melanie. "So much for your little speech the other day."

"Shut up!" I screamed at her. "You have no idea what you're talking about." I slammed my fists against the table.

In response, my mother leapt from her chair and headed to the door, demanding the rest of my family join her. I grasped her arm as she passed me.

"I told you last night this has *nothing* to do with Melanie and my relationship. I *begged* you not to pass judgment on her. She is trying to explain everything to you. You claim to be a religious woman, yet you thrive on gossip. For once in your life, listen to the truth instead of creating some warped scenario in your head."

"Ryan, that's enough," my father barked.

The room was silent. My mother returned to her seat, crossing her arms in front of her chest. From the other end of the table, my father glared at me.

Melanie wrapped her hand around my forearm and coaxed me back down into my chair. Once I sat down, she continued sharing the background story which led up to the events that unfolded yesterday. She described the necessity for money to pay bills, going to the photo shoot, learning the guy was a pervert, the lawyer, the affidavit and Jack turning over the negatives. The only piece of information she omitted was her sister's involvement.

"Could the lawyer have reproduced the pictures?" my father asked.

Melanie shook her head. "The photos I received yesterday were not the pictures turned in. The new photos were taken... after I passed out." Her gaze returned to her lap.

"I thought you were smarter than that, Melanie." Diane rested her forehead against her fingertips. "Why would you go into a strange man's apartment, and then drink alcohol."

"He said it would calm our nerves. If we didn't photograph well, he threatened not to pay us." She cried.

"We thought you knew the difference between right and wrong. How could you be so foolish?" Diane berated her daughter.

Phillip tapped Diane's arm to calm her.

"Why didn't you tell us, Melanie?" Phillip asked. "We could have gone to the police and pressed charges against this guy."

"We were at his apartment for a photo shoot, which means we authorized him to take pictures of us. We would have been eaten alive by his defense attorney."

"Where did you hear something so silly?" my father asked. "You were minors. No one would have ridiculed you."

"Your sister is an attorney, for God's sake. You could have gone to her."

I looked to Jessica, waiting for her to confess the role she played. It shocked me that she remained silent.

"I considered that," Melanie explained. "Until we were told a defense attorney would make us out to be whores."

"That's ridiculous." Phillip shook his head.

"I always considered us to be a close family. Why didn't you feel comfortable coming to *us*?" Diane looked from one daughter to the other while dabbing her eyes with a tissue given to her by my Aunt.

"I was too ashamed to tell anyone." Melanie pulled a loose cuticle attached to her thumb. "Now the whole world is going to find out."

"Do we have any idea how to find this guy?" George asked.

"The photographer and the guy in church are two different people," I explained. "Although I'm pretty sure they know one another."

"No one noticed a man dragging you into the bathroom?" Phillip asked. "Do you remember seeing him earlier, Melanie?"

"It was the blond man I pointed out in the restaurant the night my show closed," She explained. "I was gathering my things after mass when I noticed someone walk by and drop a wallet on the floor. By the time I realized it was him, he had already restrained me."

"No one heard you scream?" George asked.

"He covered my mouth before I had the chance. He threatened to shoot everyone in the church if I alerted them of the attack. I was told to wait five minutes before exiting the bathroom"

"Could it be someone we know?" Nancy asked.

"I'd like to know if anyone remembers John Barkley milling around," I told her.

"You think *John* had something to do with this?" my father retorted.

"John suggested he saw pictures of Melanie at the party the other night," I reminded my father. "A short time later, Melanie receives an envelope with a few pictures in it. That is too much of a coincidence."

My father waved his hand dismissing my concerns.

"I know it wasn't John who threatened Melanie because she would have recognized him," I continued. "But I think he *is* somehow involved."

"The picture he referred to that evening was of your mother and me. It had nothing to do with Melanie."

"How do you know that?"

"A few minutes after you walked away he remembered someone showing him a picture of mom and me. Melanie was in the background of that picture, which is why he had a difficult time placing her."

"Who showed him the picture?"

My father shrugged. "I didn't ask him."

"What are the police doing?" Phillip directed the conversation back to the pictures.

"They're interviewing the choir, the ushers, the band and anyone else we remember being at mass," Melanie told them. "They said they would dust for fingerprints, although they don't hold much hope of finding anything usable. They expect to find thousands of smudged and partial prints."

"We've spoken about security before Ryan. Have you hired anyone yet?" Diane asked.

I nodded. "I made some calls last night and expect our bodyguard shortly. He'll stay with us for the remainder of the trip. Once we return to New York, we'll meet our permanent guard."

"When do you plan on returning to New York?" Phillip asked.

"Our original plan was to leave tomorrow. With the

investigation just starting up, it may be a little longer," Melanie told them. "I'm guessing once the police gather all the information they need, we can go home."

"I want to make sure the police are doing everything they can to find this guy," I added.

Melanie's parents were still not happy by any means, but appeared satisfied with the steps taken to protect Melanie. They planned to stay in Pennsylvania until evening, hoping the police would provide an update before they left. I advised them that we do not intend to pay our blackmailer.

Frankie awoke and called Marcy from his crib. While Marcy went to retrieve him, my aunt and mother cleared the table. My mother rejected Diane's offer to help. Instead, my father suggested she, Phillip, Jessica, and Melanie go into the living room and talk. My mother stopped my attempt to join them by requesting that I help her in the kitchen.

George knew as well as I did that she intended to reprimand me for the way I spoke to her. This was his cue to disappear. I'm sure he ran to my sister warning her against coming downstairs. I also knew she would ignore him. Missing the family drama would be torture for Marcy.

I am not sure where my father went. He was no longer in the dining room, nor was he in the recliner in the living room. The man has a knack for disappearing when things get ugly.

My mother screamed and lectured me for ten minutes. She accused me of being a horrible son, and then expressed shock and despair over my self-centeredness.

She said the way I speak to her is disgusting, complained of my lack of regard for anyone except for Melanie and myself, and then accused me of turning my back on the family.

"Regardless of the last name you choose to use, remember you are a Fowler."

The rant ended with an ultimatum. I had to decide whether I wanted to be a member of the family. She would no longer tolerate me being a part-time son.

Later that evening, Melanie told me her parents called her immature and stupid. They referred to our life as *living in a fish bowl* (which neither of us can deny is true) and demanded Melanie reveal any other secrets she may be keeping.

Melanie maintained there were no more secrets and told us all that she has learned that secrets are as dangerous as lies in our business.

Unlike the way my family meeting ended, Melanie's parents hugged her, acknowledged her career path came with heartaches, and agreed that placing blame and yelling wouldn't solve any problems. Instead they agreed to help her through this ordeal without further name calling.

My mother stopped speaking to me and my father remained in hiding. Diane wasn't too thrilled with me either, at least that was the impression I got from the scowl on her face each time she looked in my direction.

Bringing Versace for walks was the highlight of my day. At times, the chill I received from the people inside the house was more biting than the frigid temperature outside.

"I'll go with you. " Melanie offered when I slipped the harness on Versace for the second time that afternoon.

"I don't think it's a good idea for you to go out, Melanie," Phillip told her.

"I need some fresh air. I don't plan on leaving the backyard." She slipped into her coat and scooped Versace into her arms.

"I can't breathe in that house," She confessed once we were outside. "I've had enough of both families. I really want to go home."

"My parents are driving Marcy, George, and Frankie to the airport in another few hours." I removed strands of hair caught in her eyelashes. "I'm sure it's just a matter of time before Jessica pressures your parents to leave. We'll get a break then."

"I need more than a couple of hours, Ryan. I want to go home." She followed Versace to the bushes.

"Give the police a few days to get their investigation underway. In the meantime we'll return to the hotel, get a massage and relax before leaving for our honeymoon."

She closed her eyes and bit her bottom lip.

"What now?"

"I sort of...um...offered airline tickets to Eve yesterday."

"Why would you do that?"

She shrugged. "I felt bad she was spending the holidays alone and suggested she visit her sons and their families."

"Okay, so we'll buy her open-ended tickets to use whenever she wants. It doesn't affect our plans. They can be mailed or e-mailed to her from the airline carrier."

"I know. I just forgot to tell you." She removed a bag from

her pocket, cleaned up after Versace and freed him from his leash so he could run. "What do we do with Versace?"

* * * *

Melanie's family left the house a short time later. We exchanged Christmas presents with Marcy, George and Frankie before they left for the airport. My parents didn't participate in the festivities.

Melanie and Marcy discussed plans for their visit to New York in March and we promised to update them on developments in the blackmail case. Once everyone was gone, we packed the few belongings I had picked up from the hotel the night before and waited for our new security officer to arrive.

Melanie could not bear to send Versace back to New York with her parents, so we planned to smuggle him back into the hotel room.

Our security officer's name was Ben. He arrived a few minutes before the Town Car we hired to take us to the hotel. Ben checked the driver's credentials, and then called a co-worker of his to tail our car.

The only person in the house when we left was Aunt Janet. She made me promise to square things away with my mother before returning to New York.

A call from the detective assigned to our case informed us police were no closer to finding the identity of Melanie's attacker. The period of time in which we had to turn the money over had expired, which meant we had an irate blackmailer. At the suggestion of the police, we hired a second security guard to keep an eye on my parents' house.

Chapter Fifteen

Melanie

I don't know that I will ever get used to having a security guard. It was awkward knowing someone was sitting outside the suite while Ryan and I skinny dipped in the pool and made love in the shower. Despite the entourage, I managed to enjoy the time with my husband without allowing the security guard or my problems to interfere.

"I'm happy to have everything out in the open—well almost everything." I confessed to Ryan as we lay in bed that night. I rested my head in the crook of his arm, entwining my fingers with his. "I hope my parents never find out that Jessica knew about this whole mess. They would never forgive her for keeping it from them."

"Imagine the car ride home had they found out? We'd hear them screaming at her from here." Ryan made light of the conversation.

The phone rang a few seconds later. I groaned at the likelihood that one set of parents was calling.

"Hello," Ryan answered. He sounded tired and for the first time I considered his feelings and realized the stress this situation placed on him.

He paused to listen to the caller, slid his arm out from under my neck and sat up in bed. "Melanie is here with me. Let me put the call on speaker."

"Hi Mrs. Carlisle," Detective Newell began. "I spoke to the two women who were photographed with you. Neither of them has been contacted, but both are pretty shaken up to learn of the photos." Paper shuffled in the background. "The lawyer who confiscated the pictures faxed me the document signed by Jack Boucher. Were you aware Mister Boucher was assaulted the day he turned the pictures over to your attorney?" He cleared his throat.

"I had no idea."

"We are going to investigate things further. One person I will be contacting is your sister."

"I'll tell her to expect your call."

"Have you made any progress with the people from my parents' church?" Ryan asked.

"A few people. So far, no one has been able to provide information. Everyone agrees there were dozens of unfamiliar faces in church that morning. No one recalls a suspicious blond man milling around. This guy may have slipped down the stairs during mass and hid somewhere waiting for Melanie. We'll be conducting more interviews tomorrow."

"What about John Barclay?"

"I mentioned your concern over the comment he made during the dinner dance. He told us a man approached him with a picture of your parents. Melanie had been in the background of that picture. The man claimed to be an old friend of your father. He asked Mister Barclay if he knew how he could find him." He hesitated a moment before continuing. "The description he provided of the stranger matches the description Melanie gave."

"How do we know he isn't more involved than he claims?" Ryan asked.

"Rest assured we are not dismissing anyone at this time. Our investigation is just beginning. We're monitoring your parents' phone lines and are keeping tabs on Mister Barclay," he told us. "Have you checked your home answering machine?"

"I checked a few hours ago. There were no messages, nor have we received any on our cell phones."

"Okay. I'll keep in touch. Call me right away should someone contact you."

"We will," Ryan promised. "Thank you Detective. Good night."

Ryan disconnected the call and resumed our snuggling position. "Hopefully the fact he hasn't made contact is a good thing." He kissed my head.

"He wouldn't have risked attacking me in public if he didn't intend on following through," I told him.

Before going to sleep, I called my sister's house to make sure she arrived home safely. She told me our mother cried most of the ride home and that she came close to confessing, but couldn't find the courage. I told her not to worry. I didn't intend to tell them of her involvement.

My next call was to Eve. I didn't want her to think I had forgotten about the airline tickets I promised her. She was more interested in hearing about the investigation. She told me Detective Newell visited her and asked me if they had any leads.

While I was speaking with her, Ryan left the bed. Moments later, I heard water running and a strong smell of lavender soap.

I was giving Eve an abbreviated version of our conversations with police when Ryan returned to the bedroom. He scooped me up from bed and carried me into the bathroom. I made an excuse to end the call and promised the tickets would arrive within the next few days. She was still talking when I disconnected the call.

Rose pedals topped our bubble bath. The floral arrangement that had been nestled in the corner of the tub was gone and I figured he used it to make our bath romantic.

After a few minutes in the water, I began to sweat. I reached past Ryan and turned the cold water on.

"I'm getting you heated, huh?" he teased.

"You always do."

A knock at the door interrupted our romantic interlude.

"Our dinner must be here." He stepped out of the tub, wrapped a towel around himself and sprinted to the door. A few minutes later, he returned balancing two trays of food. "I thought we'd eat in the tub."

"Gross!" I told him. "Why don't you set the food up in the dining area? I'll be right out."

Reluctantly he left the bathroom with our dinner. I hurried into the shower to rid my skin of the left over bubbles and slid into the hotel robe.

Ryan was on the phone when I joined him in the living room. I leaned over his shoulder to read the notes he was taking, but was unable to decipher his handwriting, so I lifted the lid off my plate, pulled off a small chunk of salmon and slipped it into my mouth. When he finished the call, he pushed the note pad and his phone to the side, broke his food open and announced he was starving.

"Who was that?"

"My agent. She was giving me information on my new movie. They begin filming in May, which presents a work conflict for me. I don't finish filming my next movie until the first week of June."

"What are they going to do?"

"The director is going to hold off shooting my scenes until June."

"That's good."

"That means I am flying from the set in Georgia straight to Germany." He screwed his mouth up, knowing I was not going to be happy with the news.

I made a pouting face. "That's going to be a long stretch for us."

"No pouting face. We knew this was going to happen before I accepted the role." He devoured a large piece of steak.

"It doesn't mean I like it."

"I don't like it either." He made a pouting face back at me. "We also discussed the blackmail issue. She says we should set up an interview to discuss the matter publicly. Beat him to the punch by going to the media before he does."

"I don't know Ryan. It was tough enough telling you and my parents." I placed my fork on the table and covered my half-eaten plate of food. "I don't think I'm ready to go public with it."

"It was just something she suggested."

"Let's hold off...at least for now."

He didn't argue, but the expression on his face indicated he disagreed with my decision.

I got up from the table and brought Versace out on the balcony. Rather than doing his business on the newspaper I set down on the floor, he sniffed around.

"My pants are getting a little snug." I changed the subject. "I'd like to work out for a couple of hours."

"You want to go to the hotel gym?"

"Not a good idea Mister Carlisle. Remember we're in seclusion. I guess I'll have to exercise in the room."

"How about racquetball? Ben can reserve a court for us. He mentioned that the manager was willing to close the gym down for an hour or two if we were interested."

I felt guilty stopping the other guests from using the gym and racquetball courts. Ryan sensed my reluctance and said we could go around five o'clock when people were at dinner.

* * * *

The next day we ate breakfast in bed, I jogged in place, did some sit ups, played with Versace and ate lunch in our room. By five o'clock I was climbing the walls and anxious to escape. I brought Versace out on the balcony to do his business, locked him in his cage, laced up my sneakers and headed out the door.

The daytime security guard had left and Ben was back at his post by the time we were ready to play racquetball. At six foot five, Ben made Ryan look short. I looked ridiculous next to him. The muscles in his dark arms bulged to the point I figured they would explode. He stood with his arms folded across his heaping chest and his head in constant motion checking the surroundings. As scary as he appeared, he was a nice man. I preferred him to the daytime guard—whose name I didn't even know.

Once we were inside the elevator, his face softened and he even smiled at something Ryan said. He instructed us to wear the hoods of our sweatshirts over our heads on the way to the racquetball courts. Black curtains hung over the glass wall of the court, shielding us from view of the other players.

Ben waited outside the room for an hour while we played game after game against one another. The fun ended when my cell phone rang and a familiar voice echoed through the receiver.

Chapter Sixteen

Ryan

Blood drained from Melanie's face. She put her cell phone on speaker. Rubber balls bouncing in the court next to ours made it difficult to hear his words, so I stood close behind her and leaned in toward the phone.

"I told you not to go to the cops."

"You held a knife to my throat and threatened my family. Did you honestly think I *wouldn't* call the police?" she told him. "Why are you doing this to me?"

"Payback for the pain you caused a friend of mine."

I pulled my cell phone out of the pocket of my sweatshirt and recorded the conversation.

"I'm guessing Jack Boucher is your friend."

Silence.

"I didn't do anything to him."

"I suppose it was a coincidence that he was beaten on the way home from your lawyer's office?"

"I had nothing to do with his beating."

"Save the bullshit. You broke my rules and now you have to pay. I found a magazine that is interested in the pictures."

I grabbed the phone out of Melanie's hand. "You're not getting a friggin' dime from us you son of a bitch. We have already gone to the press with the story and the pictures you have given us. What you have in your possession is worthless."

"Is your nephew worthless? If I don't get my money, I just might pay him a visit."

I threw the phone across the court, causing it to shatter. Ben burst into the room, his gaze moved from me to Melanie and then the broken phone pieces scattered on the floor. Without asking questions, he directed us back to our hotel room. Hidden beneath sweatshirts, we followed Ben past a small crowd of people craning their necks to see who was causing the commotion.

Melanie called the police from the hotel phone. She reiterated the conversation to Detective Newell and voiced concern for our family members. He promised to call the Nassau County Police Department asking for squad cars to patrol the homes of Melanie's family.

She followed up with calls to her parents and her sister, questioning Jessica about Jack's beating. Jessica said she knew nothing about it. Before hanging up, Melanie told her to keep the doors locked until police arrived.

Her final conversation was with my parents. The security guard we hired to watch their house had already informed them of the threat, following a call from Ben. They promised to be careful and begged us to do the same.

While Melanie spoke with our family members, I called my agent from my cell phone. She suggested I call Lacy Randolph, a public relations assistant who has handled issues for numerous actors and athletes.

Lacy listened to our predicament then told me it was not a big deal. To ensure our blackmailer didn't publish the photographs on the internet, she suggested we consider sharing our story with a respected journalist. I agreed to the interview and requested we move quickly. Lacy was located in California, so she set up a three-way call with her New York Associate, Chelsea Baker. Chelsea agreed to set up an interview with one of the major news programs.

Melanie was not thrilled with the decision to broadcast her problems. She could not grasp the understanding that this was not her fault and feared a media backlash.

"She'll make money off of this. Of course she's wants us to go public," Melanie argued. "It was difficult enough having to confess to you and my parents. Now you expect me to tell the story to the world. Those pictures are going to ruin my career."

A call from Detective Newell interrupted a brewing argument. He checked the phone records for Melanie's cell phone and learned the last incoming call originated from a pay phone located in a Tannersville Supermarket.

I told him about the interview. He was agreeable but requested that he be present. He wanted to make a plea to the public asking anyone with information on our assailant to come forward. I promised to call him with a time and location.

Melanie disappeared halfway through the conversation. When I finished the call, I searched the bathroom and downstairs. She was in the pool with her head resting on the pillowed edge and a washcloth shielding her eyes.

"I need a few minutes alone, Ryan. I'm not in the mood to discuss any of this with you right now."

With Lacy hopping on an airplane and her associate arranging for an interview, we didn't have time for Melanie to come to terms with this. "I'm sorry this is happening so fast, but we don't have any choice except to move on it."

She removed the washcloth and glared at me. "Why did you grab the phone away from me and tell him we were going to the press? He was talking to *me*. Maybe I could have changed his mind without infuriating him. Now you've fixed it so we *have* to go public with *my* private story." She let out an angry sigh. "You didn't even have the decency to discuss it with me before making the arrangements with your publicist."

I considered what Melanie was saying and knew she was partially right. I did take matters into my own hands without discussing it with her. "I'm only doing what I believe is in your best interest."

She rolled her eyes then covered her face with the washcloth. Her only response was a loud, aggravated sigh.

"I don't want that man to become rich off of naked pictures of you. I thought I was doing the right thing."

"You're my husband, not my father. I can't stand when you confuse your role."

"What does that mean? A husband is supposed to protect his wife. I'd like to believe you would have my back if the tables were turned."

She heaved another angry sigh but didn't respond.

"I am sorry for making this decision without you." There was a trace of annoyance in my voice. "Regardless of whether or not those pictures make their way to the internet, your story is going to come out. Do you want to tell it or do you want some sleazy journalist to put his own spin on it?"

She didn't respond.

"If you want me to cancel the interview, I'll do it. You just need to get out of the damn pool and speak to me."

I walked out of the poolroom, slamming the door behind me when she failed to give up the silent treatment.

I asked Ben to go outside for a smoke. I was halfway through the cigarette when Melanie appeared. My first instinct was to ask her why she's walking around alone but stopped before the words escaped my lips.

"Can I speak with you for a moment?"

I took one last drag of the cigarette and followed her inside.

"You stink." She fanned her hand in front of her face. "Since when do you smoke?"

Smoking was a habit I picked up when I was sixteen. By the time I was nineteen, I was up to a pack a day. In one of the first movie roles I landed, I was required to kiss the leading lady. She was disgusted with the smell of my breath and refused to work with me. Fearing I would lose the small movie role, I popped breath mints and swore off smoking. For the most part, I stuck with that decision. Stress is the only thing that makes me ache for a smoke.

"I smoke when I'm stressed out...*Mom*." As childish as it was, I could not help adding that little zing to the end of my sentence.

"I guess we all have our secrets," she muttered. "I'll do the interview."

"Don't do it for me Melanie." I leaned against the wall of the elevator, slid my hands into my pants pockets and crossed one leg in front of the other.

She gnawed on her cuticle. "I don't want this guy to make money off of us and I want him out of our lives. I've tried but can't come up with any other solutions."

Our conversation stalled when the elevator doors opened. We didn't resume speaking until we were inside our suite.

"Please remember this is my life." She rubbed her hands on her face. "I feel as though you are using this to gain national exposure." "What did you...I cannot believe you just said that." I swung the closet door open, removed my I Pod and a sweatshirt from my gym bag and headed for the door.

"Where are you going?" she asked.

"I cannot be around you right now."

"It's almost eight o'clock at night. You're not leaving this room without me."

I wiggled my arm from her grip and stormed out of the room.

"Word is out that you and Melanie are staying here." Ben tried to dissuade me from leaving. "News of the incident on the racquetball court has gotten around. I have been chasing people away since we returned. You should lay low."

"I need to get out of here right now and another cigarette won't help. I'm going for a run."

Ben looked at his watch. "Oh, no you're not." He pressed his large hand against my chest. "You hired me to guard both of you. I can't do my job if you keep leaving."

"For now, guard Melanie." I slid the headset into my ears and put the hood of my sweatshirt on. "I'll be back. Please keep her in the room. Don't let her wander around the hotel."

For the first fifteen minutes of my run, I didn't notice anyone or anything. I was too angry with Melanie. Her comment hurt. Taking advantage of the dark, I continued to run the deserted road. A pinching on the outside of my knee indicated I had been running a long time. My knee tends to ache somewhere around mile seven. I wanted to keep running, even though my body begged me to stop. Someone once told me a brisk walk or a run would improve your mood. I assumed they were right considering the anger had subsided. The streetlights that lit my path were now gone, indicating I was no longer on the grounds of the resort. Therefore, I turned and headed back to the hotel.

In an attempt to focus on something other than the pain in my knee, I viewed the situation through Melanie's eyes. I didn't blame her for wanting to keep this secret. The last thing I want is for the world to learn of those pictures. However, I cannot allow the man who held a knife to Melanie's throat to go without punishment. Now that he has threatened our family members, we needed to ensure *their* safety.

I had no idea who beat the photographer, but would love to shake the guy's hand. *When I get my hands on the man threatening my family, he is going to end up like his friend.*

I slowed my pace to a walk, allowing my breathing to slow. A car full of people entered the parking lot. Fearing they would recognize me, I slipped into the lobby and darted for the elevator bank.

Ben was waiting outside the room when I arrived on our floor. "She's pretty upset with me for letting you leave."

I nodded and assured him I would take care of Melanie. I prepared myself for her wrath as I entered the suite. Instead, she leapt off the couch and ran into my arms, wrapping her legs around me. It reminded me of the day I arrived home to

New York from the movie set. I would give anything to return to that day and erase this whole trip.

"I'm so sorry. I didn't mean what I said. Please forgive me. I know you would never use me to further your career. The idea you would do such a thing is preposterous." She pressed her lips against mine and hugged me tight to her body. "I would die if anything happened to you. Promise you won't go off on your own again. "

She lowered herself to the ground. The sadness in her eyes hurt me. "Can you forgive me for saying such a horrible thing?"

I wanted to forgive her but something inside wouldn't allow me. Her words were hurtful. She needed to understand that she could not say horrible things to me during an argument.

"I'm taken back by what you said. I don't know what I have done to make you believe I would use you for career gain. I would turn over the money if it means this guy goes away. You and I both know he will demand more money." I ran my hand through my hair. "Your actions indicate a lack of trust."

"I've made such a mess out of everything, Ryan." She cast her tearful eyes downward. "Rather than acknowledge my wrongdoing, I placed blame on you." A tear rolled down her cheek. "In the few weeks we've been married, I've caused problems with your family and kept a secret that can possibly cause us both a great deal of grief."

"Are you crazy?" I placed my hands on each side of her face. Pride may prevent me from forgiving her, but it didn't stop me from kissing her. "You are the best thing in my life. Nothing that has happened during this trip is your fault."

She apologized a few more times and then promised to do whatever it took to make it up to me.

By the time we woke the next morning, Chelsea had arranged for an interview to take place in our hotel. Shortly after noon, film crews took over the main floor. Detective Newell advised us he was running late and instructed us to begin the interview without him. He was speaking with supermarket employees while waiting for a copy of the security tape. Officers were searching credit card receipts hoping to find something.

"I'm glad he is on top of things," she said.

The mood remained tense between us. "Do you have anything to wear?"

She shrugged. "A revealing dress. Not something I want to wear for this type of interview." She walked over to her suitcase and rummaged through it in search of the perfect outfit. "I'm thinking this turtleneck sweater and a pair of jeans with my brown high-heeled boots."

I nodded in agreement with her wardrobe choice and searched my own bag for something to wear, settling on a black sweater and a pair of jeans.

* * * *

Chelsea Baker was a twenty-three year old woman with big breasts, bold blond hair, and a tiny business suit. She resembled a stripper rather than public relations professional.

We spent a half hour reviewing questions for the interview. For some reason Chelsea touched my leg every few minutes, something Melanie hadn't missed.

Chelsea hadn't been successful reaching the other two women and therefore, didn't want them mentioned during the interview. While we did need to provide background, she reminded us to choose our words carefully, considering no one filed criminal charges against Jack Boucher over the incident. Earlier in the day, we decided against televising the pictures. Rather, Detective Newell discussed the legal ramifications involved in publishing sexually explicit pictures of minors.

Melanie's mood fell when the producer came to collect us. I stood up from the makeup chair and walked over to her, placing my hand on her shoulder. It took a few minutes for her to gather herself before heading to our interview. When we took our seats across from the journalist hired to interview us, tears flowed down Melanie's face.

Chapter Seventeen

Melanie

I could not decide if I felt sick or relieved when the interview ended. One thing was for sure, I feared a response from our blackmailer.

I was relieved Carlee's line of questioning was sympathetic rather than accusatory. I have seen news correspondents attack their guests by playing devil's advocate. She responded emphatically while I shared the events that took place the day Jack and his friends confronted me. I didn't provide details about the two women photographed in bed with me. In fact, the women were not mentioned. I discouraged Chelsea from continuing her efforts to contact them, explaining that there was no reason to drag anyone back into this nightmare.

Following Lacy's advice, my interview included necessary facts only. I explained that I learned of the modeling job through word of mouth, foolishly consumed alcohol to make the photo shoot less nerve-wracking, was drugged, passed out and while unconscious had pictures taken suggesting I had sex with several people.

The most difficult question asked of me concerned my word choice while discussing events following the photo shoot.

"You said the pictures *suggested* you had sex with others. Were you raped?"

"I was not raped," I replied without emotion.

She eyed me warily. "There was no way he could have guessed at the time that you would become a well-known actress," Carlee said. "Why would he photograph a high school girl if it weren't for sex?"

"He never did explain his motive," I told her. "I believe he used photography as a way to get unsuspecting women into his apartment. He most likely used the pictures to impress his friends or to satisfy a warped fantasy. I know for a fact that he didn't rape me."

She changed the subject when my attorney warned her against questioning rape allegations any further. "Has he done this to other women?" she asked instead.

"I have no idea." I shrugged. "This is the first time I have spoken about this matter publicly. If he *has* taken advantage of other women, I want justice for them as much as I want it for myself. The man who assaulted me and is now threatening my family, belongs in jail."

Carlee patted my hand, praising me for being brave enough to share my story. I was tempted to tell her it was not by choice, but decided against it. Instead, I mirrored her sad smile.

After the interview, I shook hands with each member of the news team and excused myself. The entire day had been an exhausting ordeal and I wanted to go to bed. Detective Newell told Ryan about the leads they were working on and asked to discuss them with us. Ryan offered to stay behind but asked Ben to escort me to our room. Ben didn't want Ryan walking around the hotel by himself so Detective Newell promised to deliver him to our room when they were finished speaking. I was annoyed when Chelsea suggested that she join Ryan and the detective. Exhaustion and body aches saved me from making a fuss. Instead, I pushed aside feelings of jealousy and anger and returned to the room with Ben beside me.

* * * *

The next morning I woke to the sound of the television playing in the living room. After stretching to remove a kink in my neck, I threw my legs over the side of the bed, walked to the window and tossed the curtains open. The clear blue sky led me to believe the worst was over. I would give anything for our lives to return to normal.

I snuggled up next to Ryan on the couch. "What are you watching?"

"I'm channel surfing." He kissed the top of my head and threw an arm around me. "Most news channels picked up your story. They're giving teasers and telling viewers to tune in to the five o'clock news for more information."

"Will the interview be on every channel?"

"Details surrounding the story will be, but not the interview."

I stretched again. "I'm hungry."

"Chelsea dropped off breakfast." He thumbed his finger toward the table behind the couch where bagels were on a platter and cream cheese floated in a bowl on ice water.

I rolled my eyes.

"What?" He smirked.

"She rubs me the wrong way."

"She was rubbing me the right way before the interview," He taunted me.

I screwed up my mouth in anger. "Did she rub your leg last night after I went to bed?"

He threw his head back and laughed. "She didn't get the chance. Detective Newell was present the entire time and then insisted on walking me to the room. She wasn't pleased."

"I don't find you funny at all."

He tightened his grip on me. "Lacy called this morning asking if we were satisfied with the way Chelsea handled things. I explained while Chelsea did a great job putting everything together I wasn't interested in having her represent us full-time."

"I didn't realize we needed a full-time publicist."

"A publicist would handle rumors and false stories printed about us. It's a good idea that we have one on retainer."

"Did she ask why we didn't want Chelsea?"

He nodded. "I told her we didn't click."

"Although I didn't like her personally, she did a good job. Hopefully her employer won't be upset with her."

"I don't think so. I praised her work." Ryan removed his arm from around my shoulders, stood up and helped me to my feet. "We can rehire her. She does give a good leg massage."

Without waiting for a response, he slapped my butt and told me to shower and dress.

"We aren't going to eat the bagels Chelsea dropped off?" I asked in an immature tone.

"Not even if we were starving." He smiled. "I was thinking we would head home."

"I would love that."

"You shower and I'll pack."

"You want to join me in the shower?"

"I would love to, but I'm dressed and my hair is done. Besides, I want to listen to the news."

"You think he really went to the press?" I dug through my suitcase for something to wear.

He shrugged. "I doubt he's smart enough to figure out how to." He made a face. "The town *is* crawling with paparazzi. I'm sure they would be happy to hear his story."

"The paparazzi can't beat out our interview, can they?"

I decided on a pair of jeans and a purple blouse.

"Not with the morning newscast airing teasers."

I could not help but feel annoyed with the people benefiting from my nightmare. So many people were excited about breaking the story, yet I wondered if any of them were interested in righting the wrongdoing against me or the two classmates who suffered the same humiliation. Had Amanda or Julie gone to the news station with this story, it never would have been picked up to air. Since Ryan Carlisle's wife was the whistle-blower, newscasters were falling over one another trying to score the story. All anyone was interested in were dollar signs, ratings and publicity from this interview. The aggravating part was that the interview would most likely peak the interest of people wanting to see the pictures we were trying to hide.

My anger subsided when Ryan entered the bathroom wearing only a seductive smile.

"I thought you already showered?" I shot him a crooked smile.

"I did." He stepped in the shower, slipping his arms around me. "Then I received an invitation I couldn't refuse."

I melted into my husband's embrace and made love to him.

Ryan suggested we move to the tub for a bubble bath, but I was feeling a little light-headed and declined the offer. "Let's just finish packing and go home."

"Do you mind spending one last dinner with my parents before we leave?"

I shook my head. "Let's order food from that Italian restaurant by their house so your mom doesn't have to cook."

My mother called to alert us to the coverage our story was receiving on the twenty-four hour news channels.

"You offered a half-million dollars for the arrest of that beast?"

"Yep."

"I wouldn't be surprised if by nightfall the man is arrested. People are sympathetic toward you."

I shared the information Detective Newell told Ryan the night before, including a conversation the police had with Jack Boucher. "Jack denies any connection to the pictures I received the other day or of the vigilante who is making threats against us. He indicated all of his photographs were turned over to my lawyer shortly after they were taken."

"What do the police say about that?"

"They believe he's lying, but have no evidence linking him to the attack or the blackmail. Based on the comments made by the blond man, police are convinced there is a connection. They are looking into the background of Jack's family members to see if anyone has a history of mental illness or a police record."

"I can't wait for this nightmare to be over," she admitted.

Especially since the threat now extends to each of you. I thought.

"We've decided to return home tonight."

"I am thrilled to hear that. What about a guard?"

"One will accompany us on the drive to New York and a second will meet us at our apartment."

"Do you need your father and me to do anything?"

"No. I'll call you when we get home. Love you, Mom."

"I love you too Melanie. Be careful."

No sooner did I disconnect the call when the phone rang again. Nancy wanted to let us know that Eve had called.

"She's says she hasn't been able to get through to your cell and would like you to call her."

"She probably wants to thank us for the airline tickets," I told her. "I'll call her."

Nancy continued telling me how disappointed Frankie was to arrive home before his Christmas presents. As the conversation continued, I felt nausea coming on. Unable to interrupt her story, I tossed the phone to Ryan and ran to the bathroom. I barely made it when I vomited. Afterward, my skin was clammy and the room spun. I curled up on the bed and asked Ryan to open the glass sliding door so I could get fresh air.

"I think Chelsea has poisoned the bagels." I teased.

"She mentioned concocting a plan to do away with you. I didn't expect it to happen this soon."

I stuck my tongue at him.

Ryan placed a whining Versace on the bed beside me. Versace licked my face a few times before turning in circles and nestled against my chest.

Ryan rescheduled our pick up time for later in the afternoon and slipped into bed, wrapping his arms around our new dog and me.

While we slept the afternoon away, our blackmailer set a plan in motion. A plan that would forever change our lives.

Chapter Eighteen

Ryan

The short drive to my parents' house was not enjoyable. Twice the driver had to pull the car over for Melanie to vomit. Earlier, she teased about Chelsea lacing the bagels. I'm wondering if her food had something slipped into it. When I suggested the idea, she laughed.

"I've been feeling something coming on since before Christmas. The stress most likely suppressed it until now."

"We can pick up the rest of our belongings from my parents' house and head straight home. We don't have to stay for dinner."

"I don't think I'm ready for that long drive," she told me. "Your family must think I'm made up of drama and bad luck."

I kissed her forehead. "Everyone knows you're a diva."

After slapping my chest, she nestled her head against my shoulder and drifted off to sleep. By the time we reached my parents' house, she was feeling a little better.

"It's happened twice today," Melanie told my mother when we arrived. "I'm afraid to eat anything for fear I'm going to be sick again."

She placed Versace's crate on the floor and let him out. Fastening his leash to his collar, she handed the dog over to me to bring for a walk.

Ben took the dog and asked me to direct him to the back door. He was not about to let either of us outside.

"Your lack of appetite might be the problem," my mother told Melanie. "You guys are so thin. I am surprised you are not sick more often." When she shared her opinion with Melanie there wasn't sarcasm in her voice or disapproval in her eyes. For the first time since we've arrived to Pennsylvania, she was concerned. "Come inside right now. I have sandwiches, soup, and salad. Let's get food into you." She motioned for us to follow her into the kitchen.

Melanie turned green watching my mother unwrap the different lunch meats.

"The dinner we ordered is going to be here in an hour or so. Don't open everything," I told my mother.

"Do you prefer beef vegetable soup or potato broccoli soup?" She ignored me.

My father picked the potato broccoli soup. Melanie refused both and so did Ben when he returned from the yard.

Although I was not hungry, I accepted it. Knowing if I also refused soup, my mother would take it upon herself to pour a bowl for everyone.

I couldn't help but tease my father as he walked around the counter piling his roll with different lunch meats.

"Does that even taste good?"

"I wouldn't eat it if it didn't." He didn't appreciate the mockery.

"I'm not sure how salami, bologna, turkey and roast beef can taste good together, David." My mother shook her head while creating the perfect roast beef and American cheese sandwich. She blanketed the meat and cheese in shredded lettuce and thin slices of tomato. My mouth watered just looking at it.

My mother must have noticed Melanie's slight green complexion, because mid-bite she lowered her sandwich and asked if there was a chance Melanie was pregnant.

Melanie shook her head and chuckled. "Ryan hasn't been home long enough for me to be pregnant."

My mother shrugged and picked up her sandwich again.

"It would be nice having another baby in the family." My father spoke into his sandwich.

"Melanie and Ryan are too young and too busy to start a family." My mother glanced in Melanie's direction then added, "Although I can't wait for babies one day."

I wondered if she added the last statement to make up for the hurtful things she said to her friend Lana at the Christmas party.

The nursing home called while we were eating to inform my parents that my grandmother was on her way to the hospital. Staff feared the cold she had over Christmas had settled in her chest.

"I hate leaving you, but we have to go." My mother whined.

"I'll call the restaurant and push the food delivery back a few hours. Go see Grandma."

"Do you want to come?" Dad asked.

"I don't think it would be a good idea for Melanie to sit in an emergency room. We don't know what is wrong with her."

"We'll take two cars this way one of us can return home and spend the evening with you."

I watched television while my parents were at the hospital and Melanie slept. We sent the security guard hired to watch my parents' house home and Ben took over his shift.

Text messages flooded my phone from worried friends and colleagues. Melanie's parents called complaining of non-stop calls from Melanie's friends checking in. They were concerned because Melanie hadn't returned text messages and calls. I called the cell phone company requesting they deliver a replacement phone to my parents' house. This way Melanie could assure her friends that she was fine. The request cost me a nice chunk of change, but it was worth the extra money to have the phone within hours.

At five o'clock, I turned on the news. Our story was the lead in. The news anchor described the attack on Christmas morning in typical dramatic fashion, following up with the blackmail demands. She turned the story over to a reporter who gave some background about the pictures and then invited viewers to watch a clip of our interview. Following the clip, news anchors welcomed an entertainment reporter to discuss the story with them.

"The couple each has new projects coming out within the next few months," the anchor began. "Sources tell us that Ryan Carlisle has just signed on for a controversial new war movie. Could this be a publicity stunt?"

"Ryan Carlisle doesn't need to create publicity for himself. He is on top of the world right now." The entertainment corresponded chuckled. "Ryan and Melanie are Hollywood's newest royal couple. The last thing they want is negative publicity and...um...this is an unfortunate and sad circumstance dating back to Melanie's teenaged years."

"Viewing that short clip everyone can see horror in their faces," the co-anchor added.

"Thank you Mary." The camera spanned back to the co-anchors. "We'll return after these messages."

I turned the television off and sunk deeper into the chair wondering if I made a mistake forcing Melanie to go to the media. I focused on ending this problem as quick as possible. I believed once the media broadcast the story, our blackmailer would disappear. I never considered that Melanie would have to relive the ordeal repeatedly with friends, coworkers, strangers, and even paparazzi. No one was going to forget this story. They would hound her about it for the rest of her life. Regardless of the accomplishments she achieves, this story will always be a black cloud hanging over her professional career.

Melanie never asked to be famous. Hollywood was not a place that interested her. She wanted to entertain people and was happiest on stage. I robbed her of the freedom to walk the streets of Manhattan without being recognized. I have dragged her into the ugly world of Hollywood, where dirty laundry is hanging for everyone to see.

In a way, my mother had been right all along. Fame is ugly and it is damaging to one's psyche. For the first time, I hated acting and the fame that went along with it. The comments my mother made all these years weren't meant to hurt me. She wanted to shake me from the fog fame has wrapped me in. The realization made me sick.

The house phone rang several times before the answering machine picked up the call. I didn't worry about it waking Melanie or consider answering it. I just remained slumped in the chair wondering if there was another way we could have handled this. Other than turning every dime we have over to the blackmailer.

I was relieved when my cell phone rang. I didn't want to think about my mistakes any more.

"Hello."

"Ryan!" My mother cried into the phone. "I've been in an accident."

"Are you all right?"

"I banged my head. Someone hit my car from behind and then took off. Your father turned his cell phone off. Can you pick me up?"

"I'll be right there."

I hurried up the stairs, taking the steps two at a time, to get Melanie. She didn't look too healthy, even in her sleep. Her skin was a sickly-white color and the garbage pail next to the bed contained proof that the virus still plagued her. Without waking her, I closed the door and hurried down the stairs. Slipping into my coat, I hurried out the front door to the car Ben was sitting in.

"Why don't you go inside and warm up. There's coffee in the kitchen," I told him.

"Where are you going?"

"My mother's been in an accident."

"You're not going anywhere on your own."

I recalled the promise I made to Melanie that I would no longer run off without protection. At the same time, there was no way I would leave Melanie in the house unattended. "Any chance we can get the other security guard back here?"

Ben made a phone call. "They can have someone here in ten minutes."

I safeguarded the house and walked the dog while we waited for the guard to arrive.

While Ben briefed the guard, I wrote a note explaining everything to Melanie and left it next to her on the bed.

A messenger approached the house on our way to the car. I tossed tip money in his direction and tucked the cell phone box under my arm, tossing it on the seat next to me.

* * * *

An ambulance and two police cars were on the scene when we arrived. I knew from the repeated phone calls I received from my mother, asking what was taking so long for me to arrive, that she wasn't seriously injured in the accident. Still, I hurried from the car to check on her. EMS workers were checking her pupils to make sure she didn't have a concussion. She held an ice pack to her lip.

"Can you believe someone hit me and then took off?" she asked me.

I shook my head and examined the car, careful not to get in the way of the emergency workers. The car had a broken taillight, a cracked bumper and the trunk was out of alignment. Thankfully, it was drivable. I wanted to get back to Melanie, not wait around for a tow truck.

"It doesn't appear you have a concussion but I still suggest going to the hospital for testing," the EMS worker told her.

"No, no, no. I'll be fine. It's just a bump," she assured him.

"I'm just shaken up."

"Are you sure, Mom?" I asked her. "How's your neck?"

"My neck is fine. My face took the beating. Damn steering wheel."

The EMS worker made her sign something waiving an emergency room visit before they left. The three of us waited in the car for the officer to finish his report. While we waited, I used the little bit of power Melanie's new phone could muster to retrieve eighteen of the fifty missed calls from her SIM card. The first three messages were from our blackmailer cursing at me for disconnecting our call. Two were from Melanie's family, four from Eve and three were hang-ups. There were a few messages from concerned friends. The seventeenth was a slow and angry message from our blackmailer scolding us for going to the media. His message ended with a warning. If we do not pay him one million dollars, our family members will suffer grave consequences.

"Your bodyguard looked ridiculous walking that dog today," he added with a sinister chuckle. "Who's at the house protecting your little dog and your slut wife while you're with mommy?"

Things happened quickly from this point. Ben instructed me to call 9-1-1, and then hurried to the squad car. A moment later, he took off in my rental car. I was furious that he left me behind and slid behind the wheel of my mother's car. She begged me to remain at the scene of the accident for fear the cop would arrest us.

"You're not supposed to leave the scene of an accident, Ryan."

I don't think she understood what was happening at home. The cop did follow with his lights and sirens blaring. I didn't care why he was following us. I had to get home to Melanie.

Parked on my parents' block was half of the police force. I skidded to a stop in front of a neighbor's house and sprinted toward the cluster of officers gathered on my parents' front lawn. Two police officers stop me from entering the house.

"This is my parents' house. I'm the person who called you." I explained to the officer.

"We need to see identification."

I removed my wallet and flashed my driver's license. "I'm Ryan Carlisle. Now get out of my way."

Detective Newell called from the front door instructing

the officers to let me pass. Neighbors questioning the police presence surrounded my mother. I pointed her out to the officers, instructing them to let my mother pass too. When I reached the living room, the detective and his partner were speaking to the security guard.

"The guy hit me with a taser gun."

I passed the scene in the living room and hurried upstairs. Officers stopped me in the hallway.

"I want to see my wife?"

"You shouldn't be here." An officer pressed his hand against my chest stopping me from walking any further.

"Where is my wife?"

"You'll have to speak to the detective."

I burst into the living room demanding someone bring me to Melanie.

The detective dropped his black notebook on to the table and stood. "Melanie isn't here."

"She was when I left." I looked from the detective to the security guard. "Where the hell is my wife?"

"She's gone."

"Gone...gone? What the frig does gone mean?"

A high-pitched scream forced me to turn.

"What have I done?" My mother cried. "This is all my fault."

Her body went limp. I grabbed her and we both toppled to the floor in the direction of the glass sofa table. I attempted to turn my body so she wouldn't hit the corner of the table. Pain sheared through the right side of my head as it made contact with the square edge. The last thing I remember was moisture splattering my face.

When I regained consciousness, a cool rag was pressed against the side of my head. My mother called out to me. She continued to apologize. I turned my head to ask why she felt this was her fault when I noticed blood streaming down her face. Two police officers insisted she lay still.

"Can you tell me your name?" a female police officer asked me.

"Ryan Carlisle."

"Where are we right now Mister Carlisle?"

"My parents' house. Why are you asking me these questions?"

"You banged your head and passed out," she told me.

Anxiety filled my chest. I assumed the sight of my mother lying there with blood on her face was the cause of my concern, but my gut argued with that theory. Trying to figure it out made my head hurt. Worse than that, I was sick to my stomach.

"Lay back and relax."

The sick feeling made me comply with her instruction. "The ambulance is on its way. We are going to get you and your mom checked out."

"Where's my wife?" I realized Melanie was the source of my trepidation. "Where is my wife?" I asked again, pushing myself off the ground.

The room was bustling with activity between the cluster of police officers and the emergency technicians who were pushing their way through the front door with huge orange boxes in their hands.

"Lay down Mister Carlisle. We don't want you to hurt yourself." The female police officer took hold of my arm.

"The security guard said my wife is gone. What did he mean by that?" I paused long enough to realize she wasn't going to answer me and her silence was pissing me off. I sat up and scanned the crowd looking for Detective Newell or his partner but couldn't find either of them. Pushing my way past the officer, I walked unsteadily out of the living room to check the other rooms.

Detective Newell was in the dining room conversing with several police officers. "Detective." I didn't wait to for acknowledgement. "Where is my wife?"

The detective turned the discussion over to his partner and guided me back to the hallway. "Where can we speak privately?" I led him down the hall to my father's office. "What the hell is going on?" I folded my arms across my chest.

"A man came to the door impersonating a police officer. When your security guard answered, he used a taser gun on him, knocked him unconscious with a chemical substance, and locked him in a closet. Melanie was gone when he came to."

I dropped down into the armchair nestled in the corner of my father's office. My head continued to pound and the urge to vomit came on hard. Leaning my elbows on my knees, I lowered my head into my hands, took a few deep breaths, and tried to process this information.

"We have every police officer in the state looking for her, Mister Carlisle." He placed his hand on my shoulder. "I'm figuring once they arrive to a location the kidnapper deems safe, he's going to make contact with us."

"There is something you need to hear." I pulled Melanie's new phone out of my pocket and played the threatening message for him. He took the phone to the officers in the dining room. While I waited for him to return, my thoughts bounced between Melanie and her parents. Although I dreaded the thought, I knew I had to call Phillip and Diane before they turned on the news.

An EMT came into the room and observed blood running down the side of my face. He told me to sit down and examined the wound. I resisted him at first but eventually complied. He determined that I needed stitches and a cat scan.

"I am not going to the hospital right now. My bodyguard and I are going to help you look for Melanie."

"We need you to be available should we receive a ransom call." The detective informed me when he returned to the room.

"I can take the call from the road. The only contact has been on Melanie's cell phone."

"We need to set up a trace, Mister Carlisle."

"What do you know about this guy?" I asked.

"A neighbor from across the street witnessed the man and your wife getting into the car. Police officers have a description of the vehicle and the individual," Detective Newell answered my question. "Road blocks are set up all over the county."

"Do you have information on the car, Ben?"

"Yes sir. I've been briefed by some police officers outside."

"Let's go."

"Mister Carlisle." The EMT pressed his hand against my chest. "You need to come with me." When I shook my head refusing the command, he turned to Ben. "I do not recommend leaving with him. He most likely has a concussion."

"Mister Carlisle." Ben stopped me. "I will work with the police and keep you briefed the entire time. Go to the hospital for a check up. Melanie doesn't need to come home to a husband with a brain injury."

"I am not going to the hospital until Melanie is found." I growled at the two men.

"Ben, are you coming with me to look for my wife?"

A young police officer appeared in the doorway. "Dispatch is on the phone with a woman who says she is following the car containing our missing person."

"Get her on speaker." The detective pushed past me and ran outside to a patrol car. "Who is this woman?" he asked the officer on the way.

Ben and I followed them to the cruiser and squeezed in between the group of police officers huddled around the radio listening to the conversation.

"What is your location?" Someone on the other end of the radio asked the woman.

"I'm on Bryant Street," the familiar voice answered.

"I recognize the voice," I whispered to Ben. "Why does she sound familiar?"

"Her name is Eve Austin." An officer filled Detective Newell in, "She said she was pulling up in front of the Fowler's house the same time our victim was tossed into the car."

I let out a sigh of relief. "She sang with Melanie on Christmas Day."

"Do you know what direction you're traveling in?" the voice on the radio asked Eve.

"Um...let me think for a minute."

"Concentrate on driving, Eve. Can you see them?"

"Yes."

"Are you still on Bryant Street?"

"Yes."

"Let me know when you see a street sign or any landmarks. I want you to tell me everything about your surroundings."

There was silence on Eve's end for a few long seconds before she responded. "Bryant Street and Grant Street."

"You're doing great Eve. Tell me about your surroundings if you can."

"A service station named Murphy's is on the left side. I am passing Blueberry Street and a drug store on my right called..."

The 9-1-1 operator spoke over Eve's voice, "All units, be on the lookout for a brown 1997 Chrysler traveling North on Bryant Street. This vehicle is in the vicinity of Blueberry Street. Person of interest is armed and dangerous. This is a hostage situation so use caution."

Silence surrounded the police cruiser as we listened to the

conversation between Eve and the operator. "Eve, are you able to read the license plate number yet?"

She told them it was a New York license plate and then read the numbers and letters. Police officers surrounding the car recorded the information into their black pads. The officer sitting in the driver's seat punched the plate number into his computer.

"It doesn't match the description of the car. We're dealing with a stolen automobile."

The detective nodded knowingly. "We're going to catch him." Detective Newell smiled.

Ben slapped my back and asked the detective what he could do to help.

"Accompany Mister Carlisle and Officer O'Brian to the hospital," he instructed.

"I need to call Melanie's parents and arrange for a plane to bring them here."

I was about to head back to the house when the operator stated she had lost contact with Eve. Detective Newell rested his head on the roof of the cruiser and punched the window. "Get her back on the phone."

Chapter Nineteen

Melanie

I leaned against the passenger door of his car praying he wouldn't kill me. At the same time, I struggled to hatch an escape plan that wouldn't get me killed. He warned me about looking out the side window.

"If I even think you are signaling for help, I will beat the shit out of you and throw your ass in the trunk. Do you hear me?"

We sped through town passing the high school Ryan graduated from, beyond the supermarket we shopped in when we arrived to Pennsylvania and past the church where I first encountered my kidnapper. I expected to see an alert flashing on highway signs advising drivers of my abduction, just as they do when children are abduction.

There was nothing, not even a roadblock. People went about their business, clueless that my life was in danger. It made me fear for Ryan's safety. Where had he been when this man broke into the house and dragged me into his car? I screamed for him, but he didn't answer. No one answered.

Tonight or tomorrow when people learned that someone snatched Ryan Carlisle's wife from his childhood home in Pennsylvania, would they recall seeing me for one fleeting moment as the car passed them?

The possibility of a rescue diminished when his car turned off the Interstate onto a more desolate road.

Out of the side view mirror, I detected a car following us. If I wasn't mistaken it was the same car I noticed behind us in town. *Someone is following us! Someone is following us!* My heart rate quickened.

In an attempt to distract him from noticing the car behind us, I rested my head against the passenger window of the smoke-filled car and moaned. My ploy was not far fetched. The smell of his cigarette, coupled with the twisting roads was making me sick.

"What's wrong with you?" He exhaled cigarette smoke, grasped my arm and shook me when I didn't answer.

"I don't feel well," I groaned.

"Too bad."

"Why are you doing this to me?"

"I've told you a thousand times...revenge."

He blew cigarette smoke in my direction and laughed when I coughed. "You could have made things so much easier by paying me. But, no, your stupid-ass husband didn't want to part with his millions. Let's find out if he's willing to hand over the dough now."

"What did you do with Ryan?" I asked, even though I feared the truth.

"I didn't do anything with lover boy. He left you to rescue his poor mother."

I wasn't sure what he meant, but was relieved Ryan wasn't harmed.

"What did you do to Nancy?"

"An unfortunate hit and run accident left her stranded. Your husband and his guard ran off to help. I guess that pretty much answers the question about the two of you drowning. It's obvious he'd save mommy."

Annoyance filled my gut.

"I had nothing to do with Jack's injuries."

I could not stop shivering and was undecided if it was nerves or the cold weather. The heat was on in the car, but I was only wearing a long-sleeved T-shirt and a pair of jeans. In an attempt to warm myself, I wrapped my arms across my chest and lifted my legs close to the car heater to warm my bare feet.

"No one knows who you are. Let me go. You'll never be found by the police."

"Don't play head games with me." He snarled his lip when he spoke. "That's what your attorney told Jack. Hand over the pictures and sign this legal document and we will not press charges. Then *bam!*" I jumped when he shouted the word and punched the steering wheel at the same time. "He was beaten on his way home."

I was tempted to proclaim my innocence once again, but

refrained. I wondered if he truly cared about Jack or if he used his misfortune to score cash for himself. The thought scared me. If this was all about the money, then my life was meaningless to this man.

"Besides, I don't believe anything you say." He removed the cigarette from his mouth and held it in his right hand. I watched the red glow, fearing he would use it to burn me.

"Until I receive the money from your big shot husband, I'm going to keep you as Jack's caregiver." He peered in the rearview mirror, groaned and pressed his foot down on the gas. "What the hell?" He extinguished the cigarette into the ashtray.

I glanced over my shoulder at the car following us and received a backhand across my face. "Who the hell told you to turn around?"

I curled into a ball and leaned against the side window. My lip stung from the slap, but I willed myself not to cry.

He slowed the car and pulled over to the side of the road. *Please don't let him shoot the other driver.* I prayed. *Please don't let him hurt me.*

I braced myself expecting the worst. He watched as the car crept past us. The way the car skulked, made it obvious that the driver suspected something. I glanced sideways but couldn't see anything through my tear-filled eyes.

"Keep going bitch," he growled as the car passed. I bit my lip worrying about his next move; cowering when he leaned in my direction. He removed a cell phone from his back pocket and dialed a number. Putting the phone to his ear, he waited, removed it, looked at the screen then redialed. He did this three times before cursing at the lack of a signal. I didn't know who he called, but had a feeling it was a good thing he couldn't get through.

He pulled the gearshift into drive and his tires spun clouds of dirt as the car skidded back onto the road. He sped up and down the hills and took the turns at a high rate of speed causing my stomach to churn. About a quarter mile down the road I noticed the car he let pass parked in the woods.

I stared at the driver as we passed hoping the terror in my face would confirm whatever suspicions made her follow us. I gasped when I recognize the eyes of the petite, older woman behind the wheel.

"I'm going to be sick," I told him, hoping he would pull over long enough for help to arrive. Eve found us, I was confident someone else would too.

He leaned over the back seat of the car and felt around the floor until he found an empty garbage bag.

"Throw up in the bag."

I sat up, raised the open end of the bag to my mouth, and actually barfed. He groaned, lowered my window, and instructed me to toss it.

"What the hell is wrong with you?" Spit flew out of his mouth as he barked at me.

"I have a stomach bug," I muttered, keeping my cheek against the open window enjoying the cool air.

"I knew I should have put you in the trunk."

I ignored him and focused on my surroundings, making mental notes of landmarks and street signs as we passed. We passed three houses set back from the road. They were a good distance apart and surrounded by woods. It would be a difficult trek without shoes, yet I made a mental note.

When we reached the end of the winding road, he made a right and traveled around a lake. The narrow block led to a one-lane bridge. On the other side of the bridge, miles of green pastures and forests replaced houses and street signs. We made a left and then a right, leading to a small farm with a decrepit red house nestled in the middle of it. He drove around back and pulled the car into an old barn, parking next to a pick-up truck with huge tires.

He walked around the car, opened my door and pulled me out by my hair, tugging so hard I lost my footing and fell on the ground. Pain seared through my head as a handful of hair came out. He yanked me off the floor and dragged me across the snow-covered ground.

We entered through the kitchen door. The inside of the house was as dilapidated as the outside. Old cabinets covered in dark contact paper hung from broken hinges. Grease and grim caked the appliances and thick dust blanketed the table. A puke-green rug covered the living room floor.

He dragged me through the room and tossed me on to a couch. It reeked of smoke, beer and dirt. The room was murky due to plywood covering the windows. Other than empty beer bottles, overflowing ashtrays and a few pieces of worn out furniture, the house was bare.

"Stay here," he told me.

"If you try to run, you'll be dead by the time you reach the door."

He removed a shotgun from the closet and carried it on his way down the hallway. The sound of his boot heel against the wood floor echoed.

I sobbed as the reality of the situation sunk in. Then I remembered Eve hidden in the woods. I hoped she had the wherewithal to write down the license plate number and note the description of the car. The thought sent my heart racing with hope that the police would soon find me.

I stiffened when I heard him approach the living room. In addition to the sound of his boots, was a squeaking sound. I turned my head in his direction and saw the wheel chair.

"I'm sure you remember Jack." He ran the wheel chair over my foot as he passed.

I cried out and lifted my foot to inspect it. The pain was horrendous, but I was able to move my toes, indicating it most likely wasn't broken.

I glanced at the thin, old-looking man before returning my attention to my foot. Jack's good looks were gone. His hair was stringy and dirty. He now had a potbelly and a mouthful of rotted teeth. Based on the stench of alcohol seeping through his skin, my guess is years of drinking booze were to blame.

"You've benefited from my photo shoot, haven't you?" Jack smirked.

I ignored the comment.

"I tried to do something positive for your career then you took my legs from me." His tone was patronizing.

"You owe me an apology."

He paused as though he really expected one from me.

"I'm giving you the chance to apologize, wipe the indignant look on your face?"

I considered my response before speaking. "I am not responsible for your accident." I eyed him pensively. "Once you handed the pictures and the negatives over to my attorney, I had no further interest in you."

"You weren't furious with me?"

"I was relieved the ordeal was over and the pictures were destroyed."

"Apparently your boyfriend held a grudge."

"I didn't have a boyfriend at the time," I snapped. "I never told anyone about you or those pictures."

"I find it strange that he was beaten on the way home from *your* attorney's office, yet you say you're not responsible," the blond man added.

I shrugged. "It was an unfortunate coincidence."

Jack closed one eye and shook his head, distrustful of my theory.

"Jack," I whimpered. "I am sorry this happened to you, but I can tell you that I had nothing to do with the attack. The situation was humiliating. I never spoke of it to my family or friends. As a matter of fact, they only learned of the photo shoot on Christmas morning when *he* held a knife to my throat."

Jack turned to the blond man, who was sitting on the arm of the chair behind him. "You put a knife to her throat, Sam?" he asked with a chuckle.

Sam shrugged. "I followed directions. I scared the crap out of her but didn't hurt her."

Jack drummed his fingers on the armrest of his wheel chair. "I wonder if your husband has returned home? We have some money to collect from him."

I would give him every dime I had to escape this putrid place. I know Ryan would do the same.

"Start dialing." Sam tossed his cell phone to me. My unsteady hands misdialed the number three times. When the call finally went through to Ryan's number, I held the phone out to them.

"You're doing the talking," Jack told me.

Sam walked over to me and put his finger in my face. "Use your words carefully. If you play games while on the call, I will kill you, then torture and murder your husband."

"Put the phone on speaker, Melanie," Jack added in a less threatening tone.

"Hello?"

The concern and tension in Ryan's voice brought me to tears.

"It's me." I whimpered.

"Melanie? Where are you? Are you okay?"

"I'm fine."

"Melanie. Can you tell me where you are?"

Jack waved his finger in the air warning me. Sam held out a piece of paper with a five-line script. I glanced at it. The two of them were insane. Sam grabbed the phone and hit me across the face with it. I cried out in pain, covering my face with one hand while holding the other arm in front of me to protect against further attacks.

"Relax Sam," Jack told him. "She can't make the call if she's dead."

Sam glared at me. "Read it a few times and we'll try again."

"He's never going to believe this," I cried.

"You'd better use those acting skills and make him believe you," Sam shouted.

I flinched when he tossed the phone into my lap. With shaking hands, I picked it up, put it on speaker, and dialed Ryan's number again.

"Hi," I whimpered.

"Melanie. Thank God. What happened?"

"I haven't been totally honest with you or the police." My stomach churned as the lies spilled from my lips. "I am responsible for Jack's injuries. I hired someone to kill Jack Boucher the day he turned the pictures over to my lawyer."

"Melanie, stop," Ryan warned. "What do they want? I'll give them anything. Just tell me where I can find you."

My lip quivered but I fought the urge to sob. "I want to give him enough money to pay for a decent caregiver. Ryan, I don't want to go to jail for attempted murder. After you turn the money over..."

Sam clenched his fist when I stopped speaking.

"I need to disappear."

"I know you're listening you piece of crap. If you hurt my wife, I swear I'll..." He stopped speaking. At first, I thought he disconnected the call, but he began talking again. "I'll give you anything you want. Don't hurt my wife." His tone was less threatening.

Jack pointed to the script. I hesitated unsure why he wanted me to continue. Ryan agreed to pay the ransom. Sam made a fist and threw his arm back in a threatening manner.

"I'm a criminal, Ryan." I struggled to keep emotion from my voice. "I wanted Jack dead for embarrassing me. I realize now how wrong it was to try to kill this man."

"Melanie, stop talking. I will get you a lawyer and we will work everything out. In the meantime, I want you home. What does he want?"

I couldn't decide if Ryan actually believed the story or if someone instructed to go along with the conversation.

I couldn't blame him if he did believe the lies. The secret I kept hidden about Jack and the pictures were trivial to me now. I should not have kept it from him.

A smack to the side of my head ended my daydreaming. "Umm..." I read from another strip of paper given to me by Jack. "I want two million dollars to help the poor man. I'll be in touch with a drop-off location."

Risking another slap by Sam, I ad-libbed. "Ryan, you know how religious I am. Please help me set things straight with God by helping Jack."

A brief silence on the other end of the phone indicated he was processing this important clue.

"I understand Melanie. I'll deliver the money wherever you want."

Sam grabbed the phone from my ear and disconnected the call.

Jack smiled. "Nice job Melanie. Now I see why you went further than the other two girls." He lit a cigarette and pointed to me with it. "Do you know the police did nothing to find the men who attacked me?"

I looked at him but didn't respond.

"While I was in a coma fighting for my life, they asked my mother who I pissed off. Sons of bitches." He released a cloud of smoke. "That's what happens when you have a rap sheet. The police don't care."

"We're hoping the little story you shared will cause the police to lose interest in you too," Sam admitted. "Hopefully they won't want to waste the money getting you back."

Jack took another drag of his cigarette, extended his neck to look at the ceiling, and exhaled a cloud of smoke.

"It isn't going to be that easy, Sam. She *is* married to Ryan f'n Carlisle. We need to take this story to the press. Let's keep the media huddled around the water cooler talking about Mister Carlisle and his lowlife wife. I want the spotlight off of the kidnapping." He stubbed his cigarette in a nearby ashtray.

"I like that idea."

Sam's face brightened at the thought. "We'll record her telling the story and e-mail it to that tabloid show on T.V. and the computer."

Jack considered this. "It's a possibility, provided you stop leaving bruises on her face." He glared at Sam. "Black and blue marks indicate coercion."

"Why did you pick me?" I asked, knowing the answer, but wanting to hear it from him anyway.

"What do you mean?"

"There were three of us. Why did you pick me over the other two?"

Jack smiled but didn't make eye contact with me. "You had the most to lose."

"You *know* I had nothing to do with the attack. I just have the biggest bank account, don't I?"

The arrogant smile disappeared. He stared at me for a few moments before answering. "It has to do with justice. I wouldn't have been anywhere near that location if it weren't for the appointment with your lawyer. I tried to do the right thing and look where it landed me." He punched the sides of his wheel chair. "Get her out of my face."

Sam grabbed me by the hair and hauled me down a flight of stairs to the basement. He sat me in a folding chair in the middle of the room and tied my arms behind my back.

"If you scream, I will stuff that towel in your mouth." He pointed to a white towel covered in a black substance. He shut off the lights and closed the door, locking it behind him.

I sat in darkness thinking about Ryan and my parents. By now, I was sure my family knew about my kidnapping. I hoped Ryan called. If they learned about the kidnapping on television, they would never forgive him.

I closed my eyes and concentrated on my thoughts. Hoping if I thought hard enough, Ryan would hear me. *I am in an abandoned farmhouse deep in the woods. Look for a single-car bridge and a lake. They have me hidden in the basement. They are going to kill me. Please find me. Please, please find me.*

Jack and Sam were speaking upstairs. Sam persisted on recording me tell their ridiculous story. Jack was leery. "They'll figure out who sent an e-mail. The cops can't prove my connection to any of this. Let's keep it that way."

"I won't use my own computer."

"Let's just think this through before doing anything."

Running water drowned their voices out, so I returned to my thoughts. I was concerned about Ryan. He blames himself for everything. I could only imagine the self-punishment he was inflicting. I envisioned the hurtful things my parents would say to him when they arrived.

"How does our daughter get abducted twice in a matter of days?" My Mother would yell. *"If I didn't know better, I'd think you were behind this. Are you trying to kill my daughter?"*

"I cannot believe you left Melanie unattended," My father would yell.

Secretly, my family may suggest the police investigate Ryan, unaware their mistake will distract police from finding me.

I spent the next hour moving my hands in circular motions trying to loosen the ropes tied around my wrists. All I managed to do is hurt my wrists.

Hours passed before the basement door opened and the light turned on. "Let's call your husband again."

"Can I use the bathroom?"

"We'll see how the phone call goes." He untied my arms and led me up the stairs. For the first time he didn't inflict pain on me.

There was heartbreak in Ryan's voice when we spoke again. In between sobs, I told him to place the money in a backpack and bring it to the campground located on Route 611. He was to enter the woods right before the guard shack, walk five hundred feet and leave the backpack on the ground. A teenaged boy would retrieve the bag.

"Ryan, the boy's mother and I will be killed if they do not get the money." I repeated my kidnapper's lies. "They have warned him about working with the police. Forewarn them not to approach the boy. Someone will be watching."

"Melanie, I'll do whatever they want," Ryan cried. "Are you okay?"

Sam disconnected the call. "Where on the page did you see the word *they*?" Sam smashed the paper in my face, deliberately hitting me in the mouth with the heel of his hand. "You stupid bitch, you just hinted to them that there are two of us."

"No I didn't." I wiped away a trickle of blood. "I'm sorry. I didn't mean to."

Jack reprimanded Sam for injuring my face once again. Afterward, he dragged me down to the basement, without a visit to the bathroom, and threw me into the folding chair. He bound my wrists once again before leaving. This time the rope was loose. After the lights shut off, I wiggled my wrists, freeing them from the rope.

It took a while before I gained enough courage to leave the

chair, knowing he would kill me for escaping. Water ran for the second time and I recognized the sound as either a bathtub filling with water or a shower. Since the water drowned out their voices earlier, I figured it would prevent them from hearing any noise I made. I tiptoed over to the wall, feeling for a weapon or a window to slip through. I felt around in the dark, but found nothing useful. I only managed to add to the collection of bruises I had gotten over the past few hours by bumping into things.

I returned to the chair as soon as the water turned off, slipping the rope around my wrists. Five minutes later the door opened and the light flipped on. I lowered my head, allowing it to dangle above my chest and pretended to be asleep. Sam muttered a few vulgar words and walked back up the stairs. I used the few seconds it took him to shut the light off to scan the room.

Once I heard the door lock, I slid the rope off my hands and picked up the dirty towel on the floor. To protect my legs and feet from further injury and to avoid making noise, I crawled in the direction of the pipe I spotted in the far corner of the basement.

I secured the pipe and the towel then crawled into a closet. My plan was to break a window after Jack and Sam went to bed so I could sneak out. Should Sam check on me before going to bed, I would attack him as he approached the closet.

The men continued their earlier conversation about calling the media. I could only make out some of the details.

"I think this is a safer plan. If we play our cards right..."

There was a knock at the door. Again the water turned on.

A while later someone turned the television on. I didn't recall a television in the living room, which meant they were most likely in a room in the back of the house. Probably down the hallway. I hoped that Jack and Sam headed to bed and would be asleep soon. Fearful the house would be too quiet once they shut the television off; I decided to move forward with my escape plan immediately.

I scurried out of the closet holding the pipe in my hand when I heard someone walking around. Moments later, water ran again. I was perplexed as to why they kept running water in the bathtub, but didn't let the mystery delay my plan. I needed to take advantage of the noise.

I wrapped the dirty towel around one end of the pipe and

rammed the window. Without wasting a moment to find out if Sam or Jack heard the shatter, I pushed the glass out of the way with the rolled up towel, hoisted myself up and climbed out of the small opening.

Running as quickly as I could, I crossed the field and slipped into the woods. Thorns and branches cut my skin as I sprinted deeper into the snow-covered forest. Tree branches scratched the palms of my hands and face as I hurried past them. I looked back a couple of times fearing the kidnappers sensed I had escaped.

Darkness prevented me from seeing the large rocks sticking out of the earth until I ran into them. This happened twice. The first time I dusted myself off and continued running despite scrapes on my knees. The second time, I flipped over the rock, banging my head on the ground.

I lay there long enough to evaluate my injuries. My shins hurt a great deal, my head throbbed and my left wrist hurt. On top of everything, the snow soaked my clothing.

Shielding myself from view behind a bush, I stopped to catch my breath. I was safe as long as I didn't see light shining in the forest. The woods were too dark to find me otherwise.

Unable to tolerate the cold any longer, I dragged myself off the ground and limped toward the opening in the trees. My body ached, making it difficult to run. I crept in an unknown direction. "Damn," I cursed when vine-like tree roots tangled around my foot and I stumbled once again. The sound of running water alerted me that I was heading toward a dead end.

I closed my eyes and recalled the mental notes I took during the drive to the farmhouse. Convinced I was walking in the right direction, I continued along the edge of the forest, prepared to hide in the trees if necessary.

Several concerns plagued me as I continued. The first was the exposure to the cold weather. At least an hour had passed since I escaped from the basement. The December air was unbearable without a coat and shoes. Now that my clothing was wet and adrenaline was no longer racing through my veins, the effects of the chilly weather were taking a toll on my body.

Another concern was my inability to move quicker. Sam could come looking for me in six hours or six minutes. I still had to travel more wide-open areas. I needed to reach them before the sun rose, but the body aches and the burn in my lungs made running difficult.

Panic set in when I noticed headlights headed in my direction. I slid into the trees and crouched down out of view.

The car passed, traveled down the road a bit, stopped, turned and passed again. I peeked around the tree hoping it was a police car. A bright light shined into the woods, indicating the driver was looking for someone...me being that someone. Each time the car passed, the motorist stopped in a different location, got out of the car, shined the light into the woods then circled around again. I froze with fear.

The car passed a fourth time. The driver stopped the vehicle fifty feet from me and scanned the forest with the flashlight. I stood completely still praying they wouldn't see me. The flashlight lit up the woods to the left of me, slowly making its way in my direction. I hunkered down behind the tree waiting for the light to pass. The searcher scanned the woods slowly, until he reached the area of the woods where I was hiding.

Chapter Twenty

Ryan

The hours since Melanie's disappearance had been the longest of my life. The police were unable to regain contact with Eve. Neither the helicopter nor the squad cars had located the kidnapper's vehicle despite patrols swarming the vicinity that Eve provided. EMS workers were concerned about the repeated blows my mother had taken to the head and brought her to the hospital for evaluation. I tried to reach my father, but couldn't get through.

Melanie's parents called from the airplane every ten minutes for an update. Diane sobbed each time she learned Melanie was still missing. To make matters worse, the police were unable to trace either of the phone calls to my cell.

I paced between the living room and the dining room, where FBI agents set up camp, waiting for an update on Melanie. The pictures Melanie received from the kidnapper on Christmas Day were sprawled across the dining room table for every man with a shield to see. Melanie would be devastated to walk in and find the display.

The media took over my parents' street. Reporters with questions bombarded anyone leaving the house. Most stations had interrupted their normal programming with special reports about Melanie's kidnapping. Other channels scrawled the information on the bottom of the screen. At first, I was angry for the intrusion, but Ben explained the more it's broadcast the better chance of receiving tips. With most of the police force and a half-dozen FBI agents sitting in the next room, there was no reason for Ben to hang around any longer, so I sent him home. He apologized profusely for letting us down. I patted his back and told him I'd call with news. Otherwise, I'd see him in the morning.

My phone rang non-stop. I answered the first dozen calls but forwarded the rest to voicemail. FBI agents prepared to trace each incoming call, only to learn it was another friend offering support. My parents' church friends stopped by asking what they could do for us. I sent a few to the hospital to keep my father company. The rest I thanked and sent home.

FBI agents tried to locate Jack Boucher to questions him further about Melanie's disappearance. His apartment was empty and the property owner maintained he hadn't seen him for days. Now that Melanie confirmed retaliation was the motive, police obtained a warrant to search his apartment, check his credit card purchases, bank accounts and cell phone numbers.

For hours, police officers combed the area Eve described. There was concern the kidnappers realized she was following them and took her hostage too. They surmised Eve might be the other person Melanie stated was in danger.

While everyone was busy trying to find my wife, I felt useless. I dropped off the money as the kidnappers instructed and spent the rest of the time waiting for another call. In the meantime, agents waited for the teenaged boy to retrieve the ransom.

I walked through the dining room to the kitchen for coffee. The guilt of consuming anything while my wife was missing forced me to dump it down the drain. On my way back to the living room, I reminded the agents about the pot of coffee in the kitchen.

I dialed my father's cell and left a message asking how my mother was making out. I ended the message by telling him Melanie was still missing. Placing the cordless phone on the table, I sank into the armchair and sobbed.

Detective Newell startled me when he charged through the front door, marching directly into the dining room. I jumped to my feet and followed him, noticing his bright-red face. I strained to hear the whispered conversation between him and the lead agent.

"We searched the entire area. There is no evidence of Eve or a struggle along the roadside."

"She never indicated an altercation with the perps." One of the agents sneered as though he was mocking the officer's intelligence.

"No. However, we did lose communication with her. When

we called back, we received a message indicating she was out of range. Our cell phones worked fine in that area. One of my officers has the same cell phone provider as Eve. He had full bars in that area," he said. "I listened to the conversation between Eve and our dispatch a dozen times. There is no mistaking the area she described to us."

"It could have been a set up. The men may have forced Eve to make up the location," one of the agents said.

"We're looking into Eve's background now," Agent Rhodes admitted.

"She wouldn't be any match for my wife," I said aloud. "Melanie is tiny but very strong. I hope you're not going to waste valuable time investigating an elderly woman. The security guard said a man took her."

"We have many people working on this case Mister Carlisle," Agent Rhodes assured me. "We are looking into the background of every person we encounter. I want to ensure we aren't leaving any rock unturned. I'm sure you can appreciate that."

* * * *

Melanie's parents arrived around ten at night. The moment they crossed the threshold they demanded answers. Agent Rhodes assigned one of his agents to brief us.

Diane and Phillip sat huddled together on the couch and listened to Agent Hobbs explain every detail of the kidnapping. Neither of them fully comprehended the severity of the situation until now.

Phillip pressed Hobbs to find out what they were doing to bring Melanie home. The agent explained that the local and state police were combing the area while FBI followed up on leads. When asked what we could do, he suggested we stay in the house and wait for Melanie's call.

"We should hang posters offering a reward," Diane said.

"Melanie's story is on every news channel. The coverage is worldwide," the agent replied.

"Can we speak to the neighbors to find out what they remember?" she suggested.

He shook his head. "FBI agents are conducting interviews with neighbors as well as those calling in with tips." Hobbs patted her hand reassuringly.

"I promise we are doing everything to bring Melanie home."

Diane, Phillip, and I sat quietly for several long minutes—each of us deep in our own thoughts and prayers.

Marcy called for an update on Melanie and my mother. She explained that the hospital wouldn't release information. Instead, they promised to forward the message to my dad.

"I'm flying in tomorrow."

"What? Why?"

"To help you and Dad," she told me. "I also want to see Mom."

"It's too dangerous for you to be here. They threatened Frankie's life. You should be home with him."

"He and George are staying with his sister. The guard you hired is with them. They're fine."

"Marcy, it's not a good idea. Things are really bad."

"George couldn't change my mind and neither can you."

I heaved a sigh.

"I want a guard to escort you here, so text your flight information to me."

"I plan on going to the hospital before arriving to the house."

"He'll go with you. I cannot believe you're coming back."

"You're welcome. I'll see you tomorrow."

"What happened to your mother?" Phillip asked, noticing their absence for the first time.

"She was in a car accident and banged her head against the steering wheel. Then when we arrived home to find Melanie... missing," saying the words aloud caused my stomach to turn. "She passed out. EMS workers took her to the hospital to have the head injuries checked out."

"Will she be okay?"

"I'm sure she will."

"It looks as though you took a nice shot to the head too." Diane noticed.

"We both fell," I told her. "Would you like something to eat or drink?" I asked unenthusiastically. "There's a pot of coffee in the kitchen along with cakes and sandwiches the neighbors dropped off earlier this evening."

They refused.

FBI agents didn't expect to hear from Melanie until morning and recommended we get some sleep.

"I can't sleep while my daughter is missing," Diane told the agents.

"Let's make posters and hang them around town tomorrow," Phillip offered. "The more exposure she gets the better off she'll be."

I led Diane and Phillip to my father's office and turned the computer on. While Diane created a missing person flier, I ran upstairs to retrieve our camera. I found it in the bottom of Melanie's duffel bag, wrapped in a sweatshirt for safekeeping. I shook my head at the realization that she must have lost the camera bag again. Before closing the bag, I removed the sweatshirt and held it to my face taking in her scent.

When I returned to the office with the camera, Phillip and Diane noticed my red, swollen eyes.

"What's wrong?" Her father stiffened.

"The camera was in Melanie's duffel bag."

I left the room to pull myself together. When I returned to the office, Agent Rhodes was speaking with Melanie's parents.

"We are going to hold a press conference in the morning," he repeated for my benefit. "We want to bring the kidnappers out of their hiding place."

Diane burst into tears over the likelihood that Melanie wouldn't be found before morning. Phillip and I carried her to the living room couch where she laid face down screaming for her daughter. I could not handle her emotional breakdown. While Phillip consoled her, I headed to my old bedroom. I couldn't help but think how safe they've kept their daughter her entire life and how three weeks after marrying me she's been taken from my childhood home and God only knows what was happening to her. I slid down the wall scrunching my body up tight. My chin rested on my knees. Throwing my hands over my mouth, I tried to stifle the screams in my throat.

Chapter Twenty-One

Melanie

The beam of the light shined on the ground next to me.

"Melanie?" a voice called out.

I stood motionless. My breathing was too heavy to hold my breath. Every time I tried, I came close to hyperventilating. Relief washed over when the beam of light traveled away from me. After a few minutes, there was darkness.

The searcher returned to the car, drove further down the road, and repeated the steps, once again calling my name. This time the voice carried through the woods.

A moment passed before I recognized the person calling out to me. Finding the energy I lacked minutes before, I slid down the small hill leading to the road and raced to my rescuer. When we made eye contact, I placed my finger over my lips signaling for her to keep quiet.

"Turn off your headlights before they see you," I whispered.

Eve complied and I hurried to the passenger side of her car. The warmth of the heater caused a burning sensation in my feet.

"I can't believe you stuck around. Where are the police?"

"I'll take you to them now."

I leaned against the headrest and released a huge sigh of relief. "How did you know I was out here?"

"I have been watching the house since you arrived. I saw something running across the property tonight and hoped it was you."

"You could have gotten yourself killed," I told her. "I was petrified he was going to kill you earlier."

"Me too." She laughed nervously. "That's why I hid my car in the trees and waited. I didn't start following you again until he reached the bridge. It took me a while to locate that farmhouse. I didn't even know if you were there. Since nothing else is around, I figured it was a safe bet."

"Where are the police?" I searched for activity on the deserted road.

"I spoke with them briefly, but lost connection once we turned off the main road. I stuck around for fear those men would relocate and I would lose you forever. My plan was to get the police tonight once the house went dark." She ran a hand over the bruise on my cheek.

"What happened to your face?"

"They hit me a few times."

"Bastards."

"My feet and my head hurt more than anything else."

She flipped on the interior light. "You're bruised from head to toe. Lie back and relax. I'm driving straight to the hospital."

"I want to call Ryan and let him know I'm safe."

"Once we get back on the main road we'll call him and the police. I don't have cellular reception now."

"Let's get going before they find us. They could come looking for me any moment." I closed my eyes. "Do you know how to get out of here?"

"Absolutely."

I looked in the backseat of Eve's old car for a blanket or jacket to warm myself. I could no longer stand the aching in my chest from the unrelenting shiver.

Eve made an unexpected turn, jerking my body to the right. I spun around, fighting off panic.

"Where are you going? You turn left to get to the highway. You told me you knew the way out of here."

"I do."

"You are driving back to the house!"

I grabbed the steering wheel.

"Let go of the steering wheel before you kill us both." Eve slapped my hands away. "It's a right to the highway. You must be disorientated."

"Stop the car!"

"Calm down Melanie. We are going to get into an accident."

"Let me drive! The highway is opposite the woods, you're heading in the wrong direction."

I slid my leg over the center console, pushing her leg out of the way and slammed my foot down on the break. The car veered onto the grass. "You're leading us back to them."

I jumped into the back seat and instructed her to move into the passenger seat.

"Hurry!"

When she didn't move, I pushed her small body over and leaped into the driver's seat. It astonished me that she continued to argue with me.

"I'm sorry Melanie."

"Don't apologize Eve, just move." I pulled the gearshift into reverse and stomped on the gas. Once I was facing in the correct direction, I shifted into drive and sped away.

I considered turning the headlights off, just to be safe, but navigating unknown roads in the dark, at seventy miles per hour was difficult.

We raced by the open field and approached the one-lane bridge in a matter of minutes. Eve was chattering about something, but I was not paying the least bit of attention. My focus was on escaping this deserted area.

We crossed the bridge and passed the three houses set back from the road. Headlights of a truck traveling in the opposite direction blinded me as it approached. I shielded my eyes in an effort to see the road in front of me. The car beeped as it passed, decreased speed and made a U-turn.

Eve turned to get a look at the vehicle behind us.

"You'd better stop Melanie. Sam is behind us. God knows what he'll do once he catches us."

"That's not him." I shook my head. "There's a pick-up truck behind us. You're more paranoid than I am."

"It's Sam, Melanie."

"What makes you so sure?"

"He and Jack drove off in the same truck a few hours ago."

I recalled the pick-up truck parked in the garage. "You're right." Anxiety bubbled inside my stomach.

I refused to allow panic to ruin my chances of escaping. Instead, I concentrated on the road. We were only a few miles from the Interstate. We would be safe then. Sam wouldn't dare hurt us on a busy roadway. Still, something didn't feel right.

"Are you listening to me, Melanie?"

"Not now Eve," I admonished her. "I need to concentrate. Please be quiet."

I pressed my foot on the gas, accelerating the car to fifty miles per hour and then sixty. We zipped past the forest of trees in pursuit of freedom from my kidnappers.

The trees reminded me of a comment Eve made when she found me. My heart tightened. *I stuck around for fear those men would relocate and I would lose you forever. My plan was to get the police tonight once the house went dark.*

Why didn't she call the police when Sam and Jack left in the pick-up truck? How did she know they had left me behind? How did she know their names? I never mentioned Jack's name to her.

It took a few moments for me to comprehend the situation. *Eve witnessed the kidnapping, followed us to the farmhouse, failed to go for help, saw me escape, found me in the woods, knows the names of my kidnappers and....*

"You?" The word sounded more like an escaped breath.

"Sam wants to kill you. I talked him out of it so far. You aren't the monster I imagined all these years. I had hoped things wouldn't turn out badly." The expression on her face suggested that option was no longer on the table.

"The running water in the house was meant to prevent me from learning your role." My heart pounded wildly in my chest as I figured it all out. "I don't understand. Why are you doing this to me?"

"My sister is Jack's mother. That makes me Jack's aunt."

For the first time I observed a calculating person behind those sweet old-lady eyes.

"His mother died of a stroke two years ago. She had been in poor health a good portion of her life and was on heart medication from the time she was forty-three. You can imagine the strain her body suffered caring for a crippled adult child." She shook her head. "I'm sure Jack deserved the beating he received. He always was a troublemaker."

Eve waved her finger in the air. "My sister didn't deserve the pain his disability caused."

"How many times do I have to tell you," I slammed my hand against the steering wheel. "The beating wasn't my doing."

"You're a liar." Eve shouted. "Now you have to pay for the pain my sister endured." She grabbed the wheel, trying to force me into the lake. I slapped her hand away then glanced in my rearview mirror to check on Sam.

She continued with her story as if we were taking a leisurely drive.

"We've been following you for more than a year.

Unfortunately for us, your husband's newfound fame brought droves of paparazzi along with it. Having them follow you every day made it impossible for us to get close enough." She shrugged. "So I decided to get to you through your family. I tried to befriend your parents but they aren't very social. What do you expect from New Yorkers?"

"Ryan's parents were much warmer. Nancy and Dave will befriend anyone associated with their church. I joined a few of the groups Nancy is involved with this past summer. While we weren't exactly friends, I knew she wasn't fond of her new daughter-in-law."

She paused long enough to let the comment linger in the air. As ridiculous as it sounded, it hurt me to hear my mother-in-law openly discussed her ill feelings toward me.

"I must say the family drama did make me question the likelihood you and prince charming would visit. I was about to give up, then I heard Ryan and his new bride were coming for Christmas. Nancy was so excited. So was I."

I struggled to concentrate on the road ahead.

"Now that you are wealthy, we decided taking your money would be almost as gratifying as breaking your beautiful body in two–which was our original plan."

"You make me sick."

"Speaking of sick, wasn't it convenient that the lead singer of our choir fell ill right before Christmas?" She chuckled. "I was worried for my health considering I dropped by the old bat's house on Christmas Eve. I hope she didn't get sick from something I added to her food."

If I weren't petrified of crashing the car, I would have punched her.

"Jack isn't a victim. He was the monster who caused me ten years of suffering. He brought his own problems on. He caused his mother's death. The anger that consumes you should be directed toward Jack."

"How dare you?" she shouted at me. "You were the whore who went into his apartment and then made up lies to cover your shame."

"I could have him arrested. I saved us both public humiliation by asking the lawyer to solve our problems in private."

Eve removed a cell phone from her coat pocket. "I'm growing bored of this game, Melanie. This is your last warning. Pull the damn car over."

"Never."

With death closing in on me, rage replaced fear. The only chance of surviving was to fight. I had lived in fear of Jack Boucher for ten years. He wouldn't rob me of my future with Ryan or my family.

I grabbed at the cell phone, causing the car to swerve. Eve moved her hand closer to the window waiting for cellular service. I reached for the phone a second time. The swerving motion alerted Sam that we were fighting. His truck picked up speed and rammed the back of our car, jolting us both forward.

My head hit the steering wheel and for a moment or two, my vision blurred. The strike also affected Eve. She shot forward, slid out of the seat and banged her face against the dashboard. The phone dropped to the floor.

Blood poured out of Eve's nose, over her mouth and spilled on her light-blue coat. I steered the car with my left hand and held Eve with my right hand, preventing her from reaching the phone. She grabbed my hand and bit down. I responded by backhanding her in the mouth. When that didn't stop her, I punched her in the head until she passed out. Her body slumped in the front seat. The possibility that she was dead sickened me.

Her phone lit up and chimed, indicating cellular service. I swerved back and forth until the phone slid closer to me. Eve fell over and moaned.

Bending down, I swiped it off the floor just as it rang. Spelled out on the phone screen was Sam's name.

"Back off Sam. I'll kill her."

He threatened to do horrific things to my dead body once he caught me.

"Just let me go. You're the only person the police can't attach to this crime. Eve and Jack are both going to jail."

The phone went dead. I held my breath waiting for his next move. He eventually backed off and his truck sat idle on the road.

I reduced my speed and dialed 9-1-1. Checking my rearview mirror, I noticed Sam's headlights were gone.

"9-1-1. What's your emergency?"

I wanted to remain calm, but was no longer capable. Speaking the words into the phone, my tone was frantic. "My name is Melanie O'Shaughnessy and I've been kidnapped."

"Do you know your location?"

"I don't know where I am. I'm driving on a dirt road not far from the highway. I'm in Eve's car. I can't remember her last name. My husband is Ryan Carlisle. His family will know her name. One of my kidnappers is behind me."

"Describe the area for me Mrs. Carlisle."

Hysterical words spilled from my mouth. "I think I'm traveling southbound. There's a pond to my left and trees to my right. The highway is on the other side of the trees. There's a huge field and a farm with an old red house and a barn. There are woods behind the farmhouse and some houses on the other end of the woods." I checked for Sam in my rearview mirror again. There was total darkness behind me.

"How far are you from the highway?"

"Not too far. I'm close to the turn leading to the service road."

The closer I got to the service road, the more apprehensive I become. *If he turned around, I should see taillights.* I convinced myself he most likely shut his lights to make himself invisible. He was aware I had Eve's cell phone and would undoubtedly use it to contact the police."

"Can you put the phone on speaker?"

I looked down at the glow of the screen. "No. This isn't my phone. I'm afraid of cutting you off. Connection goes in and out in this area."

"We don't want that to happen. I need more information from you."

"Okay." I was breathless. A mixture of fear and excitement filled my chest.

"Can you tell me how fast you're driving?"

"Sixty."

"I want you to slow the car down to forty-five. You're driving too fast right now. Is anyone following you?"

"No. He was behind me but now he's gone."

"Keep driving Melanie." She instructed. "How far are you from the service road?"

"I'm reaching the turn now."

"Good. Describe your surroundings. We want road signs, exit numbers, street names or whatever landmarks you see. In the meantime we are searching cell phone towers for your location." The operator's tone was firm but calm. "Once we've determine your position, a helicopter will hover above your car and you'll hear police sirens approaching. Whatever you do—do not stop until the squad cars reach you. What kind of car are you driving?"

"I'm not sure...an old one. The car belongs to Eve. She orchestrated the kidnapping. She's Jack's aunt."

"Okay. We have her information. How are you doing?"

"I'm slowing down to make the turn."

"Great job Melanie. Keep talking to us."

Bright lights appeared in my rearview mirror, blinding me. "Oh, my God!" I screamed as Sam's truck slammed into the back of my car.

He pulled alongside me and sideswiped the driver's side, pushing me down an embankment. I grasped the steering wheel in an attempt to regain control, but it was too late. I no longer had a hold over the car or my destiny.

My body stiffened as the car rolled once...twice...three times before colliding into a tree. The movement was swift but painful. The horrific sound of metal slamming against the ground ceased and now everything was still. Images formed in my head. My parents. Jessica. Birthday parties. Elementary school. High school prom. Graduation day. My apartment. The stage. Meeting Ryan. Our wedding.

The warmth of the fire felt good against my raw, frostbitten skin. I prayed the smoke took me before the flames burned my flesh.

Death would have been easier to accept if I had a few minutes longer with Ryan. I would have spent the time wrapped in his arms, expressing the joy he had brought to my life. I yearned to tell my family I loved them. That was no longer a possibility.

Chapter Twenty-Two

Ryan

There was a lot of whispering in the dining room, which angered Phillip. We could tell something was wrong. Agent Rhodes promised to speak with us, but had yet to step away from the conversation. While I understood they were discussing business and not ordering lunch, we feared the worst. Unable to wait another minute of awful suspense, Phillip stormed into the dining room demanding the agents update him.

Agent Rhodes followed us into the living room and suggested we take a seat. Phillip and I lowered ourselves on to the couch beside Diane.

"Eve Austin is related to Jack Boucher," He blurted.

The news stunned me. It didn't make sense.

"Who is this woman?" Diane asked.

"How is some church lady from Pennsylvania involved with Jack Boucher?" Phillip asked after I explained how Melanie and Eve met.

"She moved from New York to Pennsylvania four months ago," Agent Rhodes explained.

"Have you arrested her?" Diane asked.

"No one has seen or heard from her all day."

"Do you know the man who took Melanie from the house?" Phillip asked.

"We are working on a lead from a supermarket purchase he made a few days ago."

"Anything else?" I asked.

The agent hesitated then shook his head. "We're trying to find out who he is. We believe the three of them are together."

"You're no closer to finding her, huh?" Phillip groaned.

"I realize things aren't coming together as quickly as you'd like but I promise we are working hard to find her." The agent motioned with his hand to a young, petite woman with blond hair. "I would like to introduce you to Doctor Reyes."

Doctor Reyes resembled a schoolteacher more than an FBI agent. She wore her hair tied into a tight bun, wore glasses and was dressed in a grey suit.

She smiled and extended her hand in our direction. Diane was the first to shake hands with her. Phillip reluctantly shook her hand. I did the same.

"I am a psychologist working with the FBI. I specialize in helping families through ordeals such as this one. I'm here to get you the information you are seeking and to help you understand the steps FBI agents are taking to rescue Melanie."

Doctor Reyes invited us to return to our seats. Phillip refused, making it clear he was not accepting of this young woman. I slid into the armchair I'd been occupying most of the day. Diane sat on the couch.

Doctor Reyes patted Diane's hand. "Agent Rhodes and his team are good at their jobs. They know exactly what to do to get Melanie back home."

"Will they get her back home in one piece?" Phillip glared down at her.

"Phillip, stop," Diane begged him. "She's trying to help."

"We've looked into the background of Eve Austin and Jack Boucher. Other than a few minor brushes with the law, neither of them have a criminal record or history of violence." She informed us. There is no record of mental illness on file. These are two people looking for a payday."

"How do we know the man who took her from the house won't hurt her?" I asked.

"That's a fair question." She nodded. "We are confident the man who kidnapped Melanie is taking direction from one of the other two. He is most likely the least intelligent of the three and promised a great deal of money to help them out. Neither Eve nor Jack have a history of kidnapping."

"What about the man who threatened her by knife point?" Phillip asked.

"We've searched our database using the picture of the man in the supermarket surveillance, the same man believed to have removed Melanie from the house. So far, we haven't found a match...which is a good thing. It leads us to believe this third person also lacks a violent or criminal past."

"Or maybe he just has never been caught," Phillip said.

"Try to keep yourself from that negative place, Mister O'Shaughnessy," she told Phillip.

"Agent Rhodes," a young, red-haired agent called into the dining room. "May I speak to you for a moment?"

Phillip and I made a beeline for the entryway to find out what information the redheaded agent wanted to share. Doctor Reyes hurried from the couch, grabbing our arms to stop us.

"We'll be right back," I told her while gently removing my arm from her death grip.

"Why don't we stay here and speak a little longer," she suggested with an annoying smile plastered across her face.

"Diane will greatly benefit from speaking with you. I need to find out what's going on."

"Mister Carlisle, Agent Rhodes will share information with you as soon as he gets the chance. I was asked to communicate with you so the agents can continue working on the case without interruption."

Her words stopped me in my tracks. As badly as I wanted to find out what the redheaded agent wanted to tell Rhodes, I didn't want to delay them from finding Melanie. I yanked my arm out of her grip for a second time and returned to my chair. Phillip didn't give up as easily. I could not hear what she was saying to him but know she was speaking in a firm voice.

My attention was on the agents speaking in the dining room. I couldn't hear a word they were saying nor could I read his lips. I studied Rhodes' face waiting for him to react to the information. His face is was blank slate. This relaxed me a bit. I imagined if the news was about to destroy our lives, his expression would give some indication.

Agent Reyes tried to get my attention, but I had no interest in anything she had to say. I watched Agent Rhodes and the others slip headsets onto their ears. After a few minutes, his eyes widened and his lips curved upward, almost into a smile.

My heart pounded as I stared at them. I wondered if Phillip was paying attention but couldn't pull my eyes away to find out.

Agent Rhodes removed the headset, slammed it down on the table and cursed. Another agent lowered his head and ran his hands through his black hair. I jumped up from the chair and flew into the dining room before Doctor Reyes realized what was happening. Someone was standing to my right about a step behind. From the heavy breathing, I imagined it was Phillip.

"What the hell just happened?" I demanded.

At first, they ignored me. When Phillip reiterated the question, the redheaded agent looked to Rhodes for approval to speak. While the rest of the agents hurried out the front door, the redheaded agent walked us back to the living room.

Expecting the worst, we sat on each side of Diane. The agent sat on the wood coffee table, an act that would anger my mother under normal circumstances.

"A 9-1-1 operator just received a call from Melanie."

I held my breath waiting for him to continue. Diane, who didn't see the reaction inside, grew optimistic.

"She told the operator she escaped her kidnappers and was driving Eve Austin's car. We were successful at tracing the call and agents are on their way to the location we have pinpointed to search for her."

Doctor Reyes touched my arm and flashed her dimwitted smile in our direction. Diane hugged Phillip, kissed me and cried.

I looked at Phillip and knew he witnessed the same scene I had in the dining room. I hated to rob Diane of the optimism but couldn't sit here and pretend everything was all right.

"The agents were pretty upset with that phone call." Out of the corner of my eye, I saw Phillip grasp his wife's hand. "What happened at the end of the call?"

The agent tugged the collar of his dress shirt, an obvious sign he was uncomfortable with my question...or about to lie. "We lost contact with her. She must have driven into a dead area. Dispatch is trying to regain the connection while our agents drive to the location."

Jessica burst through the front door with Lewis and Lori in tow. Tears spilled down her cheeks as she scanned the room. Once she made eye contact with Diane, she ran into her mother's arms.

"Her face is on every magazine cover in the world, how is it no one has seen her?"

Diane comforted her daughter, while Phillip took Lori into his arms to calm her crying. Lewis looked as though he didn't know what to do.

I returned my attention to the agent. "Why did they lose

cell phone contact with Melanie?" I asked. "Don't lie to me this time."

"She's in an area with few cell phone towers."

"Bullshit. Detective Newell said that every one of his officers had cellular connection in the spot Eve led them. How is it that *you* keep losing contact with people?"

"Eve provided phony information. She purposely sent us to a different location."

The information shocked me.

Doctor Reyes placed an arm across my back. "I know how difficult this is for you, Mister Carlisle. I realize you and your father-in-law don't always like our answers but I promise we are doing our best to get Melanie home safely."

I leaned against the wall and crossed my arms in front of my chest. "Do you really think she's going to be okay?" I struggled to keep emotion in the back of my throat.

"I am very optimistic," Doctor Reyes responded.

I walked into the hallway to gather my thoughts. From the dining room, I heard the red-haired agent tell another that he was going to the scene.

"I'm coming with you," I told him.

"You should stay here," Doctor Reyes told me.

"Not a chance."

Within seconds, Phillip was by my side. He removed our winter coats from the closet and tossed mine to me.

"You'll be in the way," Reyes told us.

"I'm going. Please move out of the way." Phillip and I pushed past her. Reyes prevented Diane and Jessica's attempts to follow. She told them they were not going on a rescue with a child. Phillip instructed Lewis to stay behind and keep an eye on everyone.

* * * *

The agent refused to take us to the scene so we followed behind in my rental car. I spent most of the drive pleading with God to protect Melanie. The rest of the time, I apologized to him for skipping mass and for every other thing I've done wrong in my life.

The police scanner buzzed with officers shouting directions to one another. The road was blocked off when we arrived. My palms were sweaty and my heart pounded so hard,

I could feel it in my ears. Through the trees, I saw flashing lights, smoke and heard commotion. In the distance was a flurry of urgent voices. We pushed past a traffic jam of fire trucks, ambulances and police cars as we neared the end of the road. The heavy smoke burned my throat. Through the trees flames shot into the air. I sped up from a brisk walk to a jog, unable to take my eyes off the fire. I had no idea if Phillip was with me or not and I didn't waste time to find out.

Caution tape strung across the area and several burly police officers prevented me from getting closer to the car burning on the side of the road. Paramedics removed a man from the cab of a pick-up truck that had fallen into a ditch. I was relieved Melanie wasn't in the mangled truck.

Annoyance grew inside me as I considered the possibility that this accident was blocking the way to Melanie. I grabbed the closest officer asking where I could find the FBI agents en route to pick up my wife."

"This is an accident scene. I don't know anything about your wife."

I searched frantically for the FBI agent we followed, regretting that I ran ahead without him. I turned to another officer and asked the same question. Again, he could not provide answers.

My heart dropped when I made out Agent Rhodes and Detective Newell standing with a cluster of officers a few hundred feet from the burning car. I shifted my gaze to the car, squinting to make out the silhouette in the front seat. Frozen in place, I watched firefighters extinguish the flames. Agent Rhodes walked over to the car, covered his mouth and nose with a white cloth and peered inside. He then lowered his head and ran his fingers through his hair.

"God, please no." Phillip cried out behind me.

I was too stunned to speak or cry. I felt the urge to puke, scream, punch something and run, all at the same time. I stared in horror at the charred body.

Several long minutes passed before Agent Rhodes spotted us standing behind the caution tape alongside police officers and ghouls who had stopped off to witness this gruesome scene. His hands were deep in his pockets when he approached Phillip and me.

"Why don't you drive back to the house with me?"

I could not take my eyes off the emergency workers who

covered the car with a white tarp in order to hide the death inside.

"Please tell me it isn't her," my words were a high-pitched whine.

"Let's go back to the house." Agent Rhodes led Phillip and me to his car.

"The media is here," someone whispered to Agent Rhodes.

"Gentlemen, we need to leave right away. The media is here. Neither of you need cameras and microphones thrown in your face right now."

"Give me your keys," the redheaded agent said. "I will have someone drive your car back to the house."

Members of the media corralled at the end of the road. Even though they were a good distance away, I heard them shouting questions to officers on their way to the scene. A large SUV moved through the crowd and drove up alongside us. Agent Rhodes opened the door and ushered us into the back seat.

"Is Melanie in that car?" I asked again.

Agent Rhodes turned with a grim look on his face. "We won't know until DNA tests are taken."

"You believe it is her, don't you?" Phillip cried.

"We've confirmed the car belongs to Eve Austin. Just before we lost contact with Melanie we heard sounds consistent with a car accident."

I lowered my face into my hands. It was not possible that Melanie was dead. She was too young. We had yet to go on our honeymoon.

I could hear Phillip whimpering but was unable to console him. I wasn't able to do anything. I couldn't deal with the lies we had been told. She was supposed to come home. Doctor Reyes said cases similar to Melanie's have a high success rate. She was supposed to come home.

"The man the rescue team was helping was one of the kidnappers, wasn't he?" Phillip was enraged. "They tended to that son of a bitch while my daughter burned to death?"

Chapter Twenty-Three

Ryan

An anonymous source who could not keep their mouth shut, reported Melanie's death to the media. Videos of the smoldering car filled the airwaves.

Fearful that Diane and Jessica would suffer a mental breakdown, Lewis contacted their family doctor requesting tranquilizers for the two women. The entire world was familiar with the story, so the doctor didn't hesitate to comply with the request.

Our cell phones rang non-stop with grieving friends asking how they could help. After the first hour, I turned Melanie's phone off. The only reason I hadn't turned mine off was on the slight chance the police were wrong about Melanie and she called. I didn't bother to answer my parents' home phone. I listened to messages long enough to make sure it wasn't my father calling, then turned the volume down. Most calls were from their friends checking to see if the stories about Melanie were true.

Melanie's family and I clung to one another and cried for hours. The only time I left the room was to answer my father's incoming phone call. My father wept openly when I confirmed the news. Like me, he held on to a glimmer of hope that it was a mistake.

"If I hadn't called you after my accident, you and Ben would have been at the house. He could have saved her," My mother wept into the phone.

I told myself the same thing a hundred times since Melanie's disappearance. *I could have saved her if I hadn't gone to the accident scene.* Hearing the words spoken aloud was painful. Although it wasn't my mother's fault, it made me resent her that much more.

I slumped into the kitchen chair. I felt numb and that was

a good thing. The person I loved most in the world was gone. We were supposed to grow old together. It wasn't fair that our forever only lasted a short time. I couldn't help but wonder why her life was cut short.

Resting my head against the wall, I thought about the night I gave Melanie the ring. I smiled at the memory. She was so excited with the ring. I could not believe she was gone.

"It isn't fair. It isn't fair. It isn't fair!" I screamed.

I picked up a vase full of flowers and threw it across the kitchen. The vase shattered into small glass fragments on the counter and the floor. The bouquet of winter flowers and water scatter about, soaking my parents' wood cabinets.

I walked over to the window and punched a hole through it. Blood poured down my arm.

Doctor Reyes, Phillip, and Lewis burst into the kitchen and restrained me. "Hurting yourself and destroying your parents' house won't ease the pain," Doctor Reyes told me. "Sit down Mister Carlisle."

Lewis and Phillip each grabbed an arm and guided me to a kitchen chair. Phillip gasped when he noticed blood on his hand and his white shirt. "You're bleeding."

I looked at my blood soaked arm. "I guess so."

Phillip tossed me a dish towel then hurried to the sink to wash his hands. Doctor Reyes dialed 9-1-1 but I told her to stop. "It isn't bad."

I spent the next few minutes pulling shards of glass from my skin.

"Would you get the first aid kit?" I asked Lewis. "It's in the medicine cabinet in the bathroom down the hall."

He left the room in search of the kit.

"Would you like some water?" Doctor Reyes asked.

I shook my head.

"I understand how difficult this for you." Doctor Reyes rubbed my back.

"I don't understand why this happened. It should have been me. I wish it was me."

* * * *

Doctor Reyes left the house sometime in the late afternoon. She promised to return the next morning. Before she left, we ordered food, but never ate it.

I polished the cabinets with wood cleaner and tried to doctor up the dent the vase left. Then I boarded up the broken window.

Rhodes and another agent returned to the house later in the evening to pack their equipment. Rhodes assured me their departure didn't mean the investigation was completed.

"We will continue the investigation from our office. We will not rest until we apprehend Eve and Jack. I'm so sorry Mister Carlisle."

A police officer guarded the house for the night. Diane curled up on the couch with her head resting on Phillip's lap. Jessica sat in the wooden rocking chair my grandfather made for my parents the year I was born. The medicine left her in a daze, prompting me to question Lori's safety in her arms.

Versace yelped from his crate until I took him out to the yard. While he roamed outside, I gathered the firewood my father cut earlier in the week.

I returned to the living room with Versace in tow to build a fire for Melanie's family. Lewis was sitting in a chair with Lori in his arms. I offered Lewis and Jessica my old room. I then pointed out Marcy's old bedroom to Phillip. He refused the room telling me he didn't want to disturb Diane. Nor did he want to leave her in the living room alone.

It dawned on me that my sister was on her way and wondered where she would sleep. I decided to stay in my parents' room until she arrived, if Melanie's parents were still in the living room, I'd move into Marcy's old bedroom.

Lewis and I carried the toddler bed from my parents' room to the bedroom upstairs. Melanie's duffle bag was on the bed. Next to it was the sweatshirt I removed earlier when I was looking for her camera. I zipped the bag and placed it in the closet, then tucked the sweatshirt under my arm before returning downstairs.

A special news report flashed across the television screen. Video of a wheel chaired man in police custody played while newscasters reported that Jack Boucher was taken in for questioning earlier this evening.

"Police interrupted a press conference Jack Boucher had arranged to take place in his apartment tonight," The woman reported. "We do not know why Mister Boucher scheduled the press conference. He is a suspect in Melanie O'Shaughnessy's kidnapping case. An autopsy is scheduled to take place sometime in the next forty-eight hours to determine if the charred remains removed from the burning car belonged to Mrs. O'Shaughnessy." Our wedding picture filled the television screen. "Earlier this month Melanie O'Shaughnessy married movie star Ryan Carlisle."

Phillip and I looked at one another incredulity. "Are you going to call?" he asked me.

I nodded and reached for the phone. "Detective Newell, this is Ryan Carlisle."

"He was brought in for questioning two hours ago." He offered the information without me having to ask. "Police nabbed him the moment he arrived home."

"Was Eve with him?"

"No. He wheeled up to the door on his own. He said he was out for a stroll."

"For three days?"

"He didn't know we were keeping an eye on the place."

"Has the other man confessed?"

"He isn't talking."

I shared the information with Phillip and Lewis before heading to bed. We had watched the news for hours and I was tired of hearing the different perspectives of news anchors and lawyers. Lewis must have felt the same because he channel surfed the moment I left the room.

I considered locking Versace in his cage for the night, but decided against it. Like Diane, I didn't want to be alone. I climbed into bed, nestled Versace next to my body and slipped the sweater between my head and pillow. Every time I closed my eyes, I saw the burning car and the silhouette of the body inside. I forced the image out of my head and thought about the day I arrived home before Christmas. Visions of both events filled my head until I fell asleep.

Someone touched my arm and called out to me, "Ryan? Ryan? Wake up." I dreamed it was Melanie and the thought made me smile.

Sadness consumed me when the dream slipped away and I returned to a conciseness state. It wasn't Melanie calling me. It was Marcy. Marcy scooped Versace into her arms trying to stop him from barking.

"Are you okay?" She sat down on the bed. "You were crying."

"What time is it?" I rubbed my face.

"After midnight. My flight was delayed. I just arrived."

"Is Melanie's family still up?"

She shook her head. "Lewis is up. Everyone else is in bed."

"Have you spoken to Dad?"

She nodded. "I called when I landed. They gave mom a sleeping pill. He plans to stay the night. They'll be home tomorrow." She pet Versace's head. "When was the last time you ate anything, Ryan?"

"I'm not hungry. The dog could use some food." I kicked my legs over the side of the bed and sat up.

"You want me to help you change the sheets?"

"I'll make up the couch. You go back to sleep."

"I was just resting here for a little while. I'll sleep on the couch."

Marcy shook her head. "The couch is fine for me. You stay here."

"Melanie will be upset with me for letting you sleep..." I stopped mid-sentence, realizing Melanie was no longer able to be upset, happy, sad or excited. Tears spilled from Marcy's eyes.

"You are lucky to have met and fallen in love with her. She was beautiful inside as well as outside." She sniffled. "I'm so grateful we had the opportunity to spend Christmas with the two of you. I really liked her."

"Melanie liked you too. She wants to plan a trip to Florida so we can spend more time together."

Tears continued to spill down Marcy's face. "I would have liked that."

I wanted to ask her to stop using the past tense when discussing Melanie, but didn't have the strength. Instead, I told her that I hoped it was still a possibility.

* * * *

The next morning I woke up to the smell of bacon, coffee and eggs. A moment before I opened my eyes I imagined Melanie lying next to me. The only thing in bed with me was Versace. He managed to steal the sweatshirt from my pillow and made a bed out of it.

"You miss her too, don't you?"

I carried the dog into the kitchen. Diane was nursing a cup of coffee while the others ate breakfast. I couldn't help but notice that her face aged ten years since she arrived. Everyone at the table looked older.

I opened the back door and followed Versace into the yard. After he did his business and ran around for a while, I carried him into the house and locked him in his crate. Lori was disappointed with my decision but I didn't care. I would lose it if he got hurt or ran away.

"Have you heard from the FBI?" Phillip asked.

I shook my head. "They told me it may take a few days. Agent Rhodes promised to expedite things. Right now they're waiting for her dental records from the dentist."

I dug my tongue into my cheek, fighting the urge to cry.

Marcy instructed me to pour myself a cup of orange juice and sit down at the table. The omelet she was making was almost ready and she wanted me to eat. I poured a glass of juice and carried it to the table. A short time later, Marcy placed my breakfast in front of me. She scolded me for playing with the food. I forced myself to take a bite and immediately felt like I would throw up.

"I remember the first time Melanie stepped on stage." Diane broke the silence by sharing a memory. "She was three years old and had been taking dance lessons for four months."

Phillip smiled at the memory.

"Her first recital was the night before Father's Day. I paid a fortune for the gold bodysuit covered in ruffles and sequence. We pulled her hair into a knot on the top of her head and curled long pieces of hair so they cascaded down her back. I remember her asking me to take her picture. She was thrilled to be in the show."

"At that moment we knew she would be a star," Phillip added.

Diane expelled a sad laugh. "She got on stage and twirled and moved her body the way she had been taught during dance class. Unfortunately, she was three beats ahead of the other dancers...and the music. She hadn't quite mastered listening to music."

"She didn't dance well until she was a teenager," Jessica added.

"Was she born with singing talent?" Marcy asked, settling down at the table with a cup of coffee.

"She used to win chorus solos every year when we were in elementary school," Jessica told her. "Of course her voice wasn't anywhere as magnificent as it is now."

"I never should have let her go to that performing arts school. She would be here if she finished high school on Long Island."

"You can't think that way," Lewis told her. "You'll drive yourself crazy if you over analyze every decision you've made in your lifetime."

Phillip rubbed his wife's back. "Melanie was born to be an actress. Nothing would have stopped her."

Doctor Reyes said it was healthy to talk about Melanie. I disagreed. The anger building inside of me caused my nerve endings to flair. If I sat at the table any longer, I thought I might explode.

The conversation changed to hotel searches. Melanie's family planned to stay in Pennsylvania until the autopsy results came in. They didn't want to make work for my mother, so they searched for a hotel.

Versace's barking released me from unpleasant thoughts. Phillip retrieved him from the cage and took him outside. Once Versace had relieved himself and exercised, he settled on Lori's lap.

"I will keep an eye on the dog," Phillip promised.

I couldn't understand why he was being so kind to me.

"Do you like the puppy?" he asked Lori.

"Can we get a one?" Lori asked her parents.

"We already have a dog, sweetheart."

"I want another one."

Versace's ears perked up and he tilted his head to the side. A moment later, he jumped off Lori's lap and ran to the front door.

My father entered the house, looking as bad as everyone else did.

"Any news from the medical examiner?" he asked.

I shook my head.

Phillip shook my father's hand. "How's Nancy?"

"Her head is feeling better. She's having a hard time with…" He was unable to finish his sentence.

Marcy slipped past Phillip and me and hugged my father. "I'm picking up clothing for your Mom. They're releasing her a little later today."

"I'll go back to the hospital with you," Marcy told him. "First, I want you to eat."

Ignoring his pleas to let him be, Marcy led my father into the kitchen and made him breakfast. Melanie's family asked about my mother's prognosis.

"She has a hairline fracture on her skull."

I had no idea.

"She blames herself for everything. Says if she hadn't called Ryan for help..."

"No one blames her," Phillip assured him. "The only people to blame are the ones who took her."

I left the table to walk Versace. "Ben is due to arrive soon. Please listen for him."

My father wanted to come with me but I told him 'no'. "It's too cold outside. Mom won't be able to take care of you if you get sick."

* * * *

Versace ran around the yard as quickly as his tiny legs carried him. While he played, I sat down on the picnic bench and thought about my wedding day.

Melanie walked up the aisle flanked by her parents. The sun crept in just before the mahogany church doors closed causing Melanie to glow. When I told her about the glow later that day, she told me the sun hadn't caused the glow. It was me, standing at the Altar, waiting to marry her.

The memory was too much for me. I puked in the corner of the yard.

"Ryan." Marcy stuck her head out the back door.

"Leave me alone for a few minutes please."

"The police are here. They want to speak to you."

* * * *

The officers were waiting in the kitchen. Melanie's family looked as though they were about to pass out.

"I'm almost afraid to hear anything you have to say," I told Detective Newell.

"You'll all be happy with this news," he told me. "The woman from the car was not Melanie. The bones were riddled with osteoporosis. The brittle bones could not possibly belong to your wife." He beamed. "This is a preliminary report, but the medical examiner is confident the body belongs to a woman much older than Mrs. Carlisle."

Chapter Twenty-Four

Melanie

I had one of those dreams that wake you up from a deep slumber, and then continue when you return to sleep. Ryan and I were sitting on the beach of a beautiful Island. A man in a white suit was mixing drinks behind a bar that was set up on the sand. He smiled at me.

Ryan and I held hands as we watched the waves roll in and back out to sea. He asked if I wanted to go swimming but I was too tired to get up from the lounge chair. For some reason I was in the fetal position rather than stretched out on my back. I wore a white two-piece bathing suit with red polka dots scattered across it. Ryan was dressed in black swimming trunks with a green palm tree on the leg. I felt anxious and wondered why I was not enjoying the honeymoon we had longed to take together. I wanted to cut the vacation short, but was too tired to move.

I was also thirsty. That uncomfortable thirst that leads to a headache and nausea. The thought no sooner entered my mind when the bartender appeared with drinks for us. For some reason he was wearing winter gloves.

"Aren't you uncomfortable wearing winter gloves?" I asked with a chuckle.

"This drink will chill you to the bone," he answered with his face awkwardly close to mine, leaving the smell of his breath behind. He then straightened his body and walked away.

I looked over at Ryan and rolled my eyes at the man's absurd comment, but found Ryan immersed in his beer and not paying attention to me. I gazed to the ocean and sipped my drink through a straw. The pink mixture did nothing to relieve my thirst, but the coolness of the glass did cause my hand to ache. I placed the glass in the sand beside me and rubbed my hands together. The chill ran up my arm, down my torso, through my legs and stopped at the ankle. For some reason, my feet burned.

Now I understood why the bartender wore gloves when he delivered the drink to me.

"This drink is making me cold." I shivered.

"I'm surprised you're not frozen," Ryan responded in a voice that was not his own. I turned to face him and noticed he was no longer wearing a bathing suit. Rather, he was dressed in a ski jacket, black knit cap, boots and winter gloves. "I'm going to get you a blanket. You're going to freeze to death out here."

"Don't leave me," I cried. I wanted to follow him but could not get my body to cooperate. Instead, I curled up tighter trying to keep warm.

He wrapped one blanket tightly around my feet and then covered my body with a second one.

"We're going to get you out of here."

I opened my eyes and realized EMS workers surrounded me. We were crammed in a dark, tight area. "Where's my husband? Why am I here?"

A dark-skinned man with beautiful brown eyes smiled at me. "We're trying to figure that out. What are you doing outside in the middle of the night?"

"I'm on vacation."

"This is some crazy trip you've booked." He laughed. "I would demand a refund."

I winced when he touched my head.

"What's your name?"

"Melanie O'Shaughnessy." Realizing most people do not recognize that name, I corrected myself. "Melanie Carlisle. I just got married."

The smile on his face turned into a shocked expression. He reached for the walkie-talkie attached to his shirt. "Our squatter is Melanie Carlisle."

In the distance, I heard someone shout, "We've found Melanie Carlisle."

"Hello Mrs. Carlisle. My name is Frank."

For the first time, I realized Frank and I were huddled in the backseat of a car.

"A lot of people have been looking for you."

"I was on the beach with my husband. He went to get me a..."

Something didn't seem right. "Was I on the beach?"

"You're in Pennsylvania," Frank told me. "You have a bump on you head and some contusions, most likely caused by the car accident. My friend Larry and I are going to bring you to the hospital." Larry opened the passenger door and slipped in the backseat with Frank and me.

"How did I get inside this car?"

"You must have been looking for a warm place to sleep or to hide out."

This made no sense to me. Why would I climb into a stranger's car?

"Do you feel pain anywhere?" Larry asked.

"My feet burn."

"Anything else hurt?"

"I'm tired and can't stop shivering. My shoulders and back ache."

"I'll get the neck brace and back board," Larry told Frank.

"Don't leave me." The thought of being alone terrified me.

"I'm not going anywhere," Frank said. "I'll stay by your side until we arrive at the hospital."

"I don't remember being in a car accident. Is my husband okay?"

"Your husband is fine and so are you. Just relax." He patted my shoulder.

When Larry returned, the two men slid a board under my back and strapped my head to something hard and uncomfortable. Once inside the ambulance, they wrapped a warming blanket around me, slipped an oxygen mask over my face and hooked me up to an IV. The fluids pumping through my veins made the chill worse.

On the short ride to the hospital, they checked my vitals and asked if I felt warmer. I did, but could not stop shivering.

"Was my husband in the accident?"

"No. He's most likely on the way to the hospital to see you."

The whole situation was confusing. I could not figure out how I wound up in the back seat of that car. I closed my eyes and forced myself to remember.

After several minutes, I recalled the car flipping-each time it rolled onto its roof I lifted out of my seat. I remembered tightness across my chest and my shoulder. The horrific sound of the car banging against the ground replayed in my ears.

I dug deeper into my memory bank, eager to remember. I smelled the fire and remembered how desperate I was to get out of the car.

Someone screamed my name. Who? The windows were broken yet the door wouldn't open. I struggled to remove the seatbelt, slipped out the window then tried to rescue someone.

The body was laying over the center console, half in the front seat and half in the back. Once I climbed out, I leaned inside the window and pulled the woman into the driver's seat. The smoke choked me and the flame was burning my skin.

The man who hit us opened the door of his truck and attempted to get out. He threatened to kill me if I let her die. The woman's foot was stuck between the driver's seat and the console. I tried but couldn't free her foot. I knew I had to get away from the man, so I ran. He screamed for me not to leave her in the car. He said he would track me down and kill me.

"The man in the truck and the woman in the car were trying to kill me," I blurted. "The crash wasn't an accident. They were trying to stop me from leaving. I just can't remember why?"

"You're safe now."

I closed my eyes and recalled running along the dark road until I found a row of houses. No one answered at the first house, even though the lights were on and the driveway had three cars parked in it. I couldn't run any more. I was so tired. I pulled the handles of each car until I found an unlocked door. It was so cold and my feet hurt. I would never have made it to the next house, so I climbed in and hid.

Two police officers greeted me when I arrived to the hospital. Their grins were wide as they announced how relieved my family was. Nurses ushered them away before I had the chance to ask questions.

A group of doctors and nurses tended to me for what seemed like an eternity. When they stepped away, I heard whispering on the other side of the curtain. People were speaking about a kidnapping and before long, I realized I was the subject of their conversation. It explained why the man in the truck frightened me so much. I also understood the reason my family was relieved.

The nurse informed me that my family was in the waiting

room and asked if I was up for visitors. I nodded despite exhaustion. As hard as I fought off sleep, my eyes closed shortly after seeing my husband's handsome, but bruised face.

Chapter Twenty-Five

Melanie

I slept most of the day and night. When I woke the next morning, Ryan and my parents were sitting in chairs on each side of me. Jessica and Marcy were at the end of the bed talking quietly and my father was snoozing in a chair.

"Hi."

They jumped in reaction to my greeting.

"Hi baby." Ryan kissed my head and smiled. "How are you feeling?" Tears filled his eyes.

"Melanie," My mother sobbed. "We were so scared."

"They took a lot of tests. What's wrong with me?"

"They're treating you for dehydration and a concussion," my father began. "Your white blood cells are off, which is probably due to that virus."

"Is that all?"

Ryan cleared his throat. "You also have frostbite on your feet."

This news frightened me. I pulled the blanket away to check my feet. Something warm and pulsating covered my legs. "Please tell me nothing has been amputated."

A doctor slipped into my room. "You're awake?"

"Are my feet going to be okay?"

He made a face. "You don't beat around the bush do you?"

"She's a dancer," Jessica told him.

"Magazines in the doctor's lounge keep me up to date with her career." He turned to me. "You're responding well to the hypothermia treatment. We have covered you with a heated blanket to regulate your temperature. It will most likely be removed in a few hours." He paused. "You have second degree frostbite on your feet. You must remain in bed for the next few days. We don't want the blisters to break and get infected." He squeezed in between my mother and me to examine my fingers, which were sticking out of a pink cast. "You also have a broken wrist and a concussion from the car accident. Over all you're a lucky woman. You went through a scary ordeal."

"Will I dance again?"

"I'm doing everything in my power to ensure you recover fully. In the meantime you need to rest."

Ryan lowered the bed rail and kissed me after the doctor left. "The doctor saved one more prognosis for me to share."

"What?" I feared the worst.

"Not only were you strong enough to survive a car accident and frigid temperatures...our baby is just as strong."

"What are you talking about? What baby?" I stared at him. "I'm...pregnant?"

"You are." Ryan smiled.

I scrunched my face up in a questioning expression. "How can that be? You've only been home a week."

He whispered, "Turns out we had a shotgun wedding and didn't know it."

"Is the baby okay?"

Ryan's smile diminished slightly. "The doctors are cautiously optimistic."

"I can't believe a pregnancy would survive everything I've been through."

My mother rubbed my bandaged head. "It's a miracle."

* * * *

FBI agents stopped by my room to speak to me. They wanted a statement while it was fresh in my mind. I agreed as long as Ryan remained in the room. He told me he didn't intend to leave my side.

They questioned me for over an hour before nurses asked them to leave. By the time we were through, I was an emotional wreck. Every second of the nightmare returned to my subconscious. The kidnappers' faces are all I saw when I closed my eyes. When they weren't haunting me, the accident was. I struggled to believe Eve was the mastermind behind the whole thing. Who would believe she could be so cunning?

Ryan's parents visited after the agents left. They granted five minutes. During their visit, I learned Nancy was also in a car accident. An accident caused by my kidnapper. It was a ploy to separate Ryan and me.

"I am so sorry for the pain I have caused," Nancy said. Her swollen, red eyes displayed guilt and devastation. "I am a stupid old woman who cannot accept that her children are gown and no longer need their mother meddling in their lives."

I smiled but didn't respond.

"I am sorry it took this...this tragedy to make me realize how perfect you and Ryan are for one another." She squeezed my good hand. "I want us to be a family. Do you think you can forgive me?"

"I want to forget this entire trip. Let's pretend it never happened and start fresh," I told her.

Nancy's expression brightened when Ryan and I shared our news of the pregnancy. Despite her concerns over us having children, she was delighted. So was Dave.

After everyone left, I invited Ryan into my bed. He lay on his side and curled himself into me.

"You look as bad as I do. What happened to you?" I ran my finger across the cut on his head.

"I learned that I can't live without you." He touched my face with his bandaged hand and smiled. "I mentally and physically fall apart."

"Have you been checked out by a doctor?"

"I'll have it looked at. For now I just want to stay here with you."

Ryan slept soundly. I figured it was the first time he slept since I disappeared. It was also the first time in a week that I felt safe.

I grasped a firm hold of his shirt and buried my face into his chest, just to drink in his scent. Before long, I was dreaming about the baby we created together.

When I woke up hours later, the thermal blanket was gone and Ryan sat in a nearby chair. His head rested on my mattress and our hands remained entwined.

The next morning we received a visit from Ben and the security guard Ryan hired to stay with me that afternoon. They informed us Jack was cooperating with police and hoping for a plea deal.

We also learned that Eve suffered a broken neck in the accident. The autopsy report reported there was no smoke in her lungs, indicating she was dead before the fire started.

No matter how evil she turned out to be, I was relieved she hadn't died because I left her in the burning car.

I rubbed my flat belly, thinking of my new pregnancy and how my baby could have lost its life as easily as Eve slipped away. I reminded myself not to allow negative feelings to consume me. Unlike Eve, I did survive and so did my child.

Sam maintained his innocence, despite Jack's confession and my statement to police.

Our families returned the moment visiting hours began. They brought trays of fast food and soft drinks with them. They wanted to spend the afternoon with Ryan and me, as long as I was up to the company.

Three hours into the visit, my eyes burned with fatigue. I was exhausted but told myself I had a lifetime to sleep. Many times during my ordeal I feared I would never be with Ryan or my family again. The fact I survived the cold, the accident, and the kidnapping was a gift. There was no way I would turn my loved ones away.

The staff paraded in and out of my room with floral arrangements, balloons, fruit baskets, and candy from our friends and coworkers. Jessica and Marcy marveled at the famous names on the gift cards. For security reasons, Ben prohibited presents from fans from entering my room. Instead, I received an inventory of names and gifts.

Ryan and I read hundreds of get-well cards together in the evening after everyone went home. Our new publicist issued a statement on our behalf thanking the FBI, police officers, firefighters, EMS workers, doctors, and nurses for their hard work. She expressed our gratitude for the prayers, gifts, and support from our fans. Our short statement concluded with a request for privacy.

My family returned to the Fowler's house to pack the belongings they purchased during their stay in Pennsylvania. They were finally relocating to a nearby hotel.

The next day our family members returned for a short visit. Although police assured us the nightmare was over, Ben helped them navigate their way through the news reporters gathered outside both the hospital and Nancy and Dave's house.

"You're supposed to be resting," Dave reminded Nancy a few hours after their arrival.

My parents followed his lead and prepared to leave. They asked if I was up to an evening visit. I wasn't, but didn't have the heart to tell them. They promised the nighttime visit would be short too. Regardless of their intentions, I knew they would return in an hour and stay until security threw them out.

Lewis lifted a sleeping Lori from the foot of my bed so Jessica could pour her into her pink winter coat.

"Lewis, please ride with my parents to their hotel room," Jessica said. "I want to speak with my sister before we head home."

Lewis shot her a look of annoyance, which she ignored. He kissed me goodbye and instructed me to follow the doctor's instructions.

"The police questioned me about the assault Jack received outside my office," she began after the others left.

A chill ran through me. Part of me wanted to tell her to stop speaking for fear police would arrest her. The other part wanted to know the truth. I would never be angry with her. She is my sister and from the time we were kids, she has been my protector.

"I wanted to smack the smug look off Jack's face the day he came to my office with his ripped jeans and flip flops," Jessica continued. "He was such an arrogant bastard. He acted as though he was doing *us* a favor by turning over the pictures. He didn't show an ounce of remorse." The memory had her seething with anger. "We should've had him arrested." She took a breath. "He deserved the beating. I only wish I could take credit for it."

I was relieved she hadn't been involved.

"The police questioned Dad about it too. He was furious when he learned I helped you. Of course, I am to blame for everything that happened this week. I've been sick about it and haven't spoken to him since."

"I'll straighten everything out with Dad." I sighed. "Jessica, I'm sorry I put you in this position."

She waved her hand dismissing my words. "I'm not telling you this to upset you. Dad says foolish things when he's angry. He'll apologize once he has a chance to think about it." She smiled. "I wanted you to know I wasn't involved in the assault."

I extended my arms welcoming her in for a hug. "Thank you for wanting to beat him. I'm happy you didn't."

The hospital obstetrician interrupted our moment to examine our unborn child.

With a quick kiss to Ryan and me, Jessica grabbed her coat and left.

In addition to the examination and some more blood work, they took a sonogram of our tiny baby. The doctor estimated I was six weeks pregnant.

"You must have gotten pregnant the day I returned home before our wedding."

"My father took your comment better than I expected." I laughed. "I was afraid he would throttle you when you referred to our beautiful wedding as a shotgun wedding."

"Under normal circumstances he may have."

"Everything looks good," the doctor told us. "Your body has gone through a great deal of stress. I don't see any evidence that your injuries affected the baby. If you have any problems, call me right away." He removed a pad from his pocket. "I'm going to start you on pre-natal vitamins. Take one every day. If they make you sick, take them at night." He wrote the prescription, tore it from his pad, and handed it to me. "If you need the name of an obstetrician, call my office and we'll recommend someone."

He handed me three pictures of the baby growing inside of me.

The baby resembled a small shrimp

"I think Shrimpee resembles me." Ryan announced after the doctor left. Without taking his eyes off the sonogram picture, he settled down next to me on the bed and pointed out the resemblances, beginning with his nose.

"Hopefully he isn't as crazy as you." I laughed.

A week ago, Ryan freaked over the thought of having children and trying to balance everything. Although I do believe he was thrilled, I could not help but wonder when reality would sink in.

"Our plans have changed a little. Does it freak you out that we're going to be parents?"

He kissed me and then kissed my stomach.

"My priorities changed over the past few days. I prayed for one more day with you so I could tell you how sorry I was for being a horrible husband. I've repeatedly neglected you by putting my career first." Tears filled his eyes. "I got my second chance and want to make every day the best I possibly can. I'm dropping out of my next two movies."

"The war movie you just signed on for?"

He nodded.

"No, no, no, no..." I pleaded. "That will open all sorts of doors for you. I don't expect you to drop out of any movies. You'll throw your whole career away."

He shrugged. "I've made enough money to help us live comfortably. I am not going to some other country to shoot a movie while you're in New York. Marriage is not supposed to be a husband on one end if the world and his wife on the other. I'm no longer using the phone and e-mail as our means of communication." He continued shaking his head. "I'm most certainly not going to watch the birth of our first child on the internet. You realize I'll be in Germany when the baby is born, right."

"Your plan leaves this baby with two unemployed parents. I can no longer fulfill my contract. There is no way I can perform pregnant or with damaged feet."

"Your feet will get better."

"Even if my feet fully recover by the time I am due back at work, I'll still be pregnant." I reminded him. "Besides, I don't want to spend all day and night at the theater leaving our newborn with a nanny. I've always planned on taking a break after we have children." I smiled at him. "I'm thinking Germany would be a nice place to rest during my pregnancy. I'm sure we can arrange to return to New York in time for the birth."

"What happens after the baby is born and I have to pack up and return to Germany?"

"I'm not due until September. Filming may be completed by then. Maybe they'll even adjust the schedule and allow you to finish early." I kissed him. "If I'm right, the army movie will win you awards."

"What happens in a year from now?"

I cupped his cheek. "Hasn't this week taught us to stop trying to plan every moment of our lives? Life will play out the way it is supposed to. Other Hollywood couples make it work..."

"Many don't," he interrupted.

"Ryan and Melanie Carlisle and their baby shrimpee will make it work." I held up my hand the way one would while swearing in during Court. "We'll learn to juggle our careers so that we each have the opportunity to work and still live under one roof, even if that roof changes every year.

"I do like the sound of that." He smiled.

"As long as you're by my side, I'll be happy. I love you more than anything in this world." I took his face into my hands and pressed my lips against his. My chest filled with excitement and love as I thought of the child we would meet in the fall, the adventures we would experience by visiting different parts of the world, and the thought of growing old in each other's arms.

Epilogue

Following a nine-day hospital stay and surgery to remove Melanie's small toe, Ryan and Melanie returned to their New York City apartment.

Melanie remained on bed rest for another two weeks while the blisters on her feet healed. For a dancer, a toe amputation is devastating. Melanie accepted the loss and remained strong during surgery and throughout her recovery. The kidnapping and brush with death taught her that a career doesn't define a person.

The Broadway show she dropped out of planned to open on time with her understudy in the lead role. Critics predicted the show would thrive despite her absence. Neither Melanie's career nor the amputated toe took precedence in her life. The baby growing inside her was Melanie's top priority.

In March, the couple relocated to Georgia for Ryan's upcoming movie role. The paparazzi continued to photograph the pair's daily activities, but found it difficult to get an interview with the entourage of bodyguards Ryan hired to protect his wife and unborn son.

Melanie enlisted the help of a therapist to work on emotional issues in connection with the kidnapping. She rarely spoke of it with Ryan or her family. The few times family members brought up the topic, Melanie flew into a rage. Therefore, they agreed to leave the healing to the therapist. On the nights she woke up screaming, Ryan held her in his arms and ensured her safety.

Throughout the pregnancy, both sets of parents flew to Georgia to visit. Marcy and her family drove up for long weekends, every chance they got. Jessica's new pregnancy prevented her, Lewis and Lori from traveling. Instead, the two sisters spent hours on the phone discussing pregnancy and their plans for the new babies. Phillip apologized to Jessica for his hurtful accusations and father and daughter repaired their relationship.

A motorcycle accident involving the lead actor of the war film delayed production until late September. Ryan had mixed feelings about the delay. He was happy to remain in the States until after the baby's birth, but was nervous leaving Melanie and their newborn behind while he flew to Germany to film. Melanie encouraged him to go and promised to join him as soon as it was safe for the baby to travel.

They never did go on their honeymoon. Dave teased that now they are about to become parents, it would be another eighteen years before they got away alone.

Melanie agreed to give up her tiny apartment in New York City for a house on Long Island. They purchased a mansion in Upper Brookville. The home included four acres of property with a stable and plenty of room for horses. Neither was ready to jump into adopting more animals. For now, they were happy to use the large property for Versace to run on.

Dave, Nancy, Phillip and Diane were all present for the birth of their grandson, Hunter Joseph Carlisle, on August 29.

Shortly after the birth, criminal trials began for Sam and Jack. Jack received a fifteen-year jail sentence for kidnapping and extortion. The additional charge of murder and attempted murder lead to a fifty-year sentence for Sam.

The investigation into the assault on Jack ten years earlier remained unsolved. After a few conversations with Julie, her former classmate, Melanie was convinced Julie's brother was responsible for the assault. She recalled how furious he had been to learn Jack had taken advantage of his sister. While Melanie knew firsthand how dangerous it was to keep secrets, she wouldn't reveal this one secret.

The evening after Hunter's passport arrived, Melanie and her newborn son traveled to Germany. As Melanie suspected, the role made Ryan an awarding winning actor.

Five years later when Ryan began an extended work hiatus, Melanie returned to Broadway in a starring role. During the curtain call on opening night, Melanie looked into the audience at the people she loved most: Her parents, Jessica, Lewis and their two daughters, Dave, Nancy, Marcy, George, Frankie, Hunter, Ryan, and her and Ryan's two-year old daughter, Madeline Paige Carlisle.

Her final stage performance was March 25, one year to the date she returned to Broadway. The rehearsals and nighttime performances she once enjoyed were now torture. Living in

Manhattan was no longer enjoyable. She longed to be on Long Island with her husband and children. Family dinners, tucking the kids into bed each night, and spending time with Ryan were things Melanie desired. Missing Hunter's soccer games and Madeline's dance recitals were painful for her. Her priorities had changed. Family was the most valuable thing in her life.

The following summer the Carlisle family relocated to California. Ryan landed the lead role in a television series that won him seven awards over the years. In the eighth season, Melanie joined the series. When the show wrapped two years later, both husband and wife decide they had met their career goals and made enough money to keep their family secure for the rest of their lives. They left California and show business behind to raise their family, surrounded by the people who loved them most.

Ryan and Melanie opened a performing arts theater on Long Island. At six o'clock every evening the couple gathered around the dinner table with their seventeen-year-old son Hunter, fourteen-year-old daughter Madeline, and the twin sons Melanie gave birth to seven years earlier.

When they are not running to dance class and sporting events for their children, they drive to Pennsylvania to spend weekends with Dave and Nancy. While every visit is enjoyable, the entire family agrees the visit to Pennsylvania each December to cut down the family Christmas tree is their favorite.

About the Author:

Katie McKnight lives on Long Island with her husband, three sons and their boxer.

She is a member of the Farmingdale Writer's Group and the Long Island Writer's Guild. When she is not singing karaoke or polishing her tiaras, you'll find her glued to her lap top writing tories or attending online classes.

She has completed Mystery Writing and Advanced Fiction courses through Queens College and Piedmont Community College, respectively.

You can follow Katie's blog at:
http://www.writergirlkatie.wordpress.com/

Find her on Facebook at:
https://www.facebook.com/katie.h.mcknight

Check out her website at:
 http://www.katie-mcknight-author.com/

She enjoys hearing from readers and fellow authors.
Her e-mail is katieonthego@yahoo.com.

Also from Eternal Press:

Winter's Journey
by Kathryn Meyer Griffith

eBook ISBN: 9781615724604
Print ISBN: 9781615724611

Romance Suspense
Novel of 75,483 words

Was the man she loved an enigmatic hitchhiker or a murderer?

To keep the bank from repossessing her eighteen-wheeler, Baby Blue, and putting her and her daughter, Tessa, on the street, Loretta Brennan takes a dangerous job driving it into Wyoming with a winter storm approaching. All alone she worries if she can make the deadline and navigate the roads since her driving partner husband died the year before in an accident.

On her way, she feels sorry for and picks up a hitchhiker. Sam Emerson. Charismatically handsome, his moodiness hides a dark past that includes a dead girlfriend and a murder charge.

Snow, a series of trucker murders and a sinister truck begin to haunt them on their route.

She suspects Sam's aligned with the killer even as she experiences feelings for him. Is Sam a good man down on his luck or is she falling in love with a murderer?

Also from Eternal Press:

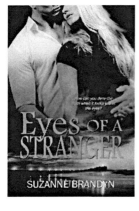

Eyes of a Stranger
by Suzanne Brandyn

eBook ISBN: 9781615726660
Print ISBN: 9781615726677

Romance Suspense
Novel of 67,472 words

How can you deny the truth when it looks you in the eyes?

When Tegan Ryan fears her secure world is about to be shattered, her nervous system takes her on a ride of a lifetime. Not only had she babbled office gossip to a stranger, she is hiding with her six-year-old son from her abusive husband.

Embarrassment floors her when she meets the new boss, sexy suited Mathew King. He is the stranger. Now she has to work for a man who chokes up all her breathing space, until she gives in to desire, just once.

Tegan always thought her son Robert had the bluest eyes ever, but Mathew presents a serious rival. As the past hurtles toward the present Tegan tries to overcome inevitable doubts and fears, but will she risk everything for the sake of true love?

Eternal Press

Official Website:
http://www.eternalpress.biz

Blog:
http://www.eternalpress.biz/blog/

Reader Chat Group:
http://groups.yahoo.com/group/EternalPressReaders

Twitter:
http://twitter.com/EternalPress

Facebook:
http://www.facebook.com/profile.php?id=1364272754

Google +:
https://plus.google.com/u/0/115524941844122973800

Good Reads:
http://www.goodreads.com/profile/EternalPress

Shelfari:
http://www.shelfari.com/eternalpress

Library Thing:
http://www.librarything.com/catalog/EternalPress

We invite you to drop in, visit with our authors, and stay in touch for the latest news, releases, and more!

CPSIA information can be obtained at www.ICGtesting.com
Printed in the USA
LVOW13s0344220813

349105LV00001B/8/P